D1634147

This edition, issued in 1962, is for members of The Companion Book Club, 8 Long Acre, London, W.C.99, from which address particulars of membership may be obtained. The book is issued by arrangement with the original publishers, Hodder and Stoughton Ltd.

Also by

VICTOR CANNING

★

A DELIVERY OF FURIES

"A blessed companion is a book"—JERROLD

A DELIVERY OF FURIES

*

VICTOR CANNING

THE COMPANION BOOK CLUB
LONDON

Made and Printed in Great Britain
for The Companion Book Club (Odhams Press Ltd.)
by Odhams (Watford) Limited
Watford, Herts
S.662.V.R.

I CAME in from the hard sunlight and paused for a moment on the edge of the great, cool pool of the hotel lobby. The pause was less for my eyes to settle to a new focus after the brilliance outside than for my mind to brace itself, without hurry, to the pleasure in this moment of coming back.

Dropping my battered leather suitcase to the tiles that spread away to the reception desk in great whorls of blue, yellow and green, I lit a cigarette slowly. Shadows passed across the gloom and, somewhere up in the roof, a great fan sucked soothingly at the air. Outside was the heat and the sunbite, the blare of horns and voices, the rattle of the trade winds in the palms, the smells of hot, dungy dust and the stale headiness of flowers and river mud; everything lush, everything bursting with life and growth and noise. . . .

I picked up my bag and went slowly across to the desk. *Hotel Polo Norte*, Barranquilla. That was the latest name for home. The clerk on the desk was new and from his face I could see that he didn't think much of me. I didn't blame him. I could see myself in the long mirror on the wall at the side of the desk. I looked like hell. My suit was water-stained and shrunk, making me look taller and leaner than I really was; a hard-looking, sun-burnt number whose brown hair needed cutting and whose chin bore a two days' growth of stubble. As I turned to the clerk I knew that he was preparing to say that there were no rooms.

"Señor?"

"Marchant." Nodding at the pigeon holes behind the boy I added, "Number 37."

The frost went from his eyes. A black hand went up for the key which had rested in its slot now for three weeks. He passed it over and raised a hand to ring for a boy to take my case. As the bell pinged, he said in proud English:

"Very welcome back, señor."

"Thank you. I want *La Prensa* and *El Nacional* for the last three days. And some soda and ice."

The entrance to the bar was flanked by two lemon trees in large marble urns. The fruit, so symmetrically posed amongst the dark green leaves, glowed with a fine polish; the polish that was over everything in the place. This was another world from the one I had just left. The last bar I had been in had been a *cantina* five hundred miles south, with the Indian proprietor asleep on the dirt floor, chicken pecking round him, the counter sour-smelling and stained with *aguardiente,* and a radio pumping out a *paso doble* that lifted the tin roof. *My Sweet Love Returns* had been the name of the bar. It was a good name, a good thought.

I moved to the doorway. From a small group around a table at the far end of the room there came a little burst of a woman's laughter. She had her back to me. I paid no attention to the others, saw no one for a while but her. Her head moved with laughter and subdued lights ran across the heavy chestnut hair. She raised an arm and the movement had all the lithe grace that took her easily through the neon-lit, martini-watered jungle of hotel bars and restaurants. The man next to her had his arm along the back of her chair. His hand touched her shoulder, rested there a moment and then drew back. I gave myself the pleasure of imagining one good firm stroke with a machete that would take it off at the wrist.

I didn't go in, not looking as I was, not wanting to meet her in a crowd. At the lift, Felipe, the attendant, gave me a nod as though I had only gone out that morning.

As he closed the door, I said. "The desk clerk is new. What happened to Fico?"

"Gone down to Puerto Colombia for better job in the *Pradomar.*"

"Any other changes?"

"No, señor. Except for new mosquito nets in all rooms. Shall I send a girl along for your things?" The old man's eyes went slowly over my battered linen suit. It had been small for me when I borrowed it. Water hadn't improved the fit.

"Don't bother, Felipe. It's going into the waste-paper

basket." I didn't offer it to him. Felipe had his pride. But I knew he would fish it out, clean it and sell it.

"You treat clothes very hard, señor." He looked down with pride at the shining brass buttons on his white drill suit, at the sharp creases of the trouser lengths. "This uniform belong to me for five years."

"Maybe I should get a job in a lift."

"Why not, señor? No troubles in a lift."

It was an optimistic statement. There were troubles everywhere. The only thing that mattered was how you took them ... thinking that, I knew I would have to be careful with Drea. Like all women she was inclined to fuss a bit when things went wrong.

The lift stopped with a sigh. The door slid back. Sunlight came through the green shutters at the end of the corridor, striping the carpet as I went along to my room.

My bag was in the room. In the bathroom, I stripped off and took a shower and then shaved, padding about the place naked, except for the bandage around the top of my right arm. The wound was a little sore still, but I couldn't be bothered to change the dressing. I put on clean pyjamas and a dressing-gown, adjusted the blinds at the window so that the room was shadowed, and then stretched out on the bed. The papers, the ice and the soda had come while I was showering. I reached out to the bedside table and filled a glass with ice and soda. The whiskey was in the cupboard by the door but I couldn't be bothered to get it. That was something I could take or leave at least, something I liked but didn't have to have. In fact, practically everything in my life was like that—except Drea. Without her when a thing was done, I could file it away into the folder marked *Experience,* strike a cash balance, sometimes red, sometimes black, and be left with the pleasure of anticipating the next thing. Happy-go-lucky. That was the way to be, committing yourself to no false stability.

Drea didn't like my way of life. There'd be trouble this time, for instance, not because the job had turned out profitless, but because of the wound in my arm. She worried about risks, about me. If she found out, I'd just have to sit tight

9

and let her have time for her anger to blow over. We loved one another; but with Drea there was no question that *she loved me for the dangers I had passed*. Or because I was happy-go-lucky. Some other witchcraft held our love.

I lay there thinking first of her, and then, because of the echoes of Shakespeare in my mind, of my father, dead now, a parson . . . and always tolerant of the break I had made from everything which had been expected of me. A shilling for every time you could cap one of his quotations. Drea and my father, both, in their own ways, disapproving. . . . But both so close.

*   *   *

Two hours later the door opened. There was the small click of the lock, a rapid filtering of light from the corridor, and then gloom as the door closed. I lay in the shadows and said nothing. It was dusk outside now. The taxis were hooting as they climbed the hill from the port, and, distantly, came the thump of a stern paddler beating up the Magdalena river. Or it might have been my heart. Knowing that Drea was standing just inside the door, listening for the sound of my breathing, I was filled with a swift affection for the river. The first time I'd seen Drea—five years ago—had been on a river boat, a shabby old tub with tall twin smokestacks, curtained decks, and the great paddle wheels going *flop, flop* at the back.

From the door she said, "Keith . . . I know you're awake."

Her voice had a vibrancy which after absence always hit me afresh.

"Who told you I was back? Felipe?"

"No. I saw you as you came into the bar door."

"You had your back to me. A man had his hand on your shoulder. Remind me to cut it off when I go down."

I heard her come forward slowly. In the darkness I reached up and found her hand, knowing it would be there in the darkness, waiting for mine. It was a cool hand, long and firm, a hand that could be commanded only at her own will.

"I saw you," she said, "in the mirror on the back wall. You looked like hell."

"I flew into Soledad, and then on by car. Quite a nice trip." When things hadn't gone well, I made a point of avoiding details with her if I could. Once the first half-hour of being together was past she let her worries for me slide. My fingers left her hand and were on the warm flesh of her wrist and arm under the loose blouse sleeve. "So you let me sleep?"

"That's what you wanted or you would have come into the bar."

"Yes," I lied, "that's what I wanted."

"Bastard. . . ."

The breath from the word moved over my face as she came swiftly down to me. She slid on to the bed at my side and my arms were round her and my lips on hers and everything was as it always had been . . . no thoughts no questions so long as her lips were on mine.

I felt her stir and lift her hand. She kissed me on the cheek, and then said, "You're all right. . . . Everything was all right?"

"I'm all right," I said lightly. "In one piece. And wanting nothing in the whole world but you—but this——"

She came back gently in my arms and I could feel the touch of her hair against my cheek. Time meant nothing. There was just Drea. Her hand came out of the darkness and moved gently across my cheek and neck, tracing with light fingers the angle of my jaw.

"Drea. . . . Wonderful Drea." I don't know whether I said it aloud. I just wanted to mark the long contentment of the darkness with her name.

Her hand moved down to my arm, moulding my flesh gently through the silk of my dressing-gown. The ceiling was suddenly faintly marked by the purple blur of light from some neon light filtering through the blinds.

I felt her hand stop, resting over the bandage under the silk. Slowly she sat up and slid off the bed and switched on the table lamp. I watched her . . . her movements full of firm, incisive grace. The light burnished her chestnut hair and up-shadowed the fine line of her cheek bones, the puma-strong loveliness.

"Take off your dressing-gown and that pyjama jacket," she said sharply.

I was back at school with the matron bawling me out.

"Why the hell should I?"

"Take them off, you hare-brained idiot." She turned away from the bed, swearing at me in Spanish, as she always did when roused.

She opened the cupboard by the door and came back with the whiskey. She poured two drinks, watching me slip out of my gown and jacket.

"You miss nothing," I said.

"Drink with your left hand." Handing me the whiskey, she sat down at my side and began to unfasten the bandage from the top of my right arm. Her fingers trembled.

"It's filthy."

"It's a strip off an underskirt."

"Who did it?"

"An Antiquenos woman. She was about ninety. A dear old soul. Wouldn't take anything for the damage to her skirt. You'd have liked her."

"Not the bandage—the wound? Hold still!"

She leaned over me, frowning as she peeled back the cloth and exposed the wound.

"It's only a bite. A mosquito bite. Don't fuss."

"A funny kind of mosquito."

"You haven't seen them all. There are eight different kinds in Colombia."

"This one was made of lead." As she bent closer to examine the wound I kissed the side of her arched neck. She shook her head impatiently, and went on, "It's clean, any-way. I'll get a fresh bandage and stuff from my office."

"Don't bother. There's all you want in the cupboard. Forget it. It's just a graze."

She stood up and swore at me again in Spanish, and then, her back to me on the way to the cupboard, finished, "God, Keith, why do you have to do this? Six inches the other way and it could have killed you!"

I tried to jolly her out of it, saying, "Six inches the other way and it would have missed me altogether. I don't try to interfere with the little chaps sitting on clouds who decide these things. They don't like it." I tried to keep it light because I hated to see her angry.

"Lord, will you ever learn? Ever be different?"

She came back, cleaned the wound and started to put on a fresh bandage. I tried to kiss her but she avoided me. But I didn't mind. I knew it would pass.

When she had finished she took her glass of whiskey and walked towards the window. Her hand went up and jerked at the blind cord. The shutters gaped and the neon light glowed on her face.

"I suppose this was Barrau?" she asked tersely.

"Yes. Straightforward job—but it turned out a shade tough."

"One day they'll carry you home."

"I could just as easily be hit by a street car."

She held the whiskey glass close to her breasts. She looked beautiful and I could see the green light flecks in her eyes, the powder brown bloom of her skin and the pull of her breasts against her blouse as she breathed hard. She had all the magic of Cleopatra for me . . . me, a third-rate Antony, but a happy one. I wanted her to be happy, too. I heaved myself up half-way, wanting to go to her but she shook her head and said:

"Stay where you are. I don't want to be smoothed down. And don't talk to me about street cars. One day some damn fool may press the button by mistake and we'll all go up. But you—you go out of your way to invite things."

"Drea—cut it out. What on earth's all this in aid of? Just a scratch on the arm. No more."

She laughed dryly. "And was the scratch worth it? What did you get out of it?"

"What do you mean?"

"You know damn well what I mean, Keith. How much did you get for the job?"

"Well . . ."

"I see, one of those. You come back here, looking as

though you've swum down the river. And not a cent to show for it. And you don't care. You put yourself in jeopardy. Get nothing out of it. And you don't care."

"It's the way I live. You know that. Oh, Drea, be sensible. Forget this." I touched my bandaged arm. "Have another drink and stop looking at me like a mountain cat that's about to go for my throat."

She shook her head angrily, "You're not going to put me off."

Just then the telephone by the bed rang and I reached out for it.

"I'm not trying to put you off," I said. "I just want you to relax."

Over the telephone came Barrau's voice, Spanish, rich with a rummy burr. "Is that my good friend Squadron-Leader Marchant?"

The last person I wanted then was Barrau and I said sharply, "This is nobody's friend and stop calling me Squadron-Leader. And go to hell, Barrau."

I heard him laugh at the other end of the line.

Drea came forward and said, "It's a pity you don't mean it. Hang up on him. Tell him you're too old for his rackets."

I grinned at her. "Thirty-odd summers. Not all of them golden, of course."

"Oh, for God's sake—what's the use of talking to you?"

At the other end of the line patient Barrau said pleasantly, "Who's with you? Drea?"

"Yes."

"I hear her voice. She is angry?"

"You could call it that."

"Tell her not to worry. This time things went a little wrong. But there is always the next time."

As he spoke I saw Drea, with a fierce shrug of her shoulders, go over to the door and put her glass down on the cupboard top. As she reached for the door handle, I called, "Hang on, Drea."

She went out without a word, slamming the door.

Barrau said, "What was that?"

14

I lay back against the pillows. When I saw her later she would have calmed down.

To Barrau I said, "That was Drea, giving me hell. She doesn't like me having bullets flying around my ears and nothing to show for it. Frankly, neither do I."

"Yes, yes," said Barrau soothingly. "It was a little unfortunate, that affair. But we both knew it might be. If it had come off, she could have had a new mink."

"Barrau, she doesn't want mink. Not that much. Now, what the hell do you want?"

He was silent, but I could hear his breathing at the other end and I could imagine the heaving of his silk waistcoat.

"Nothing," he said finally. "Nothing, except that I'd like you to call by and have a chat. Say before dinner if you can manage it."

Barrau was my business and I said, "All right. If I can manage it." I put down the receiver, and I lay back, wishing that Drea hadn't stormed out.

I picked up the telephone again and called the Boutique Ballaya in town. They had a topaz brooch that Drea had once admired. It was to have been my coming-back present, if I'd come back with money. They still had it and I told them to send it to her with some flowers. It was no good worrying about money just because you didn't for the moment have it.

"No message, señor?"

"No, no message."

2

I LOOKED in at Drea's office on the way through to the lobby, but she wasn't there. I wanted to ask her to have dinner with me. She was the assistant to the hotel manager, and she'd worked in hotels for a long time and knew the business backwards. I left a message for her and went out.

A coloured boy in red vest, white slacks, his skin grained like sandalwood, brought the car round from the garage. From the neatly trained pergola at the side of the door I snapped off a sprig of plumbago and stuck it in the lapel of my suit. It was pleasant to be wearing a suit that fitted. Beyond the drive, through the dark frieze of oleanders and palms, there was a blue upwash of radiance from the under-water lighting of the *Polo Norte*'s swimming pool. Voices and the sound of splashing came subdued across the heat-heavy evening. On the terrace away to my right a few people were already dining early. The boy descended from the seat of the car with the dignity of a Haile Selassie and the grin of a Louis Armstrong and held the door for me.

I went down the hill to the river and the port, driving easily and without hurry. The traffic thickened up as I skirted the Parque 11 de Noviembre. I had the top down and the air that came back into my face was warm and steamy, beating down as though the sky were a great damp electric blanket turned on full blast. The skirts and dresses of the women on the pavements were humid-draped about them and the men's shirts were marked with dark patches of sweat.

I came out of the Paseo Bolivar and around the Plaza by the Cathedral. A bunch of noisy youths and girls at the foot of the Columbus statue were being hustled away into the main stream of pedestrian movement by two policemen.

Barrau's place was a few blocks east of the Cathedral. How many statues of Columbus, I wondered, were there around the great blue bowl of the Caribbean? He'd certainly started something over this side. Not so long ago, this had been mud-swamp, silted, lazy river-land that suited the Indians. Now industry and its hangers-on had taken over Philip the Second's dream. Not gold and silver ingots now, but textile mills, perfumes, soaps, beers, oil and hats, flour mills, saw mills, shipyards and paint and plastics. Well, all cities were much the same to me as long as they gave me a living, and if my jobs and working hours were irregular that was the way I liked it. Drea worried over what might happen to me. So did I, sometimes. But usually I didn't give the future much thought. Why bother these days? Enjoy things while you could. And if you couldn't be lucky, at least be happy. Not that I wasn't sure that somewhere along the line my luck would change.

Barrau's offices were set in some old colonial-type buildings overlooking a small yard. The flanks of the yard were sheds, garages and three or four small hovels. An old woman sitting on a stool outside a lighted room looked up as I parked alongside her. She had a lapful of Lima beans and from the room behind her came the hot smell of tamales.

I picked out the biggest boy from the children playing in the yard and gave him a ten centavo piece to look after the car.

"Another ten when I come out," I said. "You knock the head off anyone who tries to touch the car." These children could wreck a car in a few minutes.

He nodded gravely and got into the driving seat. As I went to Barrau's stairway I heard him noisily electing lieutenants at two centavos each to walk around the car on guard duty while he lolled back against the leather.

A painted board, among others, at the bottom of the stairs announced—*L. Garcia Barrau, Importadora y Exportadora de la Barranquilla.* Just below the boards the wall was covered with *graffiti.* At the first turn of the stairs two little girls were playing with a doll. Above them in a glass-fronted wall niche was a painted plaster figure of the Madonna lit by a weak electric light bulb. Another two floors up was Barrau's brightly painted green door.

The outer office was empty, but the door to Barrau's room

17

was half open and he called to me to come in. He had his bottom in a deep leather chair and his feet on his desk. He was a big, fat sealion of a man wearing an expensive American suit of bronze silk. The stuff was like a pelt on him, as slick as though he had just come out of the sea. He rubbed his three chins with a pudgy hand and beamed a smile of welcome.

"Amigo—it is good to see you. How is the arm?"

"It's O.K."

"You are angry with me?"

"No. Things just went wrong. Nobody cheated me—unless you've become really clever."

His face saddened. "I lost money. You lost money. We close the books on it. You are sure about your arm?"

"Forget my arm. What do you want me for?"

He got up and walked to the office door, closing it with a push of his foot. "A job. Tricky, maybe. When I was asked to find someone who could set it up I naturally thought of you."

"Naturally."

He came back and sat down and began to prepare himself a cigar. "You know," he said, "that here in Colombia—by agreement with the American and British governments—the Air Force is just taking delivery of twelve new Hunter jet fighters?"

"I was reading something about it in *La Prensa*." Britain and, more particularly, America were very touchy about the increment of new weapons and military aircraft in the Caribbean area. Not that there weren't ways of getting around their embargoes. Civil aircraft, crop sprayers, helicopters and transport planes could be bought and converted. Also when British fighters were made abroad under licence in places like Sweden and Italy the British Government did not always retain rights restricting their ultimate disposal. This was the kind of business world Barrau and I could move about in blindfold.

"Well, because of the American touchiness over Castro in Cuba, and President Trujillo in Dominica, both governments made it a condition of the sale to Colombia that the

18

existing fighter planes here—which the jets would displace—must be handed back and sold only to a country which had the approval of Whitehall and Washington."

"That's the usual form." It was the old, old game. The papers were always full of the possible threats to Caribbean peace from the delivery of arms and planes to Cuba and the Dominican Republic. Behind it all, of course, was the big money, the American and British business interests and concessions. The Caribbean was the Mediterranean of the New World . . . there wasn't a situation which had plagued Europe for hundreds of years which wasn't inevitably duplicating itself under these sunny skies. In a way that was why I and hundreds like me were here. There were always eager hands around a melting pot, waiting to take a dip.

I said, "What are the planes, the ones they're kicking over to get the jets?"

"Hawker Sea Furies. Piston-engined. You know these?"

"I've flown them. Not officially." There had been some in Korea. "Even now they'd be good for a lot of work. Two 20 mm British Hispano cannons in each wing. A 2,550 horse-power Bristol Centaurus eighteen-cylinder engine. You'd probably get about 450 miles an hour out of them around twenty thousand feet."

"You remember all these things?"

"You remember the women you've slept with?"

"*Ciertamente!*"

"It's the same thing." For a moment I forgot Barrau. I was off the deck and up into the wide blue and the rolling clouds. *Oh, for a horse with wings* . . . sleeve-valved, air-cooled, and fifteen hundred miles of heaven in the tanks.

Barrau said, "Six of them are being shipped next week to Caramanga for the Republic of Cordillo. It is all approved by the Americans and the British. But not by other people."

I came back to the rat race.

"Other people," I said. "You mean Angelo Libertad and his revolutionary boys stuck away in their little corner of Cordillo?"

"It's more than a corner," said Barrau. "They've got nearly half of the island. It's a simple matter of switching these

planes two hundred miles from Caramanga to the revolutionary port of Acaibo at the other end of the island."

"Very simple," I said ironically.

"It would be done at sea. While the planes are being
shipped. It could be worked out."

"How? Bribery, or do you know a captain who's prepared
to go in for barratry?"

"Nothing like that. The captain of this boat can't be got
at. No, it would just be a straightforward take-over by you."

"By me?"

"Why not? Libertad's agent is in Barranquilla at the
moment. You could fix the details with him."

I stood up and went to the window. My lieutenant was
sitting comfortably in the car and boys and girls had joined
hands and were circling around it, chanting derisively.

"You must be off your head, Barrau. You're talking about
piracy."

"I suppose you could call it that," Barrau agreed.

"You can't call it anything else. Just plain piracy. The
moment it was done I'd have to go well away from here, and
lie low for a hell of a time. No thanks. I'm hard up and I
want to be able to go on working. Lord knows, I don't make
a fortune out of your jobs. But they all have some appearance of honesty. You go find yourself another pirate."

"I can do, I suppose. But I naturally give you first chance.
The money is very good, you know. Ten thousand American
dollars now. Forty thousand more in Acaibo when you
deliver. It is a lot of money."

"And I'd be a marked man for a long time. No thank
you."

Barrau pursed his fat lips and blew gently as though he
were fanning embers that needed careful coaxing. "Think it
over. There's no need to decide for a couple of days. Even
if you know you are going to say No—just think it over."
He stood up, smiling. "You want the beach house again?"

He had a small cottage down at Puerto and usually he
lent it to Drea and myself when I came back from a job. She
could always get away from the hotel for a few days so that
we could be on our own.

"I suppose so. But you can scrub this other thing."

"Maybe. But it is so much money, I thought I should give you the chance. You will, of course, understand that all I have said to you is in confidence."

I grinned. "Everything you say to me in this office is in confidence." I turned towards the door. "But you're way off this time."

"You may change your mind."

"Not over this."

Back at the hotel I was heading for the bar when Drea came through from the dining-room which overlooked the terrace. She was wearing a white dress and I was relieved to see my topaz brooch pinned under one shoulder.

I smiled at her and said, "Are you still slamming doors on me? Or can I say how beautiful you look?"

"I'm not sure."

"Then I must do something about it. Did you get my note?"

"Yes."

"I thought we might have a bite down at Puerto. We can stay down there in Barrau's beach hut. Can you manage that, or are you too busy here?"

For a moment I thought I caught some hesitation in her. Then she said, "No, I can get away. An hour from now?"

"Fine."

She put up a hand and touched the brooch. "Thank you for this. How the hell are you going to pay for it?"

I smiled. "Name anything you want and I'll get it—and worry about payment afterwards."

"Miracle man—that's your trouble. You've been down to see Barrau?"

"Had to clear up a few odds and ends."

"I can imagine."

"Barrau's all right. He's just doing his best in a difficult world. Out of his office he's just a happy family man, four lovely children and a wife who adores him. Just as I adore you."

"His third wife—and strictly for kitchen work." But she smiled and I felt forgiven.

"An hour from now then. I'll phone Puerto and order a table and afterwards we'll sit and watch the sea and listen to what the wild waves have to say."

I took her hand and kissed it. Her anger was gone. That was a good thing. Puerto was our special place and not built for arguments.

*   *   *

We drove down to Puerto and had dinner and then danced for a while. Then we drove out along the beach road towards Barrau's place. Somewhere along the road we drew in and stopped under a clump of palms. We sat there watching the knee-high drift of fireflies under the trees and the faint stippling of phosphorescence where the water touched the white shell beach. Drea was alongside me, happy and relaxed, and everything was perfect. I leaned over and kissed her. When, after a while, she drew her head back I saw the starlight touch her eyes, tiny points of diamond brilliance. I lit a cigarette for her and put it between her lips. She drew at it and then let the smoke go with a long sigh.

I said lazily, "This is really us. This is how it should be always. No slamming doors, no scoldings."

She nodded. "This is how it could be always if you'd be different. But you like trouble. You like uncertainty. Like living on hope."

"You mean I'm an optimist?"

"Yes. And the trouble with optimists is that they won't face facts. They're convinced that somewhere along the line a miracle is going to happen which will put everything right."

"What's all this in aid of?"

I leaned forward and kissed the sweet curve of her throat. She gave a shrug of her shoulders.

"Nothing, just talk."

I gave a little laugh and put my arm around her.

"You're not still worrying about me? I'm here, look. Right alongside you."

I reached out for her. For a moment she hung back, looking at me with an expression I couldn't quite place. Then with a sigh, as she slid into my arms, she said, "Yes, here we are. The golden moment that shuts out the future. So the world's all right and must go on that way. Oh, Keith, darling, you're impossible. What the hell do I do about you?"

I didn't try to answer that one, because it didn't seem to need an answer. Somewhere on the highway behind us a car went by with its horn blaring and its headlights probing along the low run of sand dunes. My body was suddenly hard against hers and my lips on hers and there was nothing in existence except the surrender to the golden moment. What was there to worry about? People worried too much and too often, racking themselves with cares that passed, that would have passed quicker if only they hadn't clung to them. Feeling the movement of her body against mine and her arms about me, I was content with the only miracle which a man and woman could truly know.

She eased away from me and looking down at her I bent and kissed her cheeks, her eyebrows and her lips with tenderness. She reached up gently with her fingers and touched my chin. It was a gesture so familiar . . . the feather tap of her fingers acknowledging love.

Very softly she said, "Why did you have to be on that river boat . . . Why?"

I didn't have to answer that one either. I had been. That old river boat, stern wheeling up to Bogota five years ago. . . .

Our lips came together and there were no more words.

*   *   *

Barrau's cottage was at the head of a small cove that looked north-west to the sea and to the dark line of the Isla Verde. There was a chain link fence round the property, shutting off about three acres and the beach. The cottage had a large living-room opening to a verandah that overlooked the sands, a couple of bedrooms and a kitchen. We had it all to ourselves for two days, with the world safely on the other side of the fence. Two blissful days and nights.

Drea was wonderful. She made no more reference to the trouble I had got into on my last trip. The brief storm was over and the sun shone. We kept no time-table; we bathed and ate and drank when we felt like it. Just Drea and myself, and if I was happy I also knew that I was lucky because Drea was the only woman I wanted and I blessed the moment when I had walked aboard that river boat. A man could go a lifetime and not find what I had found. When the thing happens there is no questioning it. Everything you share together takes on a beauty and rareness which makes you both unique, which shuts out everyone and everything else.

In the mornings she was lazy about getting up, and I would go down for a swim by myself and come back and make coffee to wake her. I would sit by her bed and kiss her and sleepily she would laugh at the taste of brine on my lips, and during the long day we would lie on the sand letting the sun beat at us and now and again her hand would reach across for mine and we would lie there in silence, utterly content.

On our last morning I was up early as usual and went down to have a swim, and as I came back up the beach the low sun threw long black shadows across the sand. To my surprise when I got back, Drea was up and dressed and in the kitchen making coffee.

"Good Lord, what's the matter with you?" I caught her by the shoulders and spun her round and, laughing, kissed her. "Where's my old slug-a-bed, this morning?"

She smiled and said, "I felt like getting up." Then she turned from me and went on preparing the coffee. I carried the tray out on to the verandah for her and we sat with our hands cupped round the coffee mugs, watching the day warm up.

Usually over our coffee she chatted away but this morning she was silent, just staring out to sea. I thought that perhaps she was hating the thought of going back to Barranquilla. Myself I could have stayed on the beach for ever.

I said, "Why don't you 'phone the hotel? Tell 'em you'd like to take a couple more days. They wouldn't mind."

She turned and looked at me and I caught a suggestion of her lips trembling. I put my mug down and moved to take her by the arm, but she stood up and walked a few steps up the verandah. I would have followed her, but she said:

"Stay where you are, Keith."

Puzzled, I asked, "What's the matter?"

She was silent for a while and then with an odd sort of forced calmness in her voice, she said, "There's something I've got to say to you, Keith. And I'm going to hate saying it."

I looked across at her, not understanding. Then lightly, I said, "Well let's have it then. Get it off your chest."

After a moment's hesitation she said, "Well, it's nothing very new really. It's just——"

I got it then and broke in quickly, "Oh, Drea—not that. Not on our last morning. You're not going to start fussing about this bullet business."

"That's part of it."

"But that's nonsense. We've had all that. This is our last morning here. Forget it."

She turned then and faced me squarely and her face was serious. She said firmly, "That's just it, Keith. This is our last morning here or anywhere. Keith . . ." I saw the rise of her lovely shoulders as she breathed. "Keith . . . unless you change your way of life, I'm leaving you for good."

I sat there, wondering if I'd heard her aright. Leave me for good?

Sharply, I said, "What the hell are you talking about?"

She shook her head. "You know, only you won't face it. I should have made this stand years ago. I tried to once but you came after me and I wasn't strong enough to go through with it. But I am now. No matter how much I love you, I'm leaving you unless you alter."

It was a quick outburst and it brought me to my feet, moving towards her, but she waved me away.

"No, don't come near me. Stay there."

I stood looking at her, my hands going automatically for a cigarette.

"Drea. . . . What's got into you? What's wrong with me? What's all this about change?"

"You really don't know? You really don't?" For a moment a tired smile touched her lips.

"No, I don't," I said. "I've never known a piddling little bullet scrape upset you as much as this before. It can't be that. But whatever it is, you'd better let me have it straight. What's so wrong with me?"

Her head came up, her chin firming. "Everything's wrong. The way you live, and the way you expect me to fit into the pattern. God knows, I've tried. But I can't go on like it. For five years I've been wondering what was happening to you while you were away. And when you're back, it's spoiled because I'm wondering when you will be off again. The only time I've ever been free from anxiety was after we first met and we had that holiday in St. Thomas. I've told you all this before, but you've never taken any notice. Or you haven't believed me. Keith . . ." she paused, looking frankly at me, "you've got to change. Otherwise, I'm leaving you."

"Change? But how can I? I can't be dishonest with you. People can't suddenly start being different because they're in love."

"Why can't they? That's something you can expect from love. I'm not what I was at eighteen. I'm changing all the time. Why can't you? Aren't I worth the effort?"

"Drea, you know it isn't that. I'd do anything I could for you."

"Then why should it be so difficult for you to be a little more like other men?"

A little sourly, I said, "Other men? You want a man who comes home every day from some office. Steady, reliable?"

"Why not?"

"So that's it."

I went and sat on the verandah steps, digging my toes into the loose sand at the bottom. I'd never seen Drea like this before. She'd blown me up many times. But this was different. Her mind was made up and she wasn't going to change it. Somehow I knew that even if I got near her, got my arms around her, it would mean nothing this time. She was armoured against me. And the hell of it was that I didn't really have any way in words of explaining to her why I couldn't be like other men. . . . I just didn't see life in terms of any routine, clock watching, settling down into a steady groove, putting myself into a cage where I could only prowl four steps up and four back. I hadn't thought that she honestly minded so much how I lived. I hadn't thought that her anxiety for me was more than passing, storm and then sunshine. You had to be what you were, you had to find the way which was your way. . . . I had to be on my own, indifferent, honest, maybe, but my own master. But now here was Drea wanting me to be a different person. If I didn't she would go. The last time I'd been lucky, I'd got her back. Supposing I wasn't so lucky again. But the thought of Drea leaving me was like a black cloud over the morning sun.

I looked up at her. She was keeping her eyes off me, her attention on the stretch of beach and the far run of sea.

I said, stalling, "You really mean this?"

"I do . . . God, I do. And, Keith, don't try and pretend that I don't mean it. I love you, but I can't take the waiting and wondering any longer. Do anything but these Barrau kind of jobs and I'll be with you always and through everything. But not this way. Never again."

"God, I don't know what to say to you! How can anything break us up? We'd be lost without each other."

"That's what's made it so hard for me. But my mind's made up. Don't fool yourself, Keith. I mean it. We're wonderfully in love. It's all I've ever wanted. But I can't live with it any more your way. It's up to you, Keith."

She turned slowly and came down the verandah towards me. The morning breeze teased the edge of her dress, and caught lightly at her hair. I loved her more in that moment than I had ever done before or ever thought possible. She came and sat by me and her arms were wrapped tightly across her breasts, almost as though she were cold. She was holding herself in, showing me that all the hunger of love in her, all that was between us, couldn't break out and make a nonsense of what had been said. She meant every word and wasn't going to weaken.

I put my hands on her shoulders, leaned forward and kissed her gently. But she was armed against any kind of magic.

I said, "O.K. You put it squarely. I'm not losing you. I'll just have to look round."

It sounded lame. It was lame. I was coming down with all the engines gone and the wings shaking themselves to hell. . . .

She said, "I must go and pack. I've got to be back at the hotel by mid-day."

She got up and just for a moment her hand touched the side of my cheek. I put up my own hand to catch at hers, but it was gone and I heard the verandah boards creak as she went away from me.

* 3 *

THAT afternoon I went down to the hotel swimming pool to cool off. I was feeling pretty low. I'd gone gaily along without once stopping to think about what was happening to Drea. I really had thought that she hadn't minded, that her outbursts of concern on my return from various jobs had been no more than temporary displays . . . not meaning much, just unloading the kind of tension which women so easily build up. But I couldn't believe that any longer. She really had suffered and would go on suffering. I ought to have seen that. Selfish, unobservant and taking too much for granted. . . . I lay there calling myself quite a few names.

I sprawled in a deck chair and held a magazine in front of my face to ward off any social chat from the few other people using the pool. I didn't read. I was thinking about Drea. I remembered our first meeting on the river boat . . . and later at Bogota. Almost from the start she must have been seeing just what kind of relationship she was letting herself in for. She had kept pushing the truth away, but gradually it had caught up with her until she could no longer ignore it. The first moment of hesitation, I saw now, had been in the hotel at Bogota. But then it had been no more than an instinct . . . giving out some feeble unheeded warning.

I'd made a nice little packet from my job at Bogota and had been ready to splash it. Her hotel appointment there hadn't turned out well and I knew that she was ready to leave it.

I walked into her bedroom one evening and handed her a bunch of tickets.

"I'm flying to St. Thomas tomorrow. A month's holiday." I nodded at the tickets. "There's everything there you need. The plane leaves at nine tomorrow."

She looked from the tickets to me and then walked away and fixed a couple of drinks. My heart was in my mouth. Despite all that had happened between us so far we were both unsure, both maybe still a little shy. For the last four days I'd felt that from now on everything I wanted to be and to do was linked with her. She came back and handed me my drink. I didn't touch her. We didn't kiss one another as we usually did over the first evening drink. A custom only a few days old but already a part of the thing which was building in us.

She leafed through the wad of tickets.

"St. Thomas? That's in the Virgin Islands?"

"Yes."

"You sure you've got the right girl?" She said it with a hint of a smile and her green eyes narrowed.

"Two seats. For tomorrow at nine. I know a chap up there who runs a small hotel."

She handed me back the tickets, shaking her head. "One seat. You can get a refund on the other."

I didn't argue. And she didn't turn up. But before I took off I scribbled her a note and enclosed her tickets.

The man I knew was called Marty James, an Englishman, who owned this rather run-down hotel on the eastern end of a little offshore island. He had a wife, a palish, washed-out creature. They were both good-natured, charming and inefficient. The place was no more than a comfortable, easygoing shambles which would have made a first-class tourist shudder.

Drea turned up two days later. There were no explanations. We were both committed. And for a month we lived in our own world.

At the end of the month I had a cable from Barrau. He wanted me for a job. I told Drea about it while we were having drinks on the beach below the hotel.

Drea said, "I don't want you to go."

I laughed. "Do you think I want to go? But money runs out and I've got to work to get more."

"What kind of work?"

"It's just a commission job for Barrau. Wants me to

handle the sale of some lorries in Venezuela." They weren't lorries but there was no point in Drea knowing that.

Some children were splashing about at the water's edge and their shouts were bright, echoing over the sands. A launch went by a couple of hundred yards out with a fat man in a red shirt sitting in the fishing chair.

Drea was so silent that I put my hand on her arm and said, "Cheer up. I'll do the job. It won't take long and we'll come back if you like. Or find somewhere else."

She turned to me then, giving me a long look.

"Do you remember what Marty said the other evening?"

"He says so many things."

"About the hotel, I mean."

I remembered then. Marty usually joined us for a drink at the bar before dinner. His wife didn't like the place much and he'd said that if he could get a cash offer he'd sell up and go back to England.

I said to Drea, "You know why he said that? He wants to get back to England. He knows you're in the hotel world. Probably thinks you could find him a buyer."

Drea leaned forward. "Maybe I could. This place could be a goldmine."

"You think so? Looks pretty run-down to me."

"That could be changed."

I was silent for a moment as a thought struck me, then I said excitedly: "But why not? Why don't we take it? Between us we could get it going. You could run the hotel side. And it needs a launch or a small schooner to take guests offshore fishing, charter parties to the other islands. I could do that."

"Oh, Keith . . ." the eagerness came bursting from her. "Do you mean it? Do you really think we could?"

"Sure, why not. It's the kind of job for both of us."

Enthusiastically she said, "Then why don't we go ahead, Keith? Oh, Lord—we could do it. You wouldn't know this place."

I laughed. "Must be fun to run your own show. But there's always the one snag."

"What?"

31

"Money. Marty wants cash. Twenty thousand dollars. I've got two hundred dollars in the world."

"I've got four thousand."

"It wouldn't stretch."

"Not at the moment. But Marty isn't going to sell this place quickly. If we saved for the next six months we could make half of it and get the rest on mortgage. Put the money you earn away, and we could do it. . . ."

We got quite excited and we decided to do it. But it faded. A couple more jobs for Barrau that didn't quite come off, and then a couple more, and then the whole business was forgotten. That had been five years ago.

Lying there in the sun, I heard Drea's voice from that morning saying, "The only time I've been free from anxiety was after we first met and had that holiday at St. Thomas." It was a hell of a thing to say. But I could see now that it was true. I'd forgotten all about the hotel. But I knew Marty was still there.

Remembering our past excitement it was hard to realize that I'd forgotten all that until now. If I'd really stuck into some lousy job and saved we could have had the hotel years ago. If I'd even saved some of the big money I'd earned with Barrau we could have had it. The thing had gone from my mind completely. I wondered if Marty was still there. God, what a fool I'd been.

I got up, took a plunge to cool off, and then went back to the hotel.

As I went by the desk I found myself turning aside. I went up to it and asked for a cable form. I filled it up and gave it to the clerk.

Three hours later a boy brought the reply up to my room where I was changing.

Still for sale. Twenty-five thousand. Give you a two month option for two thousand dollars. How are things? Long time no see. Marty.

I sat by the window with a whiskey and thought it over. Twenty-five thousand. I couldn't even have done it in matchsticks. Two thousand option. I had about two hundred dollars to my name.

The answer was obvious. There was one quick, direct way to what I had to have. I fenced with myself for about half an hour and then I telephoned Barrau and told him I was coming down to see him. There was no harm, anyway, in getting a little more information.

*　　*　　*

Barrau didn't show any surprise. He didn't ask any questions either about my reasons for coming back to him after turning the job down originally.

He said, "It's fifty thousand dollars gross. Ten thousand now and the rest in Acaibo. You should clear thirty thousand, at least. If you want to do it you must see Libertad's agent who is in Barranquilla at the moment."

"Where?"

"At the *Polo Norte*. It is convenient for you, no? I will give you the introduction and then I am out of it."

"Except for your commission?"

"It is small. I am just finding and introducing you."

"And the introduction at the hotel?"

"You simply write *Amairi* on the back of your card and send it up to Room 15. The rest will follow."

"What the hell does *Amairi* mean?"

Barrau gave a fat giggle. "It is the agreed code word. For use on the telephone for reference and so on. It's an anagram of *Mara II*, which is the name of the ship which carries the planes. I thought it was good."

"I'm mad about it." Barrau had a passion for mystery, code words and the secret rendezvous. Underneath his mountain of flesh was a romantic small boy delighting in a complete spy's outfit. He'd called our last operation *Salvavida*, which was Spanish for lifebelt. I'd finished up swimming three miles down river without one and with a bullet wound in the right arm.

"These precautions are necessary," said Barrau firmly.

I said, "If I do this, everything would be in my hands? Right down to the last screw? And the people I pick?"

"Everything."

I took a cigarette from his desk box and blew a smoke screen between us.

"About your commission. I pay you?"

"Yes."

"How much?"

"Fifteen per cent."

I blew the smoke away so that he could see my face clearly. "Think again."

"Not fifteen on the whole sum—but on what you make. Your expenses then are commission free. It is generous."

"Five," I said firmly. The expenses would be high and with what was left I wanted Marty's place and a small schooner or launch, and there would be other things, too.

Barrau exploded. "But this is ridiculous! Amigo, you make me angry."

I gave him a smile. We always had this pantomime.

"Five," I repeated. "Or find someone else. This isn't a job you can farm out easily. I'm taking all the risk. You just sit here."

"You are wrong," said Barrau. "There are plenty of others."

"Then you'd better find someone else." I turned and went towards the door. But I knew he would never let me get outside.

With my hand going out for the door knob he said, "All right. Seven and a half."

I turned and shook my head. "Five."

He gave in then, his plump shoulders slowly collapsing in resignation.

"As you say. Five. But this is not like you to be so hard. Think of my expenses, too."

"I daren't. It would break my heart. I'll give you a ring after I've been to Room 15. You get your commission after the job is done. If it goes wrong, we're both out."

He nodded.

I went down to my car, knowing that if I did it and it went wrong I would certainly be out. Even before I could begin I had Drea to face.

34

Back at the hotel I checked on Room 15. It had been taken two weeks previously by a Señor Gracioso Fondes from Puerto Rico. I wondered how true that was. He probably had a choice of passports. I wrote Barrau's childish code word on the back of my card and gave it to the boy to take up.

Five minutes later the boy found me in the bar and asked me to go up to Room 15.

*　　*　　*

I knocked and the door was opened. A girl stood back to let me enter. It was the sitting-room of the suite and the only light came from a table lamp by the curved settee near the window. There were some bottles and glasses on a tray on the centre table.

The door closed behind me and the girl came round the far side of the table. She stood there and fidgeted nervously.

"Señor Fondes?"

"He's not here at the moment. You are Mr. Marchant?"

She spoke English and there was no mistaking the American accent.

"I am. Where is he?"

"He's out. But it is all right. You can talk to me. Señor Barrau has already telephoned me."

"Who are you?"

"I'm sorry. Katrina Davia. You would like a drink? Whiskey?"

I nodded and watched her as she took the bottle. She wasn't used to whiskey, that was clear—or maybe she'd got the wrong impression of me. She almost filled a tumbler and hesitated with her hand on the siphon. I gave her a smile and moving forward took the tumbler and poured half of the whiskey into another glass and then filled my own with soda.

"I put too much? It is not a drink I understand."

"It's fine," I said. "When will Señor Fondes be back?"

She didn't say anything for a moment. She just stood there and looked at me over the table lamp. She was, I supposed,

35

about twenty, a tall, slim girl with dark, smooth hair tied back loosely on the nape of her neck. She was a bit coltish, but she held herself well and the green linen dress was well-cut. There was a little gold chain around her neck, dropping into the top of her dress. And she was good-looking. Not in the way that did anything for me, but in a quiet, dark, almost gentle way, like any one of a hundred girls you could see every night in any city making the walk round the plaza with their parents, eyes down, subdued, afraid to look at life until Mama told them it was safe, everything arranged for them through confirmation up to marriage.

She took the other tumbler in which half of my whiskey rested and filled it with soda. She let it swirl in too fast and some of the liquid splashed on to her hand.

"You can talk to me," she said firmly. "My name is Katrina—but not really Davia. I am the sister of Angelo Libertad." She took a sip at the whiskey and then, motioning to the settee, added, "Won't you sit down?"

I sat down and she took a chair by the table.

I said, "You speak English well." I wanted a little time. I wasn't used to doing business with madonna-eyed innocents.

"I haven't been back to Cordillo for eight years. I've been in New York. You can talk to me. It is perfectly safe."

"And Señor Fondes?"

"He went back to Acaibo three days ago. He is a cousin of mine. I have been staying here with him, but my brother needed him back. He's a captain in the People's Democratic Army."

I smiled. It was a good title for an army. The people, democracy . . . just like having a good address to impress the suckers.

I reached out for the telephone and said, "Do you mind if I make a call?"

"Please do."

I rang Barrau's number and was lucky to find him still at his office.

When he answered I said, "Barrau—you know the person I'm supposed to be meeting?"

"Of course. You refer to *Amairi*?"

"What else? Give me a description."

I heard him chuckle at the end of the line, and then he said, "She is charming. Not your type, of course. But if you look closely you will see that she has a tiny mole underneath her right ear."

I put the receiver down and said to her, "I hope you will forgive that but I have been in this business much longer than you." The mole was there.

She flushed a little and there was the hint of annoyance in her eyes.

"I told you that you could talk to me."

"I can now."

Calmly but with a hint still of nervousness she said, "You are a very suspicious person."

"Careful is the word. You have to be if you're contemplating piracy. You realize that that is what it is?"

"I want to help my brother. I realize that. Only that."

"Why did they send you? This is a man's job."

"Gracioso Fondes was going to do it. I met him here from New York with the money I've been collecting."

"Fifty thousand dollars?"

"No. Just over ten thousand. Ten is to be paid here for expenses and the rest in Acaibo. You need not worry about that. It is there waiting."

"You've thought about this thing? You know what it involves?" It was strange talking to her. All wrong. You didn't do this kind of deal with a girl who obviously was as nervous as a kitten underneath.

"It is for you to arrange. That is why you will be paid. The planes are being shipped on the *Mara II* in the next few days. All my brother requires is that the ship should be taken over when it is nearing Caramanga and then diverted to Acaibo. He is prepared to send a boat of some kind out to meet you when you are near Acaibo."

"What line is the *Mara*?"

"She belongs to the *Flota Mercante Interoceanica*. She carries cargo and a few passengers."

"I should need three men besides myself. We must go as

37

passengers and unless we can get bookings there's no point in going on with this."

"Gracioso thought of that. There is already a block booking of three cabins. Two of them are double-berth."

"Well, good for Gracioso. Are you going to be on the boat?"

"Of course. I shall give all the help I can."

"And when we get to Acaibo—what happens to the ship and the rest of the passengers?"

"The ship will be allowed to proceed when the planes have been taken off. I don't think there will be any other passengers, except the mechanic who travels with the planes. If there are they will go away with the ship. My brother is only interested in the planes."

"Who's doing the shipping over here? The Republic of Cordillo will have sent more than a mechanic."

"They have one of their Army officers, a pilot. His name is John MacIntyre Albano and he's the son of their Defence Minister."

"It's a fine name." But not unusual. I'd met this Scots-Spanish combination all over South America. "If he's on the boat I can't see your brother letting him go. He'd be too valuable."

"He won't be on it. He's flying back to Caramanga. Gracioso found this out."

And was probably disappointed, I thought. There was nothing like an important hostage in these affairs. However, I was glad he was flying. I didn't want to hand anyone over to Angelo Libertad.

I said, "You know him, this John MacIntyre Albano?"

"I have met him. Many, many years ago when I was young. He would not recognize me now."

Many, many years ago when I was young. I wondered what kind of man Angelo Libertad was to let her get involved in a business like this. I realized then why Barrau had picked me. Any other of his men would have been unable to resist some kind of double-cross. She would have had her money taken and nothing done for it. And Barrau would have lost his commission.

She said, "You will do it, won't you?"

"All right," I said. "Pay me over the ten thousand dollars and I'll give you a receipt."

"You want the money now?"

It was a silly question but I humoured her.

"The moment I walk out of here the expenses start. There isn't a lot of time. The men I engage won't wait for their money. And there are things to be bought. Do I pay for the passages, for instance?"

"I don't know."

I smiled. "Well, I suppose I do—unless Gracioso has already done that." I discovered later he'd only put down a booking fee.

She got up and went out of the room into a bedroom. I sat and sipped my whiskey and after a while she came back carrying an envelope. She'd probably had to fish her travelling case out and unlock it. The envelope was one of those tough, yellow-looking jobs in which they mail the *National Geographical Magazine*. She handed it to me and I counted it. If she was going to be in this business she must start to learn it thoroughly. Always count the money. It was fifty dollars short of ten thousand and when I told her so she looked worried and flustered in the way women do when they go through their purses after shopping and can't make out why they are short.

"I'll get the rest from my purse," she said.

"Don't bother."

I wrote her out a receipt for nine thousand nine hundred and fifty.

As I stood up I said, "If you could, why don't you go back to Acaibo some other way? I shan't really need you."

"Oh, no. . . . No, I couldn't do that."

"O.K." I reached down and picked up my glass, raising it a little to her. "Well, here's to us."

She took her own glass and drank with me and I could see the quick little wrinkle of her nose as she swallowed.

I said, "You don't like whiskey? You're not used to it?"

She smiled, a sudden frank and warming smile. "It's horrid."

"Stick to orange juice then. You don't have to drink it to impress me. You must be very fond of your brother?"

"I am. Also I believe in what he is doing."

I didn't want to argue about that. He was running a revolution in Cordillo which wasn't going any too well. There was someone who could fill me in on the details with far more accuracy than she could.

I said, "I'm staying at this hotel. I'll get in touch with you tomorrow. But for the time being if you see me around I should pretend that we have never met."

She saw me to the door, a nice, well-brought up girl who would have resented any suggestion that she wasn't capable of looking after herself, that she hadn't begun to know her way around . . . but that was what she was. She'd probably shared a flat with two other girls in New York, had a job in a shop or an office, and at night had mixed with the Cordillo expatriates, holding meetings and collecting money for her brother. She saw herself as a hardened revolutionary, with the usual rosy ideas of liberty, equality and fraternity. They were growths that didn't flourish too well under the Caribbean sun. She'd find that out in time. And because she seemed a nice creature and there was something about her that I liked, I hoped that the process wouldn't be too hard.

I went down to the hotel lobby and wrote a cable to Marty, taking an option on his place. I might have been blind about some aspects of Drea's character, but at least I knew that my only chance of going through with this was to present her with facts. Hard facts from which she couldn't escape. An option taken, and a job accepted that would bring in the money. I was doing the one thing she hated me to do, but I was going to do it for the last time.

40

4

I WENT down early the next morning to see Monk Sandoz.
As I crossed the hallway a woman came out of one of the
adjoining doors and stood at the foot of the stairs blocking
my way. She was new to me, which wasn't any surprise because I hadn't seen Monk for about three months. She was
one of his usual waifs and I could see that the old Monk
magic was working. I could not get up the stairs until she
was certain that I meant him no harm. I could think of very
few people who would want to harm Monk—but all his waifs
went this way, fiercely protective after a few weeks of his
help . . . stray dog, mangy kinkajou rescued from some
miserable side-show, parrot with a broken wing, or a girl
like this whom he'd probably picked up broke in a bar, they
all finished up by fancying that he needed more protection
than they did. Which he didn't, of course. He sent them all
on their way when they were mended or they drifted away
on their own without his noticing it. I don't think he ever
slept with any of the girls he helped. He probably meant to
but never got round to it because somewhere on the way he
was side-tracked by something that really interested him.

"It's all right," I said in Spanish. "I'm a friend of his. Is
he in?"

"He sleeps."

"I'll wake him."

She shook her head.

I smiled. "I've known him years. I've lived in this house."
As I spoke I went to the side of the stairs and looking up
shouted, "Monk!"

I had to shout twice and then heard a door open at the
top of the stairs.

"Who is it?" His voice boomed down.

"Marchant. Call off your bloodhound so that I can come
up."

I heard him laugh. Then he called, "Let him come, Valda."

She stepped aside and watched me go up the first flight of stairs. At the top of the stairs part of the landing wall had been knocked away and he'd fitted up a small aviary that looked out to the yard beyond. It had two rather sick looking Guatemala king birds in it. A sailing dinghy's mast lay up the length of the next flight of stairs and a blue sail was draped over the banisters, neatly patched in three places. Without looking I knew that the stitches would be his, small and neat like all his work; that he could be so precise with his great banana fingers always amazed me.

The door of his room was open. He was standing at a wall mirror, wrapped up in an old brown dressing-gown, and shaving with a cut-throat, his face lathered up to his ears. He grinned at me in the mirror and, screwing up his mouth sideways as he scraped away, said:

"Coffee on the table there. Help yourself. Use my cup. She brings it up every morning. Never touch the stuff as you know. But I dirty the cup to please her. You can do it for me. How are you? Lovely day. Heard you were dead. The land of rumours."

Pouring myself some coffee, I said, "She's new."

"Is she? She's from Cartagena way. Her uncle threw her out. Uncle . . ." he laughed. "The world's full of wicked uncles. Nice kid, but a hell of a cook. Thank God I don't eat at home much. Come to think of it, I don't eat much. Never got over the bottle stage."

I lit a cigarette. The coffee was bitter and strong. "When did you come out of the last one?"

He took a final flick at his face and then examined the ridge of soap-sud along the razor. "About two weeks ago. Don't drink that if you don't like it. She can't make coffee, either. Just dirty the cup. Would you believe it? In this country. Can't make coffee. Maybe that's why uncle threw her out. Poor kid. She's nice though. Sings like a canary when there's no one around."

As he spoke I was thinking that if the last drinking bout had been two weeks since, then he would be all right for my job. There were usually five or six weeks between his sprees. This job would be over in about six or seven days. Not drinking he was utterly reliable.

"Does it fit in?" he asked, watching me for a moment in the mirror and then plunging his face into the hand-basin. I didn't answer while he snorted and blew like a grampus, showering water everywhere. I wasn't surprised that he had taken the point so quickly either. The longer you knew Monk the less susceptible to surprise about him you became. He was a big, bluff-faced man, bald except for a narrow tonsure of hair which had given him the name Monk. I didn't know his real name. Even Sandoz, I suspected, wasn't accurate. I didn't even know his nationality, though it must have been some European mixture, or his history. Sometimes he said that he'd been a cashier of a store in the Bahamas and had money trouble, sometimes that he'd been a dentist and had got into customer trouble, and sometimes that he'd been a tug-boat master who got mixed up in the illegal shipping of narcotics. His best one which he swore to when he was drunk was that he'd been a curator at a zoo and had, through negligence, been responsible for the death of an old man who'd fallen into the bear pit. Maybe they were all right because in his fifty odd years he'd been everywhere and was still travelling. Some things about him, however, were certain. He was usually two jumps ahead of anything you were going to think. Sober there wasn't a mean streak in him and, drunk or sober, he'd never harmed anyone without due cause. His definition of "cause", though, wasn't orthodox.

He turned to me, wrapping his face in a towel and repeated, "Does it fit?"

I nodded and said, "Yes, but it could mean you won't be able to come back here."

He waved a big hand and his dressing-gown fell apart to show a gorilla-haired chest. "Pooh! Nothing. I can open a boarding house anywhere." Seeing his open gown he stared down at his nakedness and then patted his paunch. "Filling up. I need exercise. Thought of taking up golf again. Know I was once runner-up in the Dutch open? Fact. Haven't touched a club since. . . ." He paused and then gave a little

43

shrug of his big shoulders. "Well, tell me about it while I dress."

I told him what the proposition was and roughly how I thought we should handle it. All the time I was talking he was wandering round the room collecting his clothes and dressing. It was the untidiest room in the world. It gave you the impression that at some time or other he expected to be isolated here by some cosmic catastrophe and that he had gathered up all the odds and ends he felt might be useful for survival. There were no food stores, of course, for he wouldn't need any food. But there were a couple of crates of whiskey and a shelf full of brandy bottles. He jerked aside the bed covers looking for a neck-scarf which he had draped over the end of the bed. A cat with one battle-scarred ear drooping crawled out from the foot of the bed and, arching its back and purring loudly, began to sharpen its claws on the sheets.

"Sarah," he said, "a real old Madam."

"You can see," I pointed out to him, "that you can't come back here. Not for a long time, anyway. What about all this stuff and this house?"

"Don't worry. I'm due for a move. Valda can take over here. How much do I get?"

"You name it." I wouldn't argue with Monk over money.

"Let's see?" He picked up the cat and ran a hand over its muzzle affectionately. "Fifty thousand dollars. . . . You'll need two other people, some kind of arms, possibly the passages and Barrau's commission. Normally I'd say five thousand dollars. But this time I'll settle for two thousand now."

"What do you mean, this time?"

He dropped the cat gently to the bed and began to pull on a linen jacket over his sky blue shirt.

"You need the money more than I do. You wouldn't have accepted this otherwise. We won't argue about it. The man who's coming out best is Angelo Libertad. For fifty thousand he's getting six planes worth a damned sight more than that."

I pulled out the yellow envelope from my pocket and began to count out dollars. "Two now," I said, "and another

44

three thousand when I collect in Acaibo. No argument. What about the other two men? They've got to take orders and work fast, and they've got to look as though they're passengers. Just a couple of toughs that every shipmaster knows won't do."

He went towards the door. "I'll get the Hueica brothers. They've just sold up their taxi business and want to get back to Guatemala. They could use five thousand between them. Tomez is the brains and the mouth. Sardi is the body, the hands. They'd kill their grandmother if the price were right. But if you say go gentle, then they'll go gentle."

"I want it gentle. That way the thing will blow over quicker afterwards."

He opened the door to call for Valda but she was already coming across the landing with a cup and saucer in her hand.

"I bring a cup for your friend for coffee."

"Good girl." He took the cup and saucer and patted her on the cheek in the same way that he had fondled the cat. "Now go and tell the Hueica brothers to come up here."

"Hueica?"

"The little dark ones. Room with the broken wash-basin."

He shut the door and turned back to me.

"Another one to dirty." He filled the cup with cold coffee, swilled it round and jerked the liquid into the basin. Then seeing the yellow envelope in my hands he went on, "Count out their five thousand now and then put that away. Don't let 'em ever see your accounts." He sat down on a whiskey crate and began to roll a cigarette, doing it deftly with one hand while he looked up at me and said:

"You know the Cordillo set-up?"

"Only roughly."

"That's the word—rough. Angelo's been at it for a couple of years. It's the usual stuff. Land reform, a better deal for the peasants, abolition of privileges, Cordillo for the Cordillans. He's got some points. So have the other side. But he's too much of an idealist. That's what makes it tough for him. He's doing this on a shoe-string. If he wanted to, he could have had a dozen backers with plenty of cash—as long as he paid them off afterwards with concessions, oil rights, trans-

45

port agreements and exploitation grants. Plenty of pickings in Cordillo. But he won't do it. He's not selling out to the oil, fruit or mineral people."

"He's getting money, though."

"Sure. From the workers. Collections all over the place. But there's a bottom to that kind of well. As for the military position——"

He broke off as there was a knock on the door.

"Come in," he called.

The door opened and shut and they were in; the Hueica brothers, two small, dark-skinned little men in white suits and flowered American ties topped by neat, friendly smiles. They looked very much alike, except—as I learned when Monk introduced them—Sardi was the one with a thin pencil line of moustache. They were Guatemalan born and clearly had a lot of Indian blood. I explained to them what I wanted and that I would pay them five thousand dollars between them. Sardi said nothing and Tomez in a gentle little voice said, "Yes, señor." He took the money, counted it carefully, and then split it, handing Sardi his share. I told them to stay on tap in the house and that Monk would give them their instructions.

I finished, "From Acaibo, you find your own way home. That understood?"

Tomez nodded and said, "Yes, señor."

When they were gone, I told Monk that I would fix the passages. He could go aboard the *Mara II* tomorrow and look over the lay-out. We would make our final plan on board. It was a three-day trip to Caramanga. We wanted to take over on the second night out. That meant we could get the *Mara II* into Acaibo late the following night. The four of us could hold the ship for twenty-four hours. And it could possibly be less if Angelo sent out a boat to meet us.

When I left Monk I went to the shipping office and took up the reservations for the four of us. Señor Fondes had paid a hundred dollars deposit. I had the passage bookings for Monk and myself made out under false names. Smith for myself and Grusman for Monk. It wasn't the first time that Monk and I had travelled under false names. Barrau would

46

fix the passports. There was sure to be a lot of stir when this job was done, though I guessed it would quickly die away, particularly when Angelo Libertad's people took over and Cordillo became respectable. Anyway, I didn't want the police to be looking for Keith Marchant. Mr. Smith they could chase for ever. I asked the clerk who else was on the passenger list and he pushed it across for me to see. Señorita Katrina Davia and a Señor H. Parks were the only other two.

"Six, is that all she'll take?"

"No, señor. Twelve. But from here there are never many. She picks up more at Caramanga."

After the shipping office I went along to Barrau and found him with his bottom still in his chair and his feet on the desk.

He gave me a warm, commission-flushed smile and said, "How do you find the little señorita?"

"She's a child. Angelo wants his head examined."

"He's not such a fool. No one knows the family connection. Any of his men over here would cause comment. It was unwise for Fondes to come. Maybe that's why he changed his mind and went back. You have found the people to go with you?"

"Yes. Monk Sandoz, and a couple of brothers Hueica."

"Ah, Monk. Yes, he is all right. And the little taxi-men. They had to sell up because the big boys don't like these little operators. Don't be taken in by their smiles . . . Sardi especially. He can be very fast, like a *fer-de-lance*. And now?"

"I want false passports for Monk and myself, and arms. No revolvers. They don't impress on this kind of affair. Four sub-machine guns, not too heavy. I want them aboard in a suitcase in my cabin tomorrow evening. Locked. The key to me at the hotel. And fifty rounds for each. You can manage that?"

He nodded. "Expensive, though. One hundred dollars each. The passports come free—for you."

"Four hundred dollars? Are you mad?"

"I have to get them aboard past the customs. You know how to do that without money? Besides, why should you worry? When you get to Acaibo, you can flog them to Angelo's people at a profit. The current rate for what you

47

want is about a hundred and twenty dollars a gun over there."

I paid him four hundred dollars. By the time I had paid the hotel option, and a few other debts, including Drea's topaz brooch, I was going to step aboard the *Mara II* with very few dollars in my pocket. However, once in Acaibo things would be different.

As I was about to leave, Barrau said, "Where do you go after this is all over?"

"I can't come back here, and I don't want to. From Cordillo I shall go on to Haiti—it's less than a hundred miles north. I'll work something out from there. I'll send you your commission."

"This I know . . ." He stared at the end of his pointed black crocodile skin shoes on the desk. "You need this money bad, eh?"

"Why do you say that? I always need money."

"But not so bad that you beat me down so much on commission. That is not like you."

"Times are hard," I said.

He shook his head, his chins flopping loosely. But he said no more.

I went down the stairs past the poorly lit Madonna and out into the yard. There were no children about and the heat came up off the stones full of smells. The old woman of the Lima beans stood in the doorway of her hut and watched me climb into the car. She came slowly over and held out her hand. I gave her twenty centavos, but I wasn't sure whether it was just charity or whether she felt there had been an unspoken agreement between us for looking after the car.

I drove slowly down to the docks and found the *Mara II*. I didn't want to go aboard yet. I just wanted to have a look at her. I parked alongside a warehouse and then strolled across the rail tracks.

She was a biggish cargo boat. By the look of her she hadn't long had a repaint and her single stack was banded with the house colours of blue and maroon. The bridge and cabin superstructures were set well aft to accommodate a long foredeck and cargo well. Her bows went up high and sheer, giving her a racy, thrusting look.

There was an officer out on the starboard bridge wing directing loading operations. Alongside there was a lorry, just a cab with a long, articulated chassis, and squatting on it, wings dismantled, was a Hawker Sea Fury. It looked like some stranded, mutilated insect. Slings were coming down from the derricks. There was the usual shouting match between deck and quay parties, the officer on the bridge cutting in now and then with a sharp blast on a whistle. The lorry driver was in the cab, smoking and reading a newspaper.

As I went across a bunch of five or six men came from the left of the lorry and walked slowly the length of the tender, keeping about ten yards away. Two of them carried a banner supported on a couple of poles and the rest trailed behind like a church procession. The banner proclaimed— *Viva Angelo Libertad*. One of the men moved out of the file and thrust a sheet of printed paper into my hand.

I looked it over quickly. It was the usual stuff . . . the workers of Colombia protesting over the sale of planes to the Republic of Cordillo . . . planes that would be used against Angelo Libertad and the workers of Cordillo. None of the men in the procession looked as though he cared a damn about it either way and I guessed they were hired for a few centavos a day to march up and down. They went the length of the *Mara II*, then the pole bearers were relieved by two others. They turned and came back again. They made a sad little procession and no one was taking any notice of them. In this and all the other countries out here few workers cared a button about other workers. If you had a job, you stuck to it because there were plenty of others waiting to take your place. No revolutionary movement stood a chance unless the big boys—the generals, the business men and the politicians —were behind it.

The procession came back past me and, to avoid them, I went forward a few steps. As I did so a man came round the lorry cab and danced up to me, frowning, and growled in English, "Get back there, you! If you want to start bloody

49

agitating, bloody agitate somewhere else. I've got enough on my hands without having to be pestered by you bastards. Workers! Hell's bells, I thought the English workers were bad enough—but this lot!"

He was a short, square-faced man, restless as a pug-dog, and with bushy, sandy eyebrows, and he wore a shiny navy blue serge suit which must have been as hot as hell in this heat. I stood there, the leaflet in my hand, and tried to place his accent. It was that flat, anywhere west of London voice ... Middlesex, Surrey.

He came up closer to me and made an angry sound, and then, flapping his hands at me, said, "O.K. O.K. So you don't understand my lingo. Scarper! Vamos! And if you want to know what to do with that bit of paper in your hand I'll tell you. Bloody politics!" He looked away from me briefly as the dockhands on the lorry began to pass a sling under the tail end of the Fury's fuselage and he clucked to himself just like an old hen.

I said, "I understand the lingo all right. It's my own. And you needn't tell me what to do with the paper." I screwed it up and tossed it away.

He looked at me without saying anything. Then he shook his head and for a moment the square, wrinkled face broke into a smile.

"Sorry, guv'nor. Thought you was one of them. They get on my nerves. They've got 'em up at Soledad, too."

"The airport?"

"Yes. We're bringing this lot down from there. What a job! Excuse me——" He moved away from me and climbed up on to the lorry and pushed his way between the three men who were fiddling with the sling. Someone shouted down from the deck and the officer's whistle blew. I saw the back of his blue serge suit heave up from amongst the men and he shouted, "Hold it! What do you think you're slinging—a crate of bloody oranges? Tell that bastard not to blow his whistle until I give the sign or I'll ..." The rest was lost as he went to examine the sling fixing.

I went back to the car, smiling. Señor Parkes, without a doubt. How was he going to feel when I took his beloved

..anes from him? I'd met his kind many times amongst ground staff. They were the ones who really kept you aloft. Though never flying, they had more love for the machine than anyone else, ready to swear at any ignorant who didn't respect the beauty of their charges.

I watched the operation for a while. It looked to me as though they might get perhaps four of the planes below deck. They were just under forty feet long. Some would clearly have to be deck cargo.

*   *   *

That evening I took Drea to a place down the river for dinner. You could sit on a balcony, hung with vines, overlooking the Magdalena. The darkness over the water was studded with the lights of small craft and now and again there was the slow, brilliantly lit crawl of big stuff coming in from the sea. In the room behind the balcony was a band and we had a couple of drinks and danced for a while before eating. We didn't talk much. Since she had issued her ultimatum we had never referred to it, but it was with us both. Quite frankly I didn't know how to get things started. I'd well committed myself now. All that remained was to get her agreement.

In the end, over our coffee and liqueurs, I said bluntly, "I'm sailing for Caramanga in a couple of days."

She watched me across the table, one hand playing with her little silver cigarette lighter. She said nothing, so I went on, "I've got a job there, and I want to talk to you about it seriously, Drea."

Smiling, she said, "It'll be a change for you to be serious. And you know how I feel about your jobs. I hope it's the right kind."

I said quickly, "Let's skip that for the moment. You remember Marty's place at St. Thomas? You know, that scheme we had for taking it over . . . you doing the hotel and me running charter trips, fishing cruises?"

"I remember."

"We're as good as there. I've got a two month option on it."

Her eyes came up quickly. "It's still for sale?"

"Yes. I paid two thousand dollars for the option. It's going for twenty-five thousand. For thirty odd thousand we can fix up a schooner or launch as well."

"I'm sure we could. But where do you get that kind of money, Keith? Another miracle?"

I shook my head. "Not this time. Look, everything you've said about these Barrau jobs is right. I'll do what you say. But you've got to face the fact that places like the hotel at St. Thomas, something that we know is absolutely right for both of us, don't come along so often."

She said quickly, "Why don't you come to the real point?"

"I am."

"No, you're not. You're going round it. Keith, I'm not a fool. You hate the thought of settling down for years and working for something. Marty's place would suit us both, and you want it right away. A lovely short-cut. So how do you get the money?"

"I just want you to give me a chance. St. Thomas would be our place and we'd be together and you wouldn't have any more waiting around worrying while I was away."

"You're talking too fast, Keith! Where and how are you going to get all that money so quickly?"

"Barrau's got a job for me that would bring in all we needed." She was about to speak, but I went on quickly: "It's a simple job, too. No great risk attached to it. All I ask is that you let our old contract run for a couple more weeks. You've stood it for five years. Just let me do this one job—another two weeks at the most. It's a really big chance."

For a moment I thought she was going to stand up and walk away, but I put my hand on hers and she stayed where she was. I saw her breathe deeply, the line of her lips tightening. Then she relaxed, and her free hand went up to her cheek as though she were soothing some sudden spasm of pain.

"Keith," she said, "haven't you really got it into your head that I'm serious? Hasn't it got through to you that you can't go on relying on our love? I meant what I said the other evening. And now here you come back asking for one more mad chance to make a killing. Say I give it to you—and then it fails? I'll have had another spell of anxiety. And up you'll come again asking for another chance, and then another chance, and so it will go on."

"It won't be like that. This time nothing will go wrong. I'm just asking you to give me this one last chance."

She didn't answer for a moment. In the room behind us the band began to play a tango. A man and a woman came along the balcony, his arm around the woman's waist, and they were laughing.

Drea said, "I'm in love with you, God knows. But I'm still learning about you. The trouble is, you never learn about yourself. If you fail this time, you'll want another chance. I could want to give it to you. After all why should I try and tell you how to live? But I'm not going to let myself do it."

"You mean you won't give me this chance? You don't want me to try and get this hotel?"

"Of course I do. But not so much that I'd let you take on some job where you might be killed——"

"That's nonsense!"

"Is it? What kind of job is it? I want the truth, Keith."

"Barrau and I have fixed up an armaments deal and I've got to run the stuff into Cordillo."

"Armaments?"

"For the revolutionaries. The only snag is that there will be some temporary political repercussions. I shouldn't be able to come back to Barranquilla. But then I won't need to. We shall have the hotel. You could meet me somewhere in a week or so." I didn't want to go into details of the job. Even so she was ahead of me on that. She got up from the table and went slowly along the balcony. I followed her, my hand on her elbow. We went down a flight of steps to a small concrete pierhead by the river where there were a few boats tied up. The dank river smell was strong on the air and I found myself thinking of the old river boat going up to Bogota where I had first met her. I had to have this chance. We had to go on being together.

Without looking at me she said, "I can see you don't want

to tell me what the job really is. All right, I don't want to know. But there's something you've got to know. Something which I know about you and which you won't ever believe about yourself."

"Just give me this chance," I said.

"If I do it's for the last time. If it doesn't come off it will be the end. I shall go and you won't be able to stop me."

I put my arm around her, drawing her close to me, "Nothing will go wrong," I said tenderly. "It's a simple job. We're heading straight for that place up in the islands."

She trembled against me and then said, "But have you got it, Keith? Do you really understand? If this chance goes wrong, I'm not going to give you other chances. If this affair goes wrong—then you've lost me, Keith."

I walked her gently towards the end of the pier. "Of course I understand. But frankly, I'm not going to worry about it because nothing will go wrong. And when I'm away don't go working yourself up. . . . There's nothing to it."

She turned then, facing me, standing close to me within my arms.

"You're a liar, Keith, aren't you?" she said softly. "For so much money, this job must be dangerous. Whether I know what it is or not, I shall worry. But it's for the last time. Where do you want me to meet you?"

"In eight or nine days after I leave. I thought Port-au-Prince would be a good place. I can get there easily."

"Port-au-Prince?"

"It just happens to be the most convenient place." I knew what she was thinking. We'd been there three years before when there had been trouble between us . . . the only time until now. Our hotel room had been like an eagle's perch above the town, looking down on the blue bay of Gonave and the green and yellow plains backed by the Boutillier mountains.

"The Hotel Montana," I said. "You may have to wait around for a few days because I'll have to get a passage from Cordillo. But I'll turn up."

She came close to me, her face hidden. "I've hated saying this to you, Keith. It makes me feel bitchy and hard, but I

54

had to make you understand that no matter how much I love you I have to have something else from our love than the things I've had so far."

I put my arms around her and kissed her.

"Darling, don't worry. Everything is going to be all right." I kissed her again and then seeing how miserable she looked, I went on, laughing, "Come on, we'll open a bottle of champagne to the future and dance all night. . . ."

With a little cry she came to me then, collapsing into a fierce hungry embrace, her arms and hands hard and binding round my body. Everything was going to be all right. I was going to make it all right. I loved her and she loved me. She wasn't going to have to refuse me other chances because this was going to be a success.

*   *   *

The next two days passed quickly enough. On the first of them I telephoned Katrina Davia in her room and we had lunch in the town and I gave her a progress report. I asked her if she had any means of communicating with Acaibo and when she said she had—there was a radio ham just outside Soledad who worked for Angelo—I gave her the position and time for a meeting off Acaibo. Monk had worked this out for me. He was the man who knew all about navigation and the likely speed to be logged by the *Mara II*. I told her, too, about Monk and the Hueica boys, but that as far as she was concerned they were to remain strangers except for the normal sea-passage exchanges one couldn't avoid on a boat. As for me, there was no harm in knowing me since we were from the same hotel.

"If anything goes wrong, don't get yourself involved. You know nothing about me, except that you met me at the *Polo Norte*. Monk knows who you are, but the Hueica boys will have no idea you are anything to do with us. They'd sell you off in Caramanga to save their own hides. You've got that? If anything goes wrong—keep out of it."

She nodded a little primly and sat there as though she were being given instructions for a Sunday School treat and

what to do if she got lost. There wasn't any job comparable
to this one even in a small way which I'd ever done when at
some very early point I hadn't got butterflies in the stomach.
She was so raw at this kind of thing that, I could swear, she
hadn't even got as far as that. Which was reasonable, I
suppose. It's not until you hear your first blast of machine
gun fire, or the first dull smack of a bullet meant for you
behind your head that you acquire the grace to be scared.

But she did ask, "Will there be any shooting?"

"If there is it won't be at anyone, I hope. Just a rat-tat or
two to keep people in their places. That's all that's needed."
I hoped that this would be strictly true, but there was no
need for her to have any doubts.

We had a bottle of wine with lunch and towards the end
it loosened her up a little—or maybe she was beginning
to lose her strangeness with me and to see me as a per-
sonality not just as a name among others in a plan—for she
said:

"I suppose it doesn't matter to you which side you work
for as long as you get paid? You'd have done this the other
way round, say?"

"I would. I'm for hire. I don't involve myself in issues.
But once the contract is signed you don't have to worry. I'll
honour it."

"I don't understand. You don't seem like that at all."

"You'd like me to do it for love? The love of an idea?
Take sides?" I shook my head and beckoned the waiter over
to order brandy and coffee. "Not me. I stopped doing that
years ago."

For a moment I thought she was going to go on with her
questions. She thought better of it—but only for a few
moments—because after she'd refused a brandy and while
I was taking my first sip of mine she said:

"But there are some things you wouldn't do for money?"

Momentarily I felt I might be a man from Mars being
questioned about his general ethics. Then I realized that she
was—for all her involvement in her brother's affairs—really
new to my world and my kind of men. She had no idea how
we ticked.

56

Patiently, I said, "Well, let me think, what wouldn't I do for money? Not murder, ill treat babies or animals, steal from those who really miss it . . . quite a few things I suppose. And now, if you've finished your coffee I'll drop you back at the hotel."

There was a note from Barrau waiting for me in my room. In it was the key to the suitcase he was going to have smuggled aboard for me. The note said that he had put in three or four tear-gas grenades as a bonus, and added that he couldn't accept responsibility for their effectiveness if used because they were very old American stock, police issue from the Panama Zone.

I spent the last afternoon packing for the boat and going around town paying off my bills. I finished up at Monk's place for a final word with him. He'd been aboard the *Mara II* and had a look round. She had a Costa Rica registration and most of the crew were Costa Ricans, but the captain was a Greek, and the first mate a French-Canadian. I had a couple of drinks with him and then went back to the hotel and showered and changed.

Drea and I went down to Puerto for dinner and although we both knew that this evening was different from all the others we had spent together we made no reference to it. We laughed and drank and danced, making a hedge around these few remaining hours, looking neither forward nor back. Afterwards we drove along to Barrau's cottage and she made coffee and then we lay on the beach mattresses on the verandah. For a little while as she rested in my arms I could feel her trembling, feel something of the apprehension for us both which was awake in her. And her weakness gave me a sense of strength and almost angry determination. Nothing was ever going to part us. Nothing was going to stop me giving her the future she wanted from me. . . .

Before midnight we drove back to the *Polo Norte* and she sat in the car while I got my cases. Then she drove me down to the dock. She kissed me before I got out of the car.

"Keith, oh Keith, look after yourself."

"I'll be all right. Hang on here and I'll fix it so that you can come aboard for a last drink."

I carried my cases up the gangway to the deck and was met by a steward. I was about to ask him to bring some drinks to my cabin and for permission for Drea to come aboard when I heard the sound of a car driving off. It was Drea going. I stood there and watched the car bump across the tracks, then turn a warehouse corner and disappear.

I didn't mind. This was the way she wanted it. Hating the dragging out of goodbyes. But I would see her again in Haiti. She would always be with me. I could feel the strong chain around my heart. . . .

★ 5 ★

It was a long time before I went to sleep that night. I had a double-berth cabin to myself on the port side. I lay in the top bunk with the light off and listened to the deck noises. We pulled out about an hour after midnight and went down river. I liked moving off. I liked starting something anew. That had been my trouble. I liked new routes and a flexible time-table. I didn't want to stay on one road and pass the same places, the same people each time, every day. There was nothing you could do about it if you were really like that. I'd tried in the past. A man, everyone said, must make something of himself, carve a niche for himself, settle down and prosper. After Korea I'd flown for a time with *Aerovias Brazil,* and then with the *Rutas Aereas Nacionales, S.A.,* in Venezuela. But in the end the routine had got me down and I'd given up fighting the nomad instinct. And now, when I should have been looking forward to this trip . . . yes, looking forward, since whatever I did I had to enjoy otherwise there was no point in it . . . it was to know that too much depended on it. If I failed Drea she would go. Life without Drea. . . . Well, there had been a life without her up to five years ago. I tried to remember back past that, to the girls I'd known and loved. They were just a lot of grey shapes. What is it that one woman has, only one woman in any man's life, the woman who comes early or late and is there for ever? There was no answer to that. Only the fact. Maybe because I wasn't tied to anything else, time, place or ambition, then this one tie took on the strengths that should have gone to the others.

I went to sleep before I got too morbid. I woke early and, locking the cabin door, I checked the arms in the suitcase. They had seen some use but I worked them over, bolt and trigger action, and they were all right. I slipped a full magazine on each one and then locked them back in the case.

When I went on deck there was no land to be seen, just a smooth run of sea and a few puffs of idle cloud high up. Although I was early into breakfast the Hueica brothers were already there. The dining-saloon was small and narrow with one long run of table down it and a small cross-table at the top for the captain and his officers. The Hueica brothers sat side by side half-way down the table, looking very subdued, neat and, I felt, very much aware that they had to show their best party manners. I gave them a nod and sat down at the near end of the table. They bent over their grapefruit, two quiet little men in linen suits and flowered ties, their dark hair plastered tightly over their heads. They looked just like some brother-act, acrobats, jugglers, heading for their next booking.

The steward brought me coffee and toast and as he went away from me I heard him greet someone with *"Buenos dias, señor."*

I looked up as a young fair-haired man began to take a place opposite me. He gave me a smile as he sat down. I saw the Hueica brothers' heads swivel round for a moment to take him in and then go back like marionettes. He was in his twenties, a tall, well-set-up figure in white trousers and a blue blazer with some motif on the silver buttons which I did not recognize. He looked well-tubbed and shaved, and was good-looking in an athletic way, with a squarish, well-marked face. In England I would have put him down as public school, then one of the services, or perhaps a young city type, stockbroker, Lloyds. But his speech as he ordered his breakfast from the steward marked him as good-class Spanish. Since I had seen the passenger list and knew every-one who was to be on the *Mara II,* I decided that he was a late booking. Well, he didn't know it, but he was in for a little excitement.

And then, as I was lighting a cigarette a few minutes later to finish off my coffee, Señor Parkes came into the saloon. He still wore his navy serge suit, but as some sort of concession for being on shipboard he had white deck shoes and carried a panama hat. He sat down alongside the young man who turned to him and said in English:

"Everything all right, Henry?"

"Yes, Mr. Albano. Everything's O.K."

"Good. Now you can relax for a couple of days."

"I'll say. What a caper, eh?" He turned to the steward who had come up and went on, "Tea—and make it strong. And eggs and bacon." He glanced at the other's grapefruit. "That stuff goes sour in my stomach."

I got up to go. What was John MacIntyre Albano, son of the Minister of Defence for the Republic of Cordillo, doing on board?

As I moved, Parkes looked across to me and gave a quick, friendly nod.

"Seen you before, haven't I? Yes, of course."

"Briefly. I was on the dockside."

"That's it. Took you for one of those Libertad agitators."

The young man looked quickly up at me. I laughed. "Don't worry. Agitation's not my line." I introduced myself as Mr. Smith and he half rose and held out his hand.

"Albano," he said. "Parkes here is my right-hand man. You're English?"

"Yes."

"That's nice. I was in England for a spell, at Cranwell. We must have a chat sometime."

"I'd be glad to."

The steward came back and put a plate of bacon and eggs in front of Parkes. As I moved away I heard him saying, "Why do they have to fry 'em in this bloody olive oil? Did the same thing in Yugoslavia when I was there."

I went on deck and walked along under the bridge wing and leaned over the rail, finishing my cigarette. On the cargo deck below me were three Sea Furies, swaddled up in tarpaulins, wings gone, propellers off, looking like enormous mummies in their wrappings. They were roped down to stanchions and one of the crew was swabbing the decks between them.

John MacIntyre Albano, a nice-looking young man, a touch of Scots in him still from some distant marriage . . . the blue eyes, maybe; the square line to the top of his cheek bones. . . . And he was heading straight for Acaibo and

61

Angelo Libertad. I didn't feel at all good about that.

I flipped my cigarette end into the sea and turned away. Katrina had the cabin opposite mine. I hesitated for a moment outside the door. They were going to pay me a great deal of money for this job. Not more than it was worth, but it could be that they were, with my help, taking a quiet bonus for themselves in the shape of Albano. Perhaps I'd made a mistake about Katrina. Perhaps she wasn't as raw to this kind of thing as I imagined. I could feel my anger coming up. I knocked and she called, "Who is it?"

"Marchant."

"Come in."

She was standing by the wash-basin on the far side of the cabin, one foot up on a small stool, and she was painting her toe nails. She looked round and up to me and smiled. She made a pretty picture, young and nice looking, a pleasant girl with her pleated white skirt falling in a graceful line from the angle of her poised knee, the dark hair neatly tied back into a short tail of hair at the back of her neck.

I said, "John MacIntyre Albano is on this boat."

Her foot came down from the stool and she turned to face me, one hand going back and placing the bottle of nail polish on the edge of the basin behind her.

"He can't be. He's flying."

I went across to her and took her firmly by the arm.

"He's on board. I've just had breakfast with him. Did you know this was going to happen?"

"Of course not."

Her face was close to mine and I could see the firming of her mouth, the little movement of her chin.

"He's here. And he's going to finish up in Acaibo. You may not have known it was going to happen. But what about Fondes?"

"He didn't know, either. He expressly said that Albano was going to fly."

"I wonder. I've a damned good mind to call the whole thing off."

"But you can't do that."

"I can. Listen," I let go of her arm; "this job is big enough by itself. If it comes off I'm going to have to tuck myself away for quite a while until it blows over. But if anything happens to Albano it will take ages to blow over. You don't think your brother is just going to let Albano go . . . sail out in the *Mara II* when he's taken the planes?"

She moved away from me, her hands fiddling with one another, long hands with a fresh coat of pale pink varnish on the nails. Then she turned back and her chin tilted up as she looked squarely at me.

"Which are you worried about? Yourself or Albano?"

"Both. I want this thing to go through smoothly and be quickly forgotten. That's for me. And I'm not in any kind of business which goes around body-snatching for a lot of lousy revolutionaries——"

"Don't talk like that!" she said sharply. "My brother is a man of the highest principles."

"Look, let's not argue that one. Albano's here, aboard. What do you think your brother will do with him at Acaibo?"

"I don't know."

"I do. He'll hold him. He's the son of the Defence Minister. That's a good card to have. More than that he's organizing the Republic's half-pint air force. There are six more Sea Furies to come from Colombia. Can you see your brother letting him go off to get on with that job?"

I moved away and lit a cigarette. I was pretty sure that she hadn't expected Albano to be aboard. But that didn't help me or Albano. The only thing I could do to help him was to call the whole thing off. But I couldn't do that. Maybe it was what I should have done, but I couldn't. Drea was going to be sitting in Haiti waiting for me. She meant more to me than all the Albanos in the world. I had a bad case right then of uneasy conscience. I turned back to her. A tiny edge of little teeth was biting at her lower lip and her dark eyes watched every movement I made.

I said, "How close are you to your brother?"

"Close?"

"Yes. To what lengths would he go for you?"

"He's . . . Well, he's got no one else. And neither have I.

He brought me up, saw me educated in America. Did everything for me."

"And you'd do anything for him?"

"Yes."

"How long since you last saw him?"

"Why do you ask that?"

"Just answer," I said impatiently. "How long?"

"Five years."

"And this affair has been going on actively for two years. He's been under a lot of pressure for a long time."

"Nothing could change him. He's absolutely honest and decent." There was no doubting her belief.

"He wants these planes badly. They're vital, aren't they?"

"Yes."

"O.K., then. So if you make a promise on his behalf which will get him the planes, he'll keep it?"

She saw what was coming then and just for a moment I caught the change in her face and knew what it meant. She was young and untouched, but she was learning fast. I knew exactly the doubt in her mind because I had put it there. Two years of fighting, hiding and running in the mountains can change a man, sour him up and knock the shine off his ideals.

"He wants these planes. He must have them. What promise do you want from me?"

"I'll do this job still, if you promise on your brother's behalf to let Albano go."

I was fighting to get some kind of break for Albano so that I could go on with this and get my money. I'd go on anyway, but she wasn't to know this. Barrau, Drea, a hundred other people would have seen through me right away, but not this girl, not yet. A few more years and she'd be wiser. I could see the hesitation in her.

I went on, "He never expected—according to you—to collect Albano with the planes. It won't be any hardship to let him go."

She didn't hesitate then. She said almost curtly, "I have absolute faith in my brother. And I promise. Does that satisfy you?"

64

"Yes."

"Good. And now I think I'll go and have some breakfast."

She went out quickly, leaving me standing there. But I knew she wasn't going to eat any breakfast. She just wanted to get away by herself on deck and get used to the idea of doubting for the first time someone she loved and trusted. I wasn't happy that I'd given her a push towards reality. She was out on deck now wondering whether her brother would stand by her. She would be telling herself that he would, that she had faith in him, but she wouldn't know for certain. Yesterday, she would have staked her life on it. *An unlesson'd girl, unschool'd, unpractis'd; happy in this, she is not yet so old but she may learn. . . .* Happy? Unhappy, I'd say.

I went to find Monk, not feeling that I liked myself much, and wondering just what sort of a chance Albano had. I'd done all I could for him.

Going out of the cabin I almost bumped into Katrina coming back.

"That was a quick breakfast."

For a moment I thought she was going to snap some remark at me, angry with me for making her uncomfortable, but she suddenly smiled and gave a little laugh.

"It was silly of me. I went out without any shoes on."

She looked down at her bare feet and the gleam of fresh paint on her toe nails.

I put a hand gently on her arm and said, "Don't worry. I'm sure it'll be O.K. I only wanted to get things straight."

With Monk it was different. He was lying on his bunk, smoking a cigar and reading. When I came in he rolled off the bunk and took off his glasses which were steel rimmed and repaired on one wing with a neat binding of thin copper wire. I told him about Albano and he rubbed a hand over his bald head and said:

"Changed his mind about flying. Couldn't bear to leave his babies. But he's in the soup now. Why'd they take the propellers off those jobs?"

"For slinging 'em aboard, I imagine. You can smash a propeller easily."

"Why didn't they fly them over?"

"Red tape. Barrau said the Colombian authorities wouldn't admit members of the Republic's armed forces to the country. Albano got in as a civilian member of the Ministry of Defence. I don't like this at all. Do you think Katrina will have any pull with her brother?"

"Could have. My guess is they'll do a deal. Albano goes back in exchange for one of Angelo's men. Caramanga jail is full of prisoners they've pulled in. Anyway, it's not your worry. You start that kind of thing and you'll never get anywhere. Albano's father will take care of it. A straight deal."

"I don't like him aboard, and I don't like her aboard."

I said it almost to myself but I saw his head come up sharply and he gave me a quizzical look.

"Since when have you started kicking against facts? Hold an umbrella over someone in a storm. Act of kindness. Lightning strikes the brolly and away you both go."

"That's good, coming from you. You're always hoisting umbrellas."

"Sure, but I accept the risks. You'd be surprised how many times I've had my wallet lifted. Albano's not your pigeon. Let's go over this job and settle it."

We got down to it, but all the time we were talking I was seeing that first moment of doubt take Katrina's face. I didn't think I was a sentimental type. I'd have betted against it, but there had been something in that moment which had hit me. It was going to take me a little while to push it out of my mind. Monk must have guessed it was with me for he broke off in the middle of our plans once and said:

"The trouble with you is that you've never had any children."

"What the hell's that got to do with anything? Anyway, what do you know about children?"

"Damned sight more than you. I've had four. They're great educators for an adult. Watch them grow. You see life taking over. See 'em making their own discoveries. You've pushed Katrina into making a promise for her brother which you don't think he'll honour. Probably can't because other people won't let him. He'll give her all sort of excuses, except

66

the real one. So a little bit of her faith in him is whittled away. So what? When you've been a parent you can watch the whittling go on day after day. And again, so what? That's how life is. Now, stick your nose into this and let's get it sorted out. You'd better have Sardi with you. He enjoys a bit of violence but you can keep him on a tight rein."

*　　　*　　　*

The plan we'd worked out didn't have any obvious snags. We only had to hold the *Mara II* for something less than twenty-four hours and during that time we should be in control of the bridge and the engine room. With any luck there wouldn't be need to fire a single shot in real earnest. I spent most of the morning on deck, going over all the details in my mind. Nothing must go wrong. I had too much at stake. Normally, I suppose, I would have been confident of my own planning, but then, normally, I wasn't personally so much committed. At the back of this was Drea, the hotel, our future. . . . Everything would be all right, I told myself. But it isn't what you tell yourself that counts. It's what you feel.

Here was the *Mara II* lifting and dropping her nose gently as she cut through a sunlit sea, everything going like clockwork, and me—with an empty feeling in the pit of my stomach, because this job meant more to me in terms of my own ultimate happiness than any other.

After lunch I took a stroll along the foredeck where the planes were lashed down. I met Parkes there. He was seldom very far from the planes. We chatted for a while and I learned that he had been sent out by the Hawker people to supervise the servicing of the planes before they were handed over to the Republic of Cordillo and then to help in their shipment and assembly when they reached Caramanga. He'd been all over the world doing similar jobs for his firm. But he made it quite clear that he hadn't much time for any place that was farther than fifty miles from London, and that for his money a plane was infinitely more complicated and precious than any human being. But that didn't mean

67

that he was unaware of people. If they didn't have wings that was a pity but he had a shrewd eye and he surprised me after a while by saying:

"What lot was you with, sir?"

With a smile, I said, "How on earth did you know?'

He grinned, taking off his panama and wiping his forehead with a handkerchief. There was little breeze down on the deck and the sun was striking hard down at us.

"You can tell always and no bloody mistake. Just a word here, or the way a man looks at 'em. Way a bloke's hands go out sometimes when he wants to make a point. You got it. Mr. Albano's got it, too. But not as much as you. He's young yet."

I told him the name of a squadron—not my own—and he nodded and then he turned his sharp blue eyes on me steadily and said, "You like it out here? You're out here all the time?"

"More or less. My business is here."

I wouldn't have liked to guess how much weight he gave to the word business.

"Dunno how you stand it. They're a funny lot. Never know when they're going to boil over. Even Mr. Albano, and he's got a lot of Scots blood in him, he tells me, even he . . ." He laughed quietly. "I seen him go up in the air once at Soledad over a small thing one of the men did! All he needed was a knife and the bloke would have had it. Then the next minute he's as nice as pie. Suppose that's why they have all these revolutions. Gets it out of their system for a while. What's your business?"

"I'm a coffee broker."

"You are? Well that's something. It's about the only thing they know how to make. Though I'm a tea man, myself."

When I left him I knew that in addition to the six Sea Furies, the *Mara II* was carrying ten thousand rounds of 20 mm. ammunition for the Mark 5 cannons with which the planes were armed. That was a nice little bonus for Angelo Libertad which hadn't been mentioned to me.

He must have told Albano about my service, for the young man invited me to have a drink with him after dinner that night. We talked the kind of mess talk which had filled so many of my nights in the past. He was a nice young fellow, keen and full of go. Up until now the Republic of Cordillo had been without planes and this was one of the reasons why Angelo had been able to hang on to the far eastern tip of the island. Planes were needed to help blast a way through the two mountain passes that guarded the way to Acaibo. I didn't say so, but I knew that the blasting could be done the other way round . . . out of the mountains and towards Caramanga.

"Angelo's been at this for two years, hasn't he?" I asked.

"Yes. Two years open fighting."

"What's he after?"

He had a habit of reaching up with his right hand and twisting at a stray piece of his fair hair. When his hand came down it hung for a moment in a tight ringlet and then slowly straightened out.

"Just whatever he can make for himself. He's a fake. There's a lot of talk about land reform, confiscation of sugar refineries and so on. . . . Everything to be run for the people."

"Some people must believe him. He's kept going for two years."

"That's partly the terrain, of course. But he has support, I can't deny it. Plantation workers and that kind. He's got a way with him. And I don't say that our people haven't helped. No government is perfect. There are a lot of things that need changing in the Republic. You should hear my father on the subject! But they've got to be done slowly and sensibly——"

"So that no one who matters gets really upset or suffers?"

His hand went up nervously to his curl again but he took the remark with a smile.

"You know the world. There's no such thing as a simple problem with a simple solution. But violence and revolution never help. Libertad may have started out with all sincerity. But after a few years . . . Well, you can't avoid change. And you have to pay for the support you get."

I said, "Eventually you're going to fly these planes. Shoot up those passes so your troops can go through."

69

"Yes," he said firmly. "Because I think it's the only thing to do if Cordillo is to have a real future."

"How long has your family been in Cordillo?"

"Oh, a long time. My great-great-grandfather was a Scot. He married in Caramanga, a Spanish girl. We've been there ever since. But all the boys, you know—my father, myself and brothers, have been educated in England."

At that moment Katrina came through the small lounge, searched for a moment until she found a book she had been reading and then went out. I saw Albano's eyes following her and I wondered what he would have said had he known who she was. Certainly not what he did say.

He turned to me and said, "That's the kind I like. Dark, and quiet. Wonder who she is? Davia, the passenger list says, and she's getting off at Caramanga. I don't know any Davias there. Pity it's such a short trip, I might have got to know her."

"You've still got forty-eight hours or more. Why did you come on this boat, anyway? I should have thought you would have preferred to fly?"

"Oh, I would. But the old man wired at the last moment and said he thought I should stick with the planes all the way." He laughed. "Parkes didn't like it. Thought I didn't trust him."

Going back to my cabin, although I was glad to know that the change in his plans came from his father, that Fondes and Angelo hadn't been pulling a fast one on me, I was aware of a premonition of trouble.

I hadn't been in my cabin long before there was a knock on the door and in answer to my call Katrina came in.

I said, "What have you come for? A whiskey night-cap before turning in?"

She shook her head, smiling, and said, "I just wanted to ask you if everything was all right?"

"Yes, it's all fixed."

"For when?"

"Tomorrow night."

"But when? What time?"

"Look—it's much better that you don't know. You're a

passenger. You're going to be surprised by it, too. It's safer like that. Just in case."

She had the book she had been reading in her hands still and I could see the nervous fiddle of her fingers, riffling the pages.

"Forget all about it. Until it happens," I said.

"I know." She nodded and the cabin lights streaked the black hair with gold. "It's just that I'm a little nervous. Well, not a little. Just plain nervous. After all——"

"I know. After all, you've never done anything like this before. Never been mixed up in this sort of thing. Well, if it's any comfort, I can tell you that I'm a bit nervous, too. That's how it always is. Monk's nervous and so are the Hueica brothers. We all are until the starter's bell goes. Now go and get some beauty sleep."

For a moment I thought she was going to turn docilely away. But in her movement towards the door she hesitated and her face turned back to me.

She said, "I won't be any trouble. It's just . . ." One hand made a little flutter like a bird going up and then back from a false alarm, ". . . just that I find it hard to accept that it's me here. Involved in all this."

I went over to her and put my arm round her shoulder like an old uncle.

"I know. That's part of it, too."

"You know that feeling?"

"I did, years ago. But I've grown up now." I opened the door and shook my head as she made to answer. I gave her shoulder a squeeze and steered her out into the companion-way and watched her walk across to her cabin door.

6

It had been arranged that Monk and the two Hueica brothers should come to my cabin at half-past ten the next night to collect their arms. Monk and Tomez were to go to the engine room which was entered by a small doorway leading off the main deck. Inside the doorway a steel ladder dropped sheer to the engine room and they could cover everyone there and also part of the deck through the doorway behind them. Sardi and myself were to go up to the bridge. On the way we would deal with the radio operator and smash up his apparatus. From the bridge we could cover the full run of the cargo deck and the bow space which held the crew's quarters. Once we were in possession we could hold the ship until Angelo's men met us.

At half-past nine that evening I was in my cabin waiting when there was a knock on the door. I glanced at my wristwatch. Momentarily I fancied that Monk had made a mistake in the time. But there it was, half-past nine.

"Who is it?" I called.

"Steward, señor."

"Come in."

The door opened and he came a little way in. He was the cabin steward, not the dining-saloon man. He gave me a nervous nod of his head, his hands burying themselves in the sleeves of his white jacket, a small birdy man with a skin the colour of cinnamon bark.

"What is it?"

"Many apologies, señor. But here is first mate like to talk to you."

I rolled off my bunk where I had been sprawling. The first mate came into the cabin, past the steward who backed away a little, holding the door half-closed. I'd seen him around, on the bridge and in the dining-saloon. According to Monk he was a French-Canadian. Just one look at him told me that he was a man who had no fears about being able to look after himself. He had a big, horsey face, and was tall with narrow, stooping shoulders. I didn't like the look of him and it was clear that he didn't like the look of me. He stood there with his peaked cap on still, his shirt open to show a streaking of grey hairs running up to his throat. His white trousers hadn't seen a crease for weeks.

"Monsieur Smith?" His eyes went from me and around the cabin.

I nodded. "What is it you want?"

He came forward a step so that I was almost crowded back against the bunk and said:

"The steward is going to search your cabin."

"What do you say?"

"The steward," he repeated, "is going to search your cabin."

He gave it to me bluntly: a dark, sour-looking man who acted as though he'd long ago been convinced that there was no need to be pleasant with people.

"Why should he want to do that?"

He gave an impatient grunt, and said, "Hand over your luggage keys."

"No 'please'?" I said. "No 'do you mind'? I'm not one of your crew."

"The keys." There was no shaking him.

I sat down on the edge of the bunk and said, "Look, I don't know what all this is about, but aren't you getting out of line? I'm a passenger on this ship. Even if there were a reason for searching my cases, it would take the captain personally to make me hand over my keys. Now I suggest that you get out of here."

"I'm a ship's officer. I'm acting with the captain's authority." He said it over my head, his black eyes flicking round the place.

I stood up, impatient and showing my anger, and he moved back from me, watching me, giving himself room now in case I made some move. He was wise. If he'd been alone I would have gone for him, but I knew that if I tried anything now the steward would be quickly out of the door and calling for help. I couldn't risk that. But I think my move induced him to be a little more reasonable.

He said, "We've had a radio message from Barranquilla. From the police. It states that it is thought you might have smuggled arms aboard."

"What damned nonsense."

"Let us hope so, monsieur. But we can only tell if you hand over the keys."

"And if I don't?"

A small, grey smile touched his lips. He knew I was stalling. He shrugged his shoulders and said, "I shall have to call for a couple of the crew and do it by force. Please give me the keys and if you have no arms, I apologize in advance for myself and the captain, and trust you will accept."

I was wondering what leak there had been in Barranquilla. You never could tell. Possibly Barrau had got on the wrong side of someone, or the man who had brought the case aboard had taken his money from Barrau and then, opportunist, had doubled it by going to the police.

I moved slowly away towards the far end of the cabin. My back to him, I reached up and took down my jacket that was hanging on the side of the cabin cupboard. I took the keys out of the pocket, and, turning, jerked them across to the first mate. His eyes never leaving me he reached back and handed them to the steward.

"The cases."

They were piled on the floor, three of them, at the foot of my bunk. The steward went to them and lifted the top one on to the bunk. It was unlocked and contained my clothes. He ferreted through it. The second one went on to the bunk. It was locked and held the rest of the stuff which had accumulated in my room at the *Polo Norte*. The first mate backed away casually so that he had me and the steward now in his vision. The steward unlocked the second case, examined the contents and then lifted it on to the first case. He turned and picked up the last case. I heard him grunt a little and wasn't surprised. It was heavier than all the rest. He found the key on my ring and opened it. It was a great moment.

74

The first mate cocked his head to one side, gave the case a glance and said:

"*Eh bien,* so it is true."

I shrugged my shoulders and said nothing.

"Lock it and bring it along," he said to the steward, and then to me he added. "You will come with me to the captain."

As the steward lifted the case, the first mate jerked his head at me and said sardonically, "You go out first." There was the gentle movement of his left thumb massaging the palm of his right hand as he flexed his knuckles. Come on, he was saying to himself, out of the door or make your bid.

This was the moment. I tensed myself to go for him. As I did so, stopping me, a voice from the partly open doorway to my right said, "Drop that case."

For a split second the tableau was arrested, me leaning forward on my toes, the first mate's right hand half-raised.

And then Katrina came through the doorway, pushing it closed behind her.

She must have been walking on deck before turning in because she wore a light coat, loosely open, and a yellow silk scarf was tied about her throat. Her right hand was thrust forward awkwardly and I saw the clumsy bunching of her fingers round a tiny automatic. It was the smallest thing I'd ever seen, a handbag toy . . . and, for a second or two, while we stood there immobile, I wondered if it *were* a toy, if she were taking some wild chance; I wondered, too, whether she had the faintest idea how to use it.

"Drop the case," she said again and there was no mistaking the nervous shake in her voice.

The steward half bent to obey her, beginning to lower the case when the first mate said, "Hold on to it." All the sourness of his character was in his voice. He cocked his head towards Katrina and went on, "Hand over that gun and get out of our way."

I was two yards away from her and I wanted the gun, but I knew that if I moved he would move too.

Katrina said, "Put down the case and both of you go over there." Her right hand jerked towards the far end of the

75

cabin. There was a break in her voice, and I knew she was fighting to preserve a fading resolution.

He didn't believe her. He had all my experience and more, maybe, and he knew how she stood.

He said, his voice searing with contempt, "Get out of my way, you stupid bitch!" He moved forward to her, to brush her away.

She fired. Once, and then again. Two sounds, surprising and incongruous in the small cabin; two sounds like the quick slap a salmon makes when it jumps and smacks its tail against the water.

I saw the red stain on the dirty white trousers at the top of his right leg. She'd missed with her first shot and deliberately fired again. He stood looking stupidly at her, his mouth open, and then he toppled sideways and collapsed on the floor, half-sitting, and leaning forward to press his hands to the wound.

The steward dropped the case and ran for the door. I jumped past Katrina, caught his shoulder and swung him round and then hit him hard. He went spreadeagling backwards and his head got the corner of my bunk and he slid to the floor and lay there. I spun round and took the automatic from Katrina's hand. The first mate straightened up and began to pull himself towards me. I showed him the revolver and shook my head. His face winced with his pain and he stopped moving, leaning forward again over his wounded leg and grunting to himself.

"Don't make any noise," I said to the top of his head. His cap had come off and there was a tiny patch of baldness, scurf-flaked, right at the tip of the crown. "If you do I'll treat you like the steward."

Maybe he didn't hear. He just kept his head down and I saw the blood coming slowly out over his fingers on the crumpled white drill.

I turned to Katrina. "Go and get Monk. Get him here right away. And act naturally outside. Walk, don't run." I was pretty sure that the couple of pip-squeak shots would not have been heard.

Katrina, shaken and white, said, "I was coming down the

corridor and I heard them here . . . I heard them." She looked down at the first mate in horror.

"Get Monk," I said.

But she stood there and stared at me and I knew I had to rush her. I put my free hand on her shoulder and shook her hard.

"Get Monk! Get him!" I snapped and I pushed her towards the door.

She looked at me, and then slowly nodded her head. I slipped the door open and she went out as though she were passing from a dream.

I turned, put my back against the shut door when she had gone, and pulled my handkerchief from my pocket. I tossed it down to the first mate.

"Plug it with that. You won't die."

He took the handkerchief, made a rough pad and pressed it over his leg.

"Bastard, you! Bastard!"

I didn't answer. We had nothing to say to one another. The steward was snoring on the floor as though sleeping off a long drunk.

* * *

There was no real trouble after that. Just a routine job, running a little ahead of schedule, and with all the advantages on our side. You must have the advantages, otherwise you get stuck with heroics. Bravery is all right kept in its place, but I would rather have the help of two cowards and the advantage of surprise.

Monk came back with the Hueica brothers and the cabin became an emergency ward. The Hueica brothers stripped my sheets into lengths and without a word gagged the recovering steward and bound him hands and feet, Sardi's fingers flicking the white lengths round and jerking them tight with quick little tugs, enjoying himself.

Monk slit the first mate's trouser leg and bandaged him, the big hands, slow and deft in their work, and the cigar still in his mouth which he had been smoking when Katrina

77

called him. And the first mate said nothing because he couldn't, because Monk had gagged his mouth before he concerned himself with his wound. He was tied like the steward and lifted to my bunk. When it was done and I went to open the case I saw Katrina standing inside the door still, watching it all.

I went over to her and for a second caught her chin between my finger and thumb. I tilted her head up and saw from her eyes that she was all right now. This was just curiosity . . . the trance of watching the second act, the theatre all illusion.

I said, "You go to your cabin and lock yourself in. Stay there until I send for you. We're all right now. Thanks to you."

She went out and I opened the case.

Sardi and I left Monk and Tomez on the lower deck at the entrance to the engine room. We went up to the boat deck and the bridge. The *Mara II* was running sweetly into a gentle swell, just lifting and shouldering a little, on good terms with the sea. There was a moon and a sky full of stars almost as bright as a holiday poster. A yard from the door of the radio room I stopped Sardi, putting a hand on his arm. He stood by me, whippet small and breathing easily, his moustache a charcoal brush across the moonlit face.

"Remember these . . ." I lifted my sub-machine gun, ". . . these we don't use. Unless. But a big unless."

He nodded.

I opened the door of the radio cabin and stood aside, letting Sardi go in. I stood there, watching the light up on the bridge a few yards away and the indigo and grey sweeps of the deck below and the wingless moth shapes of the Sea Furies echeloned along the cargo well. A man began to say something inside the cabin, his voice edged with surprise and then abruptly cut away. There was a sound like a woman thumping up cushions into shape on a settee. Then a few sharp crashes and cracks and the noise of glass breaking thinly. Sardi came back. His breathing was only a few points above normal. He closed the door and we went towards the bridge.

There was no trouble with the captain. He was alone on the bridge with the wheelman.

I pushed open the half-glass door and stepped into the bridge house. The captain was leaning over a chart table on the far side of the wheel. He was a Humpty-Dumpty of a man with heavily bagged eyes and a little black mourning strip of silk in the lapel of his white jacket. He straightened up and looked at me curiously, frowning.

"Passengers are not allowed up here, señor. Will you please——"

He stopped short as I slid the sub-machine gun round to cover him. Sardi went by me and a little wide to cover the wheelman.

"I am not a passenger any longer, captain. I'm taking over this ship. I have two men in control of your engine room, your radio has gone, and your first mate is a prisoner in my cabin. All I need from you is sensible co-operation for twenty-four hours. That way neither you, nor the ship, nor the rest of the passengers will come to any harm."

It was a long speech but I wanted to make all my points at once and he listened, still half erect, one hand on the chart table. He looked at me, lips pursing, deliberating, and his eyes on my gun. Then he straightened up and gave a fat shrug of his shoulders. Clearly he was a sensible man who knew his own limitations. Maybe in his own mind he had already made the hopeful reservation that *the whirligig of time brings in his own revenges.*" He was prepared to wait.

"You're Señor Smith?" he said.

I nodded.

"You will permit me to check what you have just said?"

"On the bridge phone. But move gently."

He stepped back to the telephone and gave the handle a couple of twists.

"Speak in Spanish or English," I said.

He rang again but there was no reply and I knew that he had been trying the radio operator. He rang again, three times. This time there was a reply from the engine room.

He said, "You have the same trouble down there that I have here?"

79

I could hear the engineer officer's voice, thin and nagging like a mosquito whine. It went on for some time.

The captain said, "Do nothing. Cause no trouble and obey all the bridge signals."

The voice whined and hummed again and then was cut short by the captain.

"Those are my orders."

He put the telephone back and as he did so the wheelman turned and jumped for Sardi. My eyes came back from the captain to see the wheel spin unattended and the wheelman almost on top of Sardi, a long brown hand striking downwards with a knife in it. Most other men would have been taken by surprise, even in their watchfulness, but not Sardi. *Fer-de-lance*. Barrau had said that. He melted sideways and the wheelman stumbled full length and finished up on his hands and knees. Sardi jumped behind him as he sprawled on the boards and the sub-machine gun was pointing at the back of the man's skull.

Sardi waited for the word from me.

I said, "Stand back and let him get up." I took a step forward and kicked the knife from the man's hand. "Get up."

He pulled himself up and I nodded towards the bridge door.

The captain said, "Go forward to the crew's quarters and tell them what has happened. Tell them to do nothing."

"Tell them also," I added, "that any man who shows himself on deck will get this." I tapped the stock of the gun.

When he was gone, I said to the captain, "Take the wheel. This is the course." I laid Monk's bearing written on a piece of paper by him on the chart table and watched as he retrieved the wheel and brought the *Mara II* on to her new course. Then standing behind him I said, "I want the keys of your armoury."

He gave them to me.

"Where?"

"In the locker below the telephone."

I opened the locker. There were three revolvers, a twelve-bore shot gun, and two ·303 Lee Enfield rifles. I had Sardi carry them outside and to the far end of the open bridge wing and toss them into the sea. Then I told Sardi to go down to the deck and watch the entrance to the cabin accommodations and the crew's quarters forward. No one was to be allowed out on deck. It was late and no one was likely to try to come out. They would all be sleeping by now. Every fifteen minutes he was to check with the engine room and then with me.

I was left alone on the bridge with the captain at the wheel.

He said, "Where do we go?"

"Acaibo. To unload the Sea Furies."

He slewed his head at me. I liked him for his self-control. He had himself well in hand and it must have been difficult. Taking his ship was like taking another man's wife.

"Libertad?"

"Yes."

"This is piracy."

"I suppose so."

"You must be mad."

I didn't answer. Though I could have repeated myself and said, I suppose so. But I didn't want to go into my form of madness, the kind of inflexible madness which seems saner than sanity . . . Drea waiting for me in Haiti.

He said, "Acaibo is more than twenty-four hours. What about the change of the deck and engine room watches?"

"Nobody changes."

"And here? You expect me to man this wheel for twenty-four hours?"

"At daybreak you can have the same wheelman back. He's learnt his lesson."

He looked at me, his thick neck creasing with the turn of his head, and said, "He's an honest man who tried to do his duty."

"I know. But they learn like all the other kinds."

He didn't say any more. He just kept his hands lightly, expertly on the wheel, looking straight ahead of him, out to the starlit night. Now and again I moved behind him and checked that he was still on the same bearing. And once

81

every fifteen minutes Sardi came up, quiet, puppet-faced, and moving like a shadow.

By mid-day we should be met. All that remained now was to sit out the hours. The hours to being met, the hours to reaching Acaibo and being paid, and the hours until I could make Port-au-Prince.

7

JUST before daybreak when Sardi came up I made him go forward and fetch the wheelman. When the two came back, the wheelman took over from the captain and I left Sardi to watch him.

I went down and along to the cabins, making the captain go before me. There was a smudgy blur of light creeping over the eastern horizon and the deck lights were beginning to have a dissipated look as the darkness went, like creatures caught out long after the magic hour had struck.

We went first to Albano's cabin. It was unlocked and when I switched the light on he sat up in his bunk, fair hair ruffled, the front of his silk pyjamas unbuttoned to show a brown chest.

With the captain standing between us I gave him the straight facts. He didn't get what I was talking about for a while. When he did, he exploded like a rocket and was off the bunk with his feet on the ground before the quick lift of my gun restrained him. He wasn't scared, but he had enough common-sense to hold back. He stood there with his nice, young man's face working with anger, his eyes moving from me, around the cabin, to the captain, searching for something, some way to break through. He was the other side of the coin which carried Katrina's head on the reverse. They were both idealists, both dedicated to a cause . . . both the kind who could start trouble without caring what happened to themselves.

I said, "I want your cabin key. You'll stay here until you're let out. That'll be mid-day. You won't starve."

He was silent for a moment, and the captain said, "I'm sorry, señor. You will be wise to do as you're told. There is nothing I can do."

He spoke, ignoring the captain, whipping his words at me venomously, "You swine! You dirty English swine! If you were a Libertad man I'd have some respect for you. But you're not that. You're just a rat! A money rat! So much for the planes and so much for me!"

I took it because I had to take it. All the arguments against it would have wasted too much time to set out. But I said, "I didn't know you were going to be aboard. You were supposed to fly. You should stick to your arrangements." I didn't say anything about the promise Katrina had made to me about him. He wouldn't believe it. I didn't have much faith in it myself. "Calm down and behave yourself."

"Go to fiery hell!"

"Get his key," I said to the captain.

He kept his eyes on me as the captain went to the dressing table for the key. It lay there with his loose change, a cigarette case and a lighter. "Wherever you go after this," he said, "I'll see you're found. You won't get anything out of this. Libertad's no fool. We hold many of his people. People he wants back. They'll exchange me for one of them, and one day I'll be after you. . . ." He broke off and slowly threw his head back and put his hands wearily to his forehead as though he'd been struck by some tremendous pain. And I knew he had. He had just thought of the planes and of their enormous importance to his side. He didn't look at me again. He stood there with his hands knuckled against his eyes in an anguish which had nothing to do with any anxiety for himself.

I took the key brusquely from the captain and backed out of the cabin quickly, and because I didn't want to think I just kept repeating to myself . . . Drea in Port-au-Prince. Drea in Port-au-Prince. It worked. I didn't care a damn for Albano or the tin-pot politics and struggles of Cordillo. And who the hell was Albano, anyway, to be so high and moral? If the planes had been going to Acaibo, to Angelo Libertad, then Albano would have employed me to do the job in reverse for him without a scruple. *He's an honest man who tried to do his duty.* That's how they all thought of themselves at the beginning, but once they surrendered themselves to a party, to an ambition, then the pace became too hot for them. They changed. Even his anger would change in a few

84

months, that young man's dedicating anger to follow me and find me wherever I went. Too many things would get in the way.

I locked the door on him and we went along to Parkes.

He was up and fully dressed and was writing a letter with a pencil. To his wife, maybe? He was the kind who would use a stubby pencil, distrustful of the vagaries of fountain pens. He sat there, one hand over the sheet of notepaper to protect its privacy. As I talked, he slowly licked the end of the pencil, watching me from under his bushy eyebrows.

I finished, "I'm keeping your boss locked up for a while. He's the kind that needs to cool down. But if you give me your promise to try nothing you have the freedom of the deck and holds to keep an eye on the planes. I know you check over the holding ropes each morning."

He nodded calmly, and then said, "Coffee merchant, eh? Somehow I didn't believe that. Or the Mr. Smith. I even told Mr. Albano so. You're the other kind we used to get. Plenty of guts while they were in, but when they went out . . . Itchy bottoms, keep on the move, and sticky fingers. I'm sorry for you, mister. Now get the hell out of here and let me finish my letter."

I went and there was no pretending that he hadn't got under my skin far more than Albano. Those hard blue eyes on me, unwavering from under the sandy brows, weren't easy to forget. Outside, as I turned back towards the deck, the captain said, "What about Señorita Davia?"

"We needn't bother about her. She's free to go where she wants."

I didn't explain why and he didn't ask. I stopped at the door to my cabin and unlocked it. He went in and freed the steward and then we left him to look after the first mate, locking them in again.

* * *

By mid-day we were at our rendezvous. Monk had come on to the bridge with me during the morning and the two

85

Hueica brothers had taken over the engine room. Monk was in a good mood, a cigar sticking out of the corner of his mouth, his large face dark stubbled. He took over from the wheelman, who was sent back to the crew's quarters.

The escort from Acaibo was waiting for us. It was an old three-masted motor-schooner running under a jib and a fore-sail and with the motor going. We hove-to and she came alongside. Tomez Hueica dropped a rope ladder over and ten men came aboard. Three of them were West Indian negroes and the others lighter-skinned Cordilleans. They all wore green shirts and American-pattern army trousers, carried rifles, and had bandoliers slung over their shoulders. Their leader, wearing a peaked officer's cap, came up to the bridge and introduced himself to me as Lieutenant Ocampo. He was a stiff, rather jerky little figure, very correct and curt from the importance of his mission. He saluted me with a snap that must have made his wrist ache and informed me that he was now taking over command of the ship in the name of the Democratic Army of Cordillo. I let him get on with it. Monk and I stayed on the bridge and watched the pantomime. Four machine guns were slung up from the schooner and mounted strategically about the *Mara II*. There was a great deal of shouting and one of the guns was almost dropped into the sea. Half an hour later we were on our way with the schooner some distance astern of us. I left Monk with the captain on the bridge and went down to the cabins. The first mate and the steward had been taken from my cabin. Albano and Parkes were under guard in the saloon.

I shaved and put on a clean shirt and then went across to Katrina's cabin. There was a negro guard on the door and he wouldn't let me in. He just shook his head and said that it was the lieutenant's orders.

I went out on deck and found the lieutenant.

"Why is there a guard on Señorita Davia's door?"

He stiffened his thin shoulders and said curtly, "I have strict orders, señor, from the Generalissimo that she is to be given every protection."

86

"The Generalissimo? You mean her brother?"

"No, señor. The Liberator is at the front. I speak of Generalissimo Lemaza—her brother-in-law. He is responsible for her to her great brother. It is my responsibility also. It is safer for her to stay where she is."

"Then tell your guard that I can see her."

I saw his prim mouth work a little at the suggestion of an order from me, but I didn't care a damn for his brief authority. As he hesitated, I said sharply, "I'm not going to do her any harm. I've just handed the damn ship over to you, haven't I? I've taken the planes for you. Besides, she's my friend. She can do with some company. Ask her."

"Very good, señor." But instead of moving, he hesitated again and I could see that something was worrying him. He swallowed a little, making his adam's apple wobble in his thin neck, and then said, "You did not inform me that we had Señor Albano aboard."

"You didn't ask me."

"You should have said. He is a most important prisoner. This I might not have known. I should have been made to look foolish."

"How did you find out anyway?"

"From his passport. I am careful always to check everything."

"Well, good for you." With any luck, if the revolution lasted long enough, he'd make captain one day. "Now be kind enough to ask the señorita if she would see me."

He wasn't ever going to take a liking to me, I could see that. Eventually I was allowed in to Katrina.

She had just finished a cold lunch which had been brought to her. She looked tired and I guessed that she had not slept much.

"You're hard to see," I said. "The full V.I.P. treatment."

She gave a little laugh. "It is my brother. He treats me like a baby. I must be looked after."

"I don't get it. He let's you take on this job which is

87

dangerous. But when it's over he puts a guard on you."

"No, it is logical. Before, the risk had to be taken. He could do nothing about it. But now, the moment he can do something, he does."

"Who's Generalissimo Lemaza?"

"He is my brother-in-law."

"Everything in the family."

"He married my sister. But she is long dead. She was the next after Angelo. Without Lemaza my brother would have found things difficult. Lemaza has the kind of brain for facts and figures, for supplies."

"Paymaster and Quartermaster-General. Is he the chap who will pay me off?"

"I imagine so."

"I can't wait to get to him."

I saw then that she was looking at me with the same kind of look the lieutenant had had, a question poised, waiting to be asked.

I said, "Go on. What's on your mind?"

"It is just for money? Nothing else? You do all this just to be paid? Oh, yes, I know you have said you do before. But I cannot believe it. There are other moments when it is not a part of you." She dropped her eyes from me, embarrassed by her own frankness, and touched a fork on the tray.

"Just money," I said. "It's a portmanteau word. It wraps up everything."

"Or everybody?"

"Why do you say that?"

She shrugged her shoulders, looking up at me, and said, "I know you think I am young. No experience. But I am not so young. People don't do things for things. They do them for other people, and I am sure that if you need money you do not need it for yourself."

"I need it. Let's leave it like that."

"If you say so. But I should like to have heard about it. You see I am learning fast. Last night. All this business. Learning about myself. It was me who stood in your cabin and shot at a man. I have learnt that I could do that. I have learnt how strongly I feel. I have also learnt that there are some people to whom I can speak like this. To you, for instance. But there is much more to know."

"Why?"

She turned away a little and caught gently at the edge of her bunk curtain. "Because I wish to grow up quickly."

I laughed gently, "Don't force the pace. It will all come in its own good time. What you want is some fresh air, some exercise. Shall I go and twist the lieutenant's arm and get permission."

"No, thank you."

Her face came back to me, but it was no longer the young, unmarked Madonna face, the chaperon-shadowed demureness of the evening stroll round the town square. Something had happened to her. She was waking up fast, she was finding she had a tongue to speak more than commonplaces, a mind that forced curiosity on herself, and emotions which she had to learn to handle.

I said, "If I were you I'd take three aspirins and turn in. You've had a basinful."

The age-old prescription that no one ever takes. Go to sleep and forget it.

I went up on to the bridge to join Monk. He pointed to a long green smudge away to the north.

"Cordillo. It'll be dark by the time we get there. We'll have to lay off tonight. Can't take her in at night. It's too tricky. How long do you reckon to stay in Acaibo?"

"Just as long as it takes me to collect my money."

*　　*　　*

It was dark when we got to Acaibo. The *Mara II* dropped anchor off the mouth of the harbour to wait for daylight to get into her berth. A couple of motor-boats manned by Democratic Army soldiers came out to us after about half an hour. Lieutenant Ocampo, in full and brisk command, had the companion steps lowered over the side and a little later Albano and Parkes were taken off with their luggage. I was with Monk on the bridge and heard Parkes cursing stolidly to himself. The second motor-boat took off Lieutenant Ocampo and Katrina.

I went down to the deck and met them as they were at the head of the steps.

"Am I free to go ashore?" I asked the lieutenant.

"In the morning, señor. There are rooms for you and your friends in the hotel. I go to report to the Generalissimo and then I shall be back. Señorita. . . ." He stood aside for Katrina to pass to the steps.

She looked at me and smiled and said, "I shall see you in Acaibo?"

"You're staying at the hotel?"

She shook her head. "No. I shall be with my brother. He has a house just outside."

"Señorita, please. . . ." Ocampo made a fussy movement with his arms.

I leaned over the rail and watched the smudge of wake from the motor-boat fade creamily against the dark water. A few lights showed from Acaibo and distantly I heard the sound of a car revving up and a sudden burst of shouts and laughter.

Monk and I went down to the little bar at the back of the dining-saloon and sat there drinking leisurely until it was time to go to bed. Every so often we heard a motor-boat coming out and then going back, and orders being shouted on deck. Just before we were ready to turn in an Indian came into the bar and asked for a limejuice from the steward.

He was a doctor from Acaibo and had come out to attend the first mate.

When I asked him, he said, "It is a fracture. Not so bad, señor. The bullet I have taken out. Tomorrow he shall be plastered."

They'd moved him from my cabin and the place had been tidied up. Ocampo was efficient.

The next morning Monk and I went ashore. We went off in a motor-boat while the *Mara II* was being got under way to enter. The harbour was a large semi-circular bay about half a mile across and enclosed by two encircling horns of land. On the eastern horn, at its tip, was a grey stone citadel, El Castro, which had been built in the nineteenth century. Its gun emplacements covered the harbour and the town. Acaibo itself was a straggle of houses and buildings, white, pink and brightly shuttered, that sprawled along the water front. The main plaza lay behind the houses and was dominated by an eighteenth-century church, its baroque façade flaking with old plaster. Beyond the town were foothills rising to the great mountain chain, in places five thousand feet high, that ran westwards for about fifty miles. A long, rugged, tree-covered spine which, so Monk told me, dropped away eventually to the flat savannah lands of the western part of the island which stretched another hundred and fifty miles to Caramanga. Angelo's people held a line across the mountains about thirty miles from Acaibo at a place called San Pedro de Rabosa, a small mountain town at the end of a narrow pass through which the main road ran to Caramanga. It was this pass which formed the focal point of the present fighting. Both sides had been sitting at either end of it now for over six months.

Cordillo itself had been Spanish for about four hundred years up until the Spanish-American war. When the Spaniards went out of the Colonial business it had become a Republic. Its history had followed the usual West Indian pattern; Columbus, the Spanish greed and concern for gold and harbours rather than sugar cane and tobacco; massacre and counter-massacre of the original Caribs and Spanish garrisons, the influx of Negro slaves, the mixing of blood and the more recent, less apparent, infiltration of Indian and Chinese traders . . . it was a hotch-potch, but a valuable one, even apart from its sugar and tobacco, because in the last five years offshore oil had been discovered on the north coast above Caramanga and was being worked under a concession to an American company. Monk gave me a lecture on it all the way in and he finished, "Whatever happens, it's like all the others, a sugar pot with flies crowding round the brim. From time to time a different lot of flies take over. But they're flies just the same. Sucking away and paddling their dirty feet over everything."

I said, "I just want to take my little bag of sugar and get away." The far side of the harbour under the lee of the eastern horn was crowded with schooners, motor launches and a few paint-weary yachts . . . all the night-running stuff that a place like Acaibo and a cause like Angelo's attracted. It shouldn't be hard to get a passage out.

Monk said, "Maybe I'll stay a while. History in the making. Perhaps I'd like to see that."

The hotel was in the main square opposite the church. It was called *Hotel de la Reina* and its pink façade with green shutters sloped out at an alarming angle from the flanking buildings. It looked as though it only needed someone to move impetuously in one of the fourth-floor bedrooms to send the whole affair toppling forward on its face. Across the square which was littered with market stalls, with only a narrow passage through them for cars and donkey carts, the sun was full and blinding on the ornate face of the church to the rails of which chicken were strung up by the legs for sale. A square, unadorned bell tower rose at one side of the church with two bells, one above the other, showing in the open bell turrets. Below them was a clock which had one hand only that pointed to four stubbornly unmoving. Acaibo had nothing I hadn't seen before. And even the smells were the same.

Monk and I got two rooms, vacated about an hour earlier by a couple of Democratic Army officers, leave expired, who were going back to San Pedro de Rabosa. The one from my room, which overlooked the square, had left a pile of empty crab shells and claws in the waste-paper basket, and an earlier occupant, I imagine, had pencilled an obscene drawing on the back of the door. I shoved the waste-paper basket into the corridor and hung my jacket over the drawing. The Hueica boys hadn't come ashore with us. They were waiting for the *Mara II* to berth, and had said they didn't want hotel rooms. They'd find something for themselves which was cheaper.

It was hot in the room, but I kept the window and the shutters drawn against the market noise outside and I stretched out on the iron bed. So far as I was concerned there was nothing to do until I had collected my money and could arrange to get away. Lieutenant Ocampo had said nothing to me about it. I didn't really expect anything to be done about it that day. The Generalissimo and Ocampo would be busy enough. I decided to give it a day. Tomorrow I would get busy.

That night, after dinner, I went into the bar for a drink. The bar was perched up on a bamboo pallisaded platform overlooking a long room which ran out at the back of the hotel. At the far end of the room was a three-piece band, a piano, saxophone and a guitar. Now and again a coloured woman with thin shoulders and long hands, in a black dress which she kept kicking irritably with a backward flick of one heel, came to the microphone and sang the same dreary sort of song which was no doubt being sung in a thousand other similar places at that very moment, tropical nights, silver sands, holding hands, palm trees over us, love, love until we die. . . . And about four couples danced.

"Is it always like this?" I asked the barman.

"No, señor. This is between leaves. The officers and men went back this morning. Another lot come day after this. Then you see life."

I couldn't wait.

He looked at me as he polished a glass and went on, "For you, it is better company at the *Cantina del Morro*."

"Where's that?"

"By the harbour. Plenty of men from the boats, and also some men who come to fly. Up here is only Army, and they get wild."

It was the place, I thought, to arrange a passage. Later I'd have a look at it.

Someone came up to the bar behind me and I turned and saw Parkes. He was still in his tight blue suit, sweating hard, and mopping his face. He looked tired and grim. I waited, saying nothing, not knowing how he was going to take me. But he gave me a nod as though nothing had happened between us and said, "The lassie back there would do a damned sight better if she had a voice and a body to fill her gown. Whiskey. Double, and no ice."

93

"There is no ice, señor," said the barman.

I let him get his drink and put half of it away, and then I said, "What's happened to you, and Señor Albano?"

He cocked his head at me and the blue, steady eyes were on me unblinking.

"Do you care?"

"As a matter of fact, yes."

He breathed hard and then let his shoulders slump.

"I've got a room here. The boss is being held by them. Army headquarters. Big sugar mill place outside the town. I've had a day, I can tell you. I didn't take to that bastard at all."

"What bastard?"

"General whatever his bloody name is. Dressed up like a Christmas tree and giving his orders. You're welcome to him."

"I don't know him."

"Then you've got a pleasure to come, I don't think! I don't think much of the food here, either. All fish stuff. Can't stand that fish soup."

"What's the position . . . about you?"

He began to pack a pipe that looked as though it had been buried ten years. "Simple, according to His Nibs. They're beginning to unload the planes tomorrow. They've got a strip bulldozed out of the palms, over the hill from here on the coast. I supervise everything. Unloading, assembly and tests. When that's done I can go. With a bonus if I like to take it. Told him what he could do with the bonus. My firm would play hell, and I don't want his dirty money." He looked frankly at me as he said this, and I realized that although he was prepared to talk, prepared to have me even buy him a drink, he still held to his opinion of me.

"And if you don't do this?"

"Simple. They shoot young Mr. Albano."

"So you're doing it?"

"What do you think? Of course I am. I don't want people shot. Besides if anyone's going to touch them planes it's going to be me. They've got a shower of mechanics up there that I wouldn't trust with a kid's sewing machine. You

94

should have seen that strip they'd bulldozed. About six hundred feet long. I asked them what the hell's good they thought that was. Six hundred feet! You could do it, just about, from the deck of a carrier. Fifteen hundred feet, I said. Not a foot less. That gives a nice safety factor. Silly bastards. Now they've got to send up to the front to get the bulldozer back. One bulldozer. A bloody Fred Karno outfit. Blimey, listen to her."

The singer was murdering a Cole Porter tune.

I said, "I hear they've got some flyers here."

"So I'm told. I can guess the type, too. Ex-Nazi boys beyond the age limit, and boozy-fingered types no airline would look at. Can't hold a glass without spilling it." He looked at my hands on the bar counter and then shook his head. "You beat me. Still, it ain't my worry."

He put his glass down and went out without saying a word. Of all the people I'd known in my years out here he was the only one with the blunt gift of being able to make me think about myself from a different viewpoint. I didn't care for it. He couldn't have made it more plain that, like Orlando, he did *desire we may be better strangers.*

But, despite him, I couldn't really feel upset. There was a fine elation in me, running sweetly and powerfully like a dynamo. I'd succeeded. I was going to have the money I needed. Drea and I were going to have the hotel. We were going to be together. I kept coming back to that thought and it was like champagne in me.

Monk came in after a while and as we stood at the bar the singer came up from the dance floor. She was a light-coloured girl, nose a little flat and a big gamin mouth. She couldn't have been twenty. Monk bought her a drink and she sighed over it with resigned, dark spaniel eyes. She'd been caught at this end of the island when the trouble started five years before, visiting her brother. He was with the Democratic Army now. She wanted to get to Caramanga and have a job in one of the real night clubs, improve herself. . . . I saw the old, paternal look coming over Monk's face as she talked to him. It was always to Monk that the waifs turned, the beaten-down ones, the hopeless, the ones who were never even going to catch the tail of their phantom ambitions. Eglantina her name was. Singing and dancing, And some of the officers were nice. But it was usually a rough crowd. . . . I left Monk talking with her and went to bed. But I lay for a long time, thinking about Drea . . seeing us together . . . together always.

★ 8 ★

By mid-day I had heard nothing from Army Headquarters
and I decided that I'd given them all the grace which could
be decently allowed. I went down to the *Mara II* to find
Lieutenant Ocampo. The harbour and dockside were the
only places where there were any signs of Army activity.
Trucks were unloading petrol from a couple of schooners.
The stuff was in old American army four-gallon jerricans
and the work was being done by a negro gang.

I met the Hueica brothers coming from the *Mara II*.
Sardi gave me a solemn little nod, and Tomez beamed a
smile. They'd found themselves a couple of rooms in some
house up by the church, so Tomez said, and hadn't decided
whether to hang on here in the hope of finding some kind of
job or to look for a passage out right away. I watched them
go off in their neat suits, walking as though they were hand
in hand. They were no longer anything to do with me.
They'd been paid and they'd done their job. That's how I
wanted it to be with me, too.

There was a large, open, six-wheeled lorry alongside the
Mara II, and they were preparing to swing off the first of the
Sea Furies. Parkes was there in the thick of the operations.
At the bottom of the gangplank was a sentry and I noticed
three others along the length of the ship. Lieutenant Ocampo
was a stickler for military precautions. I had a little trouble
getting by the sentry. He conducted me to the top of the
gangplank and then made me stay there while he sent a
message to the lieutenant. Finally I was taken to him. He'd
made temporary headquarters in the saloon and already,
army-style, he had his table covered with papers, a couple of
trays for files, and a field telephone with nice new blue and
yellow wires trailing away and out of a porthole on the
harbour side. An orderly was smacking away with intense
one-finger concentration at a typewriter on a small table by

97

the bar. On one of the saloon pillars a sheet of foolscap was stuck with scotch tape. A glance at it as I waited for Ocampo to look up from his table showed me that it was the standing orders for the ship's company while under detention in Acaibo, written in Spanish and English.

He looked up, gave a stiff, curt little sigh to indicate how busy he was, and said, "Well, señor?"

"Have you had any instructions from Generalissimo Lemaza about me?"

"No, señor. Should I?"

There was no doubt that we didn't like one another.

I said, "I have an urgent business matter to settle with him. I don't regard Acaibo as a health resort. I want to get away."

"So?"

"I'd be glad if you would telephone him and ask him to make an appointment with me."

For a moment I thought he was going to make an issue of this, but he gave that quick, bony shrug of his and reached for the telephone. While he talked I studied the standing orders. No officers were allowed ashore. All crew would be in their quarters by ten o'clock at night and must remain there until six the next morning unless they were detailed members of working parties. An efficient little man, Ocampo.

He spoke in Spanish and was having a huffy argument with someone at the other end of the line. Then there was a long silence while he waited. Another outbreak of speech from him and then he put the telephone down. I turned back to him.

"Well?"

"You are at the *Hotel de la Reina*?"

"You know I am."

"I will pick you up there at five o'clock this afternoon and conduct you to the Generalissimo.

"Good. Thank you."

I left him and went over to the *Cantina del Morro* for a drink. You went down six steps from the dockside level, through a double arched doorway and into what had obviously once been a rum or molasses store. The smell was still there, thick and strong. There was a high bar pushed to one end with a juke box close to it. The glass of the juke box had been broken. There were no records to be seen but a ginger jar full of pomegranate blossoms stood on the turntable. Fishing nets were strung along the roof and bits of seaweed and glass float-balls hung from it. There were four long tables with benches on either side and each table held a pot of flowers. The owner was a big, fleshy man in red trousers and a white silk shirt, with a large, colourless, epicene face. He looked German to me but everyone in the place called him Tino.

Monk and Eglantina were sitting by themselves at one bench. The bench nearer the bar had four men around it. One look showed me that they were the types Parkes had referred to. For a moment I went over their faces. But there was no one I knew. One wore a thick brown leather American flying jacket. They were playing cards with a quiet concentration. I knew the kind. I'd just missed being one of them. They only had two lives, one when they were aloft, and the other when the evening closed around them and they began to feel the liquor in them. Otherwise they just sat out time, waiting. Life became hell when they could no longer take-off.

Monk said, "How goes it?"

"I'm seeing the General this evening."

I ordered a rum and when Tino brought it he said, "Velcome."

"Thank you."

"You bring the planes in?"

"Yes."

"The boys are glad for you."

The boys went on playing cards.

Eglantina said, "The Generalissimo is very handsome man. But no good. Particularly with women." She'd got her hair screwed up into a bun right on top of her head and was wearing a green dress with yellow bamboo stripes across it. She had a ten-cent brooch of some blue stuff shaped like a butterfly at the neck of her dress.

I said to Monk, "When I've collected are you coming out with me?"

He leaned back against the wall lazily and jerked his cigar so that it almost burnt his left eye.

"Dunno. Think I like it here. Besides, sure to be a fuss outside about this business. Stay here and let it blow."

I looked from him to Eglantina He saw the look and grinned.

"When you go," he said, "I'll move out of *la Reina*. Child here says her brother's got a cabin up in the hills. Sit on my bottom and watch the melons grow for a while. She wants me to train her voice."

"Her voice? What do you know about singing?"

"Ran the biggest choir you ever saw once. True, she doesn't have much of a voice. But you don't need one for night clubs. Just a manner. I can give her that."

"Well, the best of luck to you."

"Brother's got a boat, too. Needs a bit of work on it. You know me and boats. When she's trained I'll take her out. None of the regulars here are allowed out. Officially."

I saw then how it was. It was Monk all over. He hadn't the least interest in her as a woman. To him she was a child who wanted a toy, the smoky tawdry glitter of a night club, wanted to get out of Acaibo. And because she wanted it he couldn't stop himself from helping her.

"He's good man," said Eglantina.

"Too good," I said.

She put her hand on Monk's arm. A simple gesture but there are about five hundred different meanings to be got into it. Hers was clear.

"Already I do anything for Mister Monk." She smiled, everything on her face breaking up into a monkey wrinkle. She really was the plainest thing I'd seen, but I liked her. If it had been left to her kind he would have been canonized long ago.

*　　*　　*

Lieutenant Ocampo picked me up at five o'clock on the

dot. He had an old, but clean and well-maintained red Ford convertible with an Army sign on one of the wings. I'd already seen it on some of the trucks. A Picasso kind of bird with a rifle in its claws. Later I learned that it was meant to be an eagle.

We sat together in the back and were driven by a soldier in a smart green tunic who kept up a steady forty irrespective of the pot holes in the road. There was little conversation between Ocampo and myself for we were bouncing up and down like sacks most of the way. We went out through the square with the horn blowing and took the slope towards the far side of the island. All the way up the bluff, on either side of the road, were little checker-board patches of cultivated ground, maize, tomato, pimento and melon. On the far side the road dipped to the sea and a long stretch of curving white sand flanked by tall palms and groves of ragged looking seagrape. The ground here was flatter than around Acaibo, running back in a small coastal plain to the foothills. A couple of miles ahead I could see a block of grey and white buildings, but before we got to them the car turned off to the left and passed through the gateway of a private drive. A sentry at the gate saluted us. A few minutes later we drew up at a large wooden house, two storied and built in colonial style, a long verandah running down one side of it and fronting an overgrown garden full of poinsettias, oleanders and stubby palms. There was another sentry at the foot of the verandah.

When we got out of the car Lieutenant Ocampo said, "You will excuse me, señor."

He stepped up to me and ran his hands quickly over my clothes feeling for arms.

"Don't worry," I said. "I'm not in the assassination business. And come to think of it, I've got four sub-machine guns and a handful of grenades back at my hotel which I'd be glad to sell to the Democratic Army."

We went up the steps of the verandah into a large hall. As we entered a man came across the hall and out past us. I looked at him and he looked at me. For a moment some dusty memory shook itself. I hesitated and I saw the same hesitation in him, the beginning of a recognition which neither of us could place. Then he was past me, down the steps and into a jeep which was parked on the gravel. I went on, seeing his face, greyish and tired with a cynical droop to one corner of his mouth. From somewhere I knew him but I couldn't place him.

I said to Ocampo, "Who's that?"

"I do not know, señor." Maybe he didn't. Sometime, I knew, the memory would come back.

A few minutes later I was with Generalissimo Lemaza.

He was sitting at a large mahogany desk. Ocampo introduced me and then retired. Lemaza placed a pair of big hands widespread on the edges of the desk, half rose and half nodded and gave me a beaming man-to-man smile. Within a few moments he'd left me in no doubt of the way in which he wanted the world to regard him . . . big, bluff and frank, an honest turn of speech, and a giant's amused, but still concerned, occupation with the complexities of the world. A giant who had taken a bunch of pygmies under his fatherly control. . . . Father Lemaza who was going to be really sorry if he had to punish anyone because it would hurt him more than them. . . . He fixed me a drink and gave me a cigarette. He neither smoked nor drank himself. He smiled as he explained, and his big teeth flashed. I had learned from Monk that he had been a dentist in Caramanga before the revolution, and a good one. Maybe all this bluff, jolly-you-along act, bags of confidence and nothing to worry about attitude, was a hang-over from those days. Just lean back, señor, open your mouth and I'll take your teeth out before you can say *Ave Maria*.

Having fixed me a drink he stood by the window and, speaking in Spanish, said, "We are grateful to you, Señor Marchant, grateful, grateful. . . . A fine job. The sinews of war. That is my concern, that was your concern. Up there—" he gestured vaguely out of the window, "they fight. Heroes everyone, but fighting is not enough. Arms are not enough, nor ammunition. They must eat, they must drink, they must be clothed, trucks must have petrol and oil, and orders are non-existent without telephones, without wires, without pen and ink." He beamed at me. "Back here, the non-combatants, the seat-polishers work and there is no glory. You agree?" He jerked the last sentence at me.

"I agree."

"Of course you agree. You are a man of sense. And there are other worries too. War is a business, revolution is a business. Money and thought, money and thought. While the campaign is being fought the political future must be planned. And let's face it, señor . . . most soldiers are children, children politically. They never grow up. But a new society does not grow up on its own like a coral reef. It needs planning." He smiled again, but shadowed the smile with a little concern. The confident planner not under-estimating anything, confident but not optimistic. On a political platform, letting fly at the plantation workers under a ceiba tree, he would have been irresistible, I could see that.

But to show him that I was no sugar worker, no peasant hungry for land he would probably never get, I said, "I've brought your planes in. I've been paid ten thousand dollars on account. There's forty thousand to come."

He came back to the desk, nodding wisely. He was quite something to look at. He wore a coffee-coloured tunic—much the same style as a British officer's dress tunic—in some soft shantung and it sparkled with silver cuff and breast buttons. The flying eagle with its rifle was on each shoulder with two stars above it. A couple of rings winked richly from one hand. From the crest of a high forehead his hair went back, short and stiff, en brosse, and the skin of his face was like pale, walnut-coloured pigskin. He lifted the lid of a fruit box which stood on the desk and put an Elvas plum into his mouth. A sweet-tooth, that was bad for a dentist.

He sat down at his desk and said, "You have never met our Leader?"

"No."

"You will. And you will make no mistake about him, Señor Marchant. You will recognize the man of destiny. Look around you in Acaibo, in the bars and on the streets, look around you here, and you ask yourself 'What is it I do not see? What is it which is missing?' Something which is

103

to be found everywhere else in the world where men fight for liberty?"

"What is it?"

"His photograph, señor. His face. Those posters with the monster face looking down at you. But not here. And why not? Because Angelo Libertad is not a face, or a figure. He is a voice and an ideal. A Power for good. The symbol of justice. Why should our men need his face on every wall? Already they carry him in their hearts. In their hearts, here." He smacked his large chest as though I might be in doubt of the exact position of the heart. As far as he was concerned I was. He had no heart, only a great bag of wind in its place. But he had a brain and I had no doubt that as Quarter-master-General he was in the top class. He could get what had to be got, and he wouldn't waste a penny over it. This show was being run on a shoe string.

I said, "Once these planes are in the air, your troubles will be over. You'll break out to Caramanga; three months from now and you'll be lords of the island, master of Cordillo...." I found myself talking like him. "Even if you could have bought those planes they would have cost you the earth. I'm a business man, General, and so are you."

He took another plum, nodded, and leaned back in his chair.

"Señor Marchant," he said, mumbling it a bit because of the plum in his mouth, "as well as a business man, you are, so I'm told, a flyer. Squadron Leader?"

"I was."

"For these planes, we have at the moment four pilots. But these men are just flyers. They have no character. They fly because they know nothing else. As a business man I would like to make you a proposition." When he got down to business the bonhomie went from his voice and there was no rebel rousing grandiloquence in his speech. Hard facts.

"What proposition?"

"I will give you command of the planes. Full command. Training, operations, and so on. You fly with them. For this you would be paid five hundred dollars a month, with a bonus of five thousand when we enter Caramanga. Wait—"

He raised his ringed hand as I moved to speak. "In addition, as you are a business man, I will be frank with you. As frank as though you were my own brother . . ." he smiled as he lapsed back into rhetoric for a moment, "for between us already I have seen that nothing but the truth can stand. We owe you forty thousand dollars. Invest them in this struggle which is on the lip of success. I personally guarantee you that you will receive your money back, doubled, when we reach Caramanga. Let us see, that would give you eighty-five thousand dollars in three months. How could any business man treat such a proposition lightly?"

"I'm not treating it lightly," I said. "Any other time and I might have accepted. But not this time. I just want to be paid and to leave."

"So you shall be."

"Good." I waited for him to make some move.

"Unfortunately, however, I cannot pay you until Angelo Libertad returns tomorrow. I need his authority——"

"Look General Lemaza, I've done this job for you. I hope you're not going to keep me hanging around."

He smiled, ignoring the irritation in my voice. "Tomorrow you will be paid. There is no question of it. Meanwhile, it won't hurt to consider my alternative offer. It merits thought. Angelo Libertad returns to Acaibo tomorrow. It would be our pleasure if you came here tomorrow evening and had dinner with us." He stood up and reached behind him for his cap, a peaked affair with the old eagle on its front, and moved towards a door on the other side of the room. "Señorita Katrina, has said she would like to see you. You will find her through here. I myself must go."

And he went, leaving me high and dry and with no option but to wait until the next evening for my money. I was full of irritation over the delay. I wanted to be away as fast as I could.

* * *

The room had a large window looking out over the garden. There were green and white tiles on the floor and the furniture was all cane, cane chairs, cane table, and the place looked bare. There was a large radio set in one corner with a great jar of canna lilies on top of it.

Katrina turned from the window as I came in. With an impulsive movement which surprised me she came quickly towards me and took my hands.

"It's nice to see you again."

"It's nice to see you." Somehow she made me feel that it had been a long time since I had seen her last.

"Can I get you a drink?"

"No thank you." I moved towards the window with her. She looked fresh and young and there was the scent of some perfume about her which was new to me. It was light and faint, retiring . . . not the kind of thing Drea would have used.

I said, "I've just had a basinful of Brother Lemaza."

She laughed. "He's a bit overpowering, isn't he? Angelo has to have someone like that. Angelo just goes ahead and does the thing which has to be done. He's no good at detail. Siles worries about that."

"He certainly does. I hope I'm not going to have trouble getting my money from him."

She turned sharply towards me. "Oh, no. No, there won't be any trouble about that."

"I'm glad to hear it."

"Angelo has promised it. That is all that is needed." She paused for a moment and then went on, "But didn't he ask you to stay on, and make you a much better offer?"

"Yes. Supreme Commander of the Air Force."

"And you're going to?"

There was no missing the enthusiasm in her voice. She wanted me to stay on.

"You knew he was going to ask me?"

"Of course. I think it's a wonderful idea. Don't you?"

"No, I don't."

"But why not?" she said, puzzled. "But you must. It's such a good offer."

"Maybe, but I've got other plans. I just want to get away as soon as possible."

"Oh. . . ." Her disappointment was obvious. "But I thought you'd be glad. It's far more money."

"I'm going to have all I need. Remember, too . . ." I gave her a smile. "I don't have the same interest in Cordillo as you. My interests are miles away from here."

She stepped back from me a pace and I saw her mouth tremble. Then she said, "Is it for someone else? For a woman, for someone you—" She went to the window and with her back to me played absently with the cord of the blinds. "I'm sorry. It is none of my business."

I would have avoided it if I could but since I couldn't I decided that it was as well to have the thing in the open. I liked her and I thought I understood exactly what had happened. She'd only just come into this new world; mine and her brother's and the General's. Everything in this new world seemed exciting, romantic, razor-edged with risk. It was new and the men in it new. No matter how hard the reality of that world was, it also bred romance for the young. It wasn't my fault if she'd taken a fancy to me.

"You needn't be sorry," I said gently. "It's a woman. I love her and she loves me. And we need money to make the thing stick. Love by itself doesn't pay any bills."

Without looking at me, she said, "Who is it?"

I told her and she nodded.

"I remember seeing her."

Remember. . . . She was always there, walking with me . . . tawny hair, that movement of her body and arms which was her alone, that voice, nothing but Drea. . . .

I put a hand on her arm and turned her gently towards me.

"It was nice of you to think of me. About the job. If I were on my own I'd probably take it. But it can't be done."

To my surprise she double-backed on me and said, "Does she know you're doing this?"

"She does," I said. "But she didn't want me to do it. I had to . . . for reasons."

"She means so much to you?"

"So much, and much more." I laughed quietly. "Don't look so gloomy. You're home, you're with your brother, and

107

he's going to get to Caramanga. You've got the whole world in front of you. You don't want to waste time on hard-bitten types like me. . . . No, no." I stopped her as she stirred to speak. "Let's have a drink together. To the future. Yours as the mistress of Cordillo."

"And yours?" She was recovering and there was a smile in her eyes.

"Just the future."

She went over to a table by the radio which was full of bottles and glasses. She fixed me a whiskey and this time she did it properly. Just the right amount, but it had to be cut with water not soda. Generalissimo Lemaza didn't have soda siphons on his list of stores.

*   *   *

Lieutenant Ocampo had gone off with the Generalissimo, but he had left his car and driver for me. The man took me back to Acaibo through the swiftly gathering darkness. In a few hours Acaibo had changed. Four lorries with men and officers on leave from San Pedro had arrived and the square and the hotel were full of them. Some of them were already well on the way to being drunk. They seemed a tough but good-natured lot and most of them carried arms. After dinner I went along to the bar. The dance floor was crowded and a bunch of girls had appeared from somewhere. Just inside the bar door was a pile of rifles against the wall with a hotel servant looking after them and on a shelf behind him an odd selection of revolvers and automatic pistols was laid out. The band had been augmented and music was pumping through the room.

Monk was sitting at a little table at the edge of the floor near the bar. I joined them.

"How did it go with the General?" he asked.

"He's going to need watching. He offered me command of the Air Force."

"You told him what to do with it?"

"Not yet."

He looked around the room. "They're really letting go,

108

aren't they? The radio's just broken the news about the planes. All the world knows now. For these lads it's only a matter of time before they hit Caramanga. When do you get your money?"

"Tomorrow."

An officer with his shirt front unbuttoned came up to the table holding a glass and swaying. He beamed at us and said, "You bring the planes. Gracioso. . . . Soon we go forward to Caramanga, to glory. . . ." He lurched sideways, spilt his drink and was swallowed in the crowd of dancers.

I looked at Monk and smiled. " 'We go to gain a little patch of ground. That hath in it no profit but the name.'"

"That's about right, too, as far as the little boys are concerned. They'll get nothing. Should read their revolutionary histories. First duty of any revolutionary leader is to destroy the political force that brought him to power. Castro did it. Angelo Libertad will. They'll get nothing. No one ever learns."

The floor trembled with the stamp of dancers, the air pulsed with the music and somewhere, far away in the smoky haze over the heads of the dancers, I heard the thin voice of Eglantina trying to sing with the band. Give me my money, I thought. Give me my money and let me get out of here.

I left Monk to keep an eye on Eglantina and went down to the *Cantina del Morro* where it was quieter. The arc lights of the *Mara II* were on and a squad of labourers was still at it, unloading the Sea Furies. I saw a bulky wingless body swing over and drop slowly towards the waiting lorry platform. In a couple of weeks, maybe sooner, the Sea Furies would be over San Pedro. The pilots in the *cantina* would be alive again. They'd be right with themselves again, doing the one thing they knew . . . coming down out of the sun with their cannons going and the earth sweeping back past them in a green, brown and yellow blur, the figures of men and vehicles coming up from insignificance to the sudden, gesturing, frantic clarity of helplessness. . . .

The flyers were still in the *cantina,* still playing cards but with more animation now that the evening and the liquor had gathered about them. Also there was the man I had passed coming out of the General's house. A small, neat looking man, Latin-American, with that tired, cynical droop to one corner of his mouth. He looked up at me and then gave a little nod. I went and sat down by him.

"It was somewhere," I said. "But I can't place it."

"Marchant?"

I nodded.

"Da Silva," he said politely. "It was two years ago in Barrau's office. There was a little trouble with a firm called *Industrias Reunidas J. da Luz.*" He had a quiet, unemphatic voice, and went on, reinforcing my memory, "Manufacturers of medicinal and industrial castor oil, glycerine, linseed . . . all the usual stuff. Labour trouble."

I remembered then. Our meeting had been brief and I hadn't been involved in the trouble. But I remembered now the things Barrau had told me about Da Silva. His easy, neat and tranquil appearance had all the deception of a shark basking in the sun.

I said, "There's no industrial or commercial trouble here."

He shrugged his shoulders. "There is trouble everywhere. My employers like to help people out of trouble. So long as they make a profit. Since you brought the planes in this could be a good investment."

"What did you think of the General?"

He didn't answer the question. He just smiled at me and said, "Let me buy you a drink."

When I got back to the *Hotel de la Reina* the door of my room was open and a drunken officer with a black eye was snoring, fully dressed, on the floor by the window. I dragged him out on to the landing. The dancing was still going on down below.

I lay in bed before sleeping, thinking about Drea. And when I slept I dreamt about her.

★ 9 ★

I HAD time to kill the next day. Now that a fresh batch of
soldiers was on leave a couple of taxis had appeared in
Acaibo. They stood outside the church, two old Chevrolets
with canvas awnings in the place of hoods. The awnings
were striped in red and gold—the revolutionary colours—
and fringed with little red tassels. Ribbons of the same colour
ran from the windscreen ends down to the radiator tip.
Along the body each one had a name painted in Spanish; the
Singing Heart that Never Tires, and the *Space Sputnik
Special.* Philosophy and Science parked side by side. I chose
the *Singing Heart.* It was driven by an enormous negro, his
face broadly divided by a smile. We took the slope out of
Acaibo in a mad, honking rush through the morning market
crowd, but long before we were at the crest the pace had
dropped to a wheezing, thrombosis-threatened crawl.

We passed the drive turning to Angelo Libertad's headquarters and a little farther on skirted the block of
cane-milling buildings which had now been turned into a
barracks. The dusty enclosure before it was wired in and
there was a little guard house at the entrance. Some soldiers
were drilling in squads on the far side of the enclosure, and I
saw two groups of men about instructors and machine guns.
The eagle flag flew from the top of the building. The sentry
at the gate waved to my driver.

He turned to me and said, "That's Ernesto. We work here
once. Start as cane cutters. But I get more brain, sir. I get
job in distillery here. He still cut cane. I still get more brain,
sir. He soldier, me owner-driver of *Singing Heart.* I call that
upward progress, sir."

"You should go far," I said.

"Yes, boss!" He nodded happily.

A couple of miles beyond the sugar-mills the road curved
back, following the shore line and meeting the long, gentle

slope of the foothills. There was a little group of houses by the sea edge and beyond them a small stone jetty. Back from the houses and running into a thickness of bushes and palms was the landing strip which had been made for the Sea Furies. A bulldozer was still working at the far end of it, lengthening the run. At this end, near the houses, a long, tall Nissen hut with a semi-circular roof had been erected. As a workshop, I guessed. Outside it, four of the dismantled Sea Furies stood in the strong sunlight and there was a working party around one of them. But I saw no sign of Parkes. He was probably down at the harbour superintending the off-loading of the last planes. I got the driver to pull up opposite the little jetty. The strip hadn't been too well planned. For take-off it meant taxiing to the far end and then making a run out to sea. It would have been dangerous to take off towards the slope of the foothills and the tall crests of the palms and trees. Just for a moment I wondered whether—if there had been no Drea—I would have got more brain and gone in for some upward progress, too.

From the air strip he took me around the northern sweep of coast, following a cliff road that dipped and soared. After about ten miles we came to a junction with a sign in English and Spanish. *No Civilian vehicles beyond this point.*

"Sometimes from here, sir, when wind right you can hear guns at San Pedro."

We couldn't hear any that day. We went away left-handed and circled back to Acaibo through the mountains, eventually coming into the town by a road that brought us to the harbour.

I had lunch with Monk, whom I hadn't seen so far that day.

He had a cut over his right eye with a piece of sticking plaster over it.

"How did you get that?"

He grinned, wrinkling his big, easy, brown face.

"The dancing got a bit rough. High spirits. Even on leave they like to fight. I got mixed up."

"You had to pull Eglantina out, you mean."

"No girl likes her dress ripped off her back."

I saw then that the knuckles of his right hand were sore and cut. I'd seen him in a fight more than once. It was an uncomfortable business unless you were on his side.

"Galahad."

He smiled. "That's me. Galahad without hair."

"Why'd you do it?"

"You're too old to begin asking *why*. Just get *why* right back. Why do you do what you do? Why'd you take this job? Ten steps out of your line. But I don't badger for reasons. You took it. Good enough for me. Reason is just a string of decoys. Compulsion is the hunter. Anyway we all finished up friends. Nice chap really. Just likes to tear dresses when he's drunk. Put him in your room to sleep it off. He wasn't in any shape to make the barracks."

"I put him on the landing. He was snoring like hell."

I slept most of the afternoon and just after six Ocampo's driver called for me to take me out to the villa. On the way out we passed the *Singing Heart* and the *Space Sputnik Special* and three army trucks coming in with their evening load of mischief. They went by in a roar of shouting and singing. Ocampo's driver turned and said, "All very happy. Soon we go to Caramanga. Soon I get sixty-six acres good land. Same for each man. Viva Libertad."

"Viva Libertad," I said. It seemed expected of me. If he ever saw his land he would be lucky. Land hunger. One of the oldest wants. One of the easiest and most effective promises to make. You shall have land if you fight for it. Usually they finished up with co-operative farms, and militant youth organizations. Co-operation and organization; maybe, subconsciously, that was what we all wanted. Anything that would dispel the loneliness of being an individual. You lived under the shadow of the Bomb always—it was easier to face the threat as one of a group. Us, not me. There was an illusion of security if you were in a crowd.

I went into the hall and an orderly showed me into the room where I had met Katrina. There was no one there. I waited, staring out of the window for a few moments. As I did so, I became aware of voices coming from behind the door that led into General Lemaza's room. I couldn't catch

113

any of the words but there was no doubt that the General was excited and doing most of the talking. Just now and again I caught the lower pitch and brief interjection of the other person. The whole thing had the feeling to me of someone making a plea, arguing some point and not getting very far with it. There was a moment when the General's voice faded into silence and then suddenly came back sharp and strong, almost angry, only to be cut off by some quiet dismissal. The room went silent and I heard a door open away to my left.

I turned and saw Katrina coming in. She wore a cool green dress with white collar and cuffs and she came smiling across to me. This time I was ready for her outstretched hands, catching them briefly and returning her smile.

"Drink?"

"Thank you."

"I'm sorry I wasn't here. But at the last moment I had trouble." She half turned to me. "The hooky things on the back of this dress. You need to be a contortionist."

"You haven't got them all now," I said.

I stepped up to her and began to fix the lowest of four hooks on the back of her dress. I could see the nape of her brown neck and the fine peak line of dark hair running up into the smooth sweep of her head. . . . Just for a moment I had a swift impulse to lean forward and kiss the back of her neck . . . for no reason at all. Out of affection, because she was a nice girl, because that little piece of exposed flesh was so womanly . . . God knows. No reason. Just a compulsion which I killed rapidly.

A few minutes later General Lemaza came into the room from his office and with him was the great Angelo Libertad. I don't know what I had expected. What I saw was someone who was the complete opposite of Lemaza, Lemaza who was dressed to kill in his silver-buttoned tunic, fresh-shaved, confident with men's cosmetics and his padding of rodomontade.

Angelo Libertad was about forty-five, lean and tall, his skin and the rather stiff, unbending movements of body and limbs giving the impression of a piece of sea-weathered drift oak. You could have knocked a nail into this man and got no sound of pain from him. He wore a khaki shirt buttoned at the neck without a tie and khaki drill trousers held by a simple brown belt. His hair was as dark as Katrina's and parted in the middle, spread away in two wings to give him an old-fashioned look. He had a short dark beard into which disappeared the deep clefts that marked either cheek. He had the trick of seeming to be always still, waiting, except for his eyes which were grey, curiously light coloured and which took in everything with a warm curiosity. He carried a cheap cane walking stick, the kind you could buy in any bazaar for a few cents, and he used it when he moved to offset a stiff left leg. The result, I learned, of a badly treated bullet wound in his early days as a revolutionary. His voice was quiet, and when he spoke English, which out of courtesy he did most of the evening, it had that singing touch, almost Welsh in its inflexion which I had noticed before in educated West Indians.

He was no self-flagellating prophet squatting on a barren mountain top. He smoked and drank and laughed, but all the same there was no mistaking his hardness, his force and determination. General Lemaza's windiness would just blow past him.

At dinner he said, "I must thank you for looking after my sister on the *Mara II*. It was not a position in which I would have willingly placed her. Let me say, though, that it might have been hard to stop her from doing it . . . she feels as I do." He smiled at her.

I've no very clear recollection of the way the dinner talk went, except that it went the way he wanted it. But very early on he said, "I understand that General Lemaza has made a proposition to you?"

"That's so."

He looked at me, put one finger on the edge of his glass and said, "Do you wish to accept it?"

"Not so bluntly, Angelo," said the General. "It's an excellent proposition for Señor Marchant. You will give him the impression that we do not want him to accept. We do, of course. He is just the man to take charge——"

Angelo shook his head. "Señor Marchant understands bluntness. Does he look like a man who would be undecided after twenty-four hours? Am I right?" He looked at me.

"Yes, you're right," I said. "To be equally blunt, I just want to be paid and to leave. I'm not interested in flying or fighting. I've had my share of both."

"And, of course, this is not your country. Why should you? Still, the General did wisely to ask you. He has his problems . . . chiefly money and supplies. You see," he smiled, "he does not have my faith. With faith all things can be accomplished."

"It doesn't buy petrol or arms, Angelo. These are the sinews of war, these are the materials of victory."

"Victory is here or it is not here." Angelo to my surprise tapped his head and not his heart. His style, verbal and gesticulatory, was quite different from Lemaza's. He looked at me and went on, "The General would finance a revolution in the same way as you float a company. Issue a prospectus, underline the prospects of future developments, and make a share issue. It is on this that we part company, because I know that the seeds of true defeat, the coming death of ideals, is in that way. This is a democratic movement, not a company. When we enter Caramanga it must be free of all debts, tied by no promises except the ones already made to our people. It is, I believe, forty thousand dollars we owe you?"

"That is so."

I saw Katrina watching me.

"Before you leave here the General will pay you the money."

"Thank you."

"You have earned it. The planes are all we need."

I said, a little stupidly maybe, but I was in the clear now and the money was coming to me so I felt I had to say it, "I never meant to bring in Albano with the planes. Quite frankly, I wouldn't have settled for that if I'd known."

"I can believe that. But there is nothing to be done about it. It was just an unexpected turn of fate. Fate must be accepted."

"You're going to exchange him?"

"I think so, eventually. But it does not concern you." And

116

in the last sentence there was dismissal, unmistakable. I was to be paid, but beyond that I had no privileges. A few minutes later he was talking about Cuba and the mistakes which had been made there by Fidel Castro since the end of the revolt, of how Castro had smashed his own movement, supported originally by moderates, and handed over Cuba's political and economical future to the extremists. He spoke with a quiet bitterness about the way the land reform law and the expropriation of land holdings had been abused by the National Institute of Agrarian Reform . . . I could see that there was no question in Angelo's mind of what should happen when they got to Caramanga. He would be master. Cordillo was going to get a new deal. Anyone who was hanging on in the hope of getting a bigger slice of victory than anyone else was in for disappointment. But even as he spoke I was thinking of dark, neat little Da Silva in the *Cantina del Morro*. Da Silva wouldn't be over here wasting his time. And looking across at General Lemaza, I didn't need to be told that just because the General had married the now dead sister of Katrina there was any deep family bond between them all. I didn't need to be told, either, that paying out my dollars was going to hurt the General. There were a hundred better ways of spending it he could think of. . . .

We went into the other room for coffee and after a little while Angelo excused himself and left us. A few minutes later the General went back to his room to work. He said, "When you are ready to leave, the car is waiting. Come to see me first."

Left alone with Katrina, I said, vaguely aware of uneasiness in me, still seeing Da Silva sitting in the *Cantina del Morro,* remembering more about him now, "Just how well do those two get on?"

"Much better than it seems. Siles worries about the small things. He needs to. My brother thinks only of the big thing. They need one another."

"And when you get to Caramanga?"

"What do you mean?"

"You heard your brother talking about Cuba. Things went wrong there. Precious little land has been distributed. But

117

the boys behind INRA are filling their wallets. And Castro is President of the National Institute of Agrarian Reform. How many men are incorruptible?"

Sharply, she said, "My brother is."

I nodded. "Yes, I think he is, more than most. I get that feeling. . . . But people aren't comfortable with men like that."

"What do you mean?"

"I'm not sure. Yes, I am. I mean that people like General Lemaza can't live with people like your brother. Only during the emergency of a revolution, of fighting. Afterwards something has to blow."

"You're wrong," she said. "I know Siles isn't a man who appeals to you. Just as I know that my brother is. But Siles is the same as everyone else in this fight. They would die for Angelo."

I said, "I don't doubt it." And when it was all over, I wondered just how different things would be—and just how many, like my driver, would go on with their "upward progress". You had to be smart to keep on the band-wagon, and ruthless. Anyway, the only thing I was concerned with was my own "upward progress". I wanted to have my money and be away. I said, "Well, I think it's time I went. I've still got some business with General Lemaza." I stood up.

She stood beside me. There was just one table lamp alight in the room and a mosquito was singing about it.

"When are you leaving Acaibo?"

"Tomorrow. There are one or two boats going out."

"I shan't see you again?"

"It's unlikely." This was going to be difficult and I wasn't sure how to handle it.

"I shall miss you."

She said it simply, and before I could help myself I had put out my hand and taken hers gently.

"I'll think of you," I said, "and I hope all goes well for your brother."

She slipped her hand out of mine and smiled and said, "It's embarrassing for you, isn't it? You must have had it happen before, surely?" The more she said the more confident she became. "I know it doesn't mean anything to you. But it does to me. You'd call it part of growing up, wouldn't you, Keith?"

It was the first time she'd ever used my name. I couldn't escape her, she didn't mean me to have an easy exit so I decided to be frank, too.

"You're dead right," I said. "It's all part of growing up. You've fallen in love with me because I happened to be around at the right moment. It could easily have been someone else." I put my arm round her shoulders and pulled her slowly towards me. I kissed her, feeling her eyelids flutter against the top of my cheek. I took my lips from hers and put my hand against the smooth run of her cheek and looked into her dark eyes.

She stepped back from me and her face was suddenly awake and she said breathlessly, "Stay here in Acaibo."

I shook my head. "I'm going." I raised her hand to my lips and kissed it. "Good luck," I said. "And thank you for trying to make me Supreme Commander of the Air Force. I could have got myself a fancy uniform like Lemaza. Ten years ago just the thought of the uniform might have decided me."

She laughed, but I could see that there was no real laughter in her. This was another moment of learning about herself; one of the romantic growing pains we all have to face. I went across to the door of the General's room, knocked and entered when he called.

General Lemaza pointed to a box file on his desk. There was no need of words. I opened it. Inside the dollar bills were neatly stacked and banded with slips of brown paper. There they were. I held down the elation and excitement in me. Drea . . . waiting in Haiti. The thing was done. No more Barrau jobs. Everything plain sailing. It was a great moment. I took the stacks out and carefully counted them. The notes were new, clean and crisp, and the flutter of their edges was the only sound in the room. When I had finished I snapped the spring-loaded lid of the box back and put it under my arm.

General Lemaza leaned back in his chair, chewing on one

of his preserved plums, and said affably, "As a business man you are making a mistake. There's a fortune to be made in this country for the wise investor."

"I don't wish to speculate."

He smiled and rubbed a hand over his broad chin and then slid it up and back over his stiff brosse. "It is a pity you would not stay. We could have worked together so well, I think."

I didn't. But I didn't say so. He held out his hand to me and then walked to the door. Before he opened it, he half turned and said, "I watched you at dinner tonight. Oh, yes, I watched. It is mostly all I can do when Angelo is present. I know your thoughts, the contrast you make between us. Even, I guess, you imagine some antagonism. That would be wrong. We are just different parts of the same symbol. He is the flag that flies at the masthead, and I am that mast, that stout pole which must be there, always there if the flag is to fly. The flag of liberty and promise."

I could have clapped I suppose at this parting oration, but I didn't. I was wondering what kind of liberty it would be. The promise I didn't even consider.

Ocampo's driver was waiting with the car. It was dark, no moon, but a sky full of bright stars that seemed too close to the earth to be comfortable. One of those tropical nights which overdid everything, too hot, the air too thick with flower scents, and the fireflies around the oleander bushes too brilliant. I sat in the back of the car with the box tucked under my arm. It was going to be under my arm or I was going to be sitting or sleeping on it until I got out of Acaibo.

As the car turned out of the drive and bumped along the road to Acaibo I was thinking of Drea. By now she was probably on the point of leaving for Haiti. She'd fly. She hated the sea. Sometime or other, I supposed, I would tell her about Katrina. She had all a woman's interest in another woman's emotions. And for a while, because I was relaxed now, and could detach myself to some extent from myself, I tried to imagine what it might have been like if there had been no Drea. Maybe I wouldn't have been so avuncularly amused by Katrina. The fondness in me for her, which must have been maddening because she didn't want such an innocuous response, might have been passed over quickly. She was quite unlike Drea. Drea, out of her love, demanded. In a way she led me and I followed. But Katrina would have followed because she couldn't escape her own nature. No matter what I did or where I went she would have followed. . . .

Half-way up the slope to the hill above Acaibo the car began to splutter, spitting back through the carburettor and finally stopped. The driver got out and fiddled around under the bonnet for a while and I sat in the back smoking. He made a few adjustments and tried to start her again. She refused to come to life. I got out.

"What's the trouble?"

He turned his hands slowly palm upwards.

"It is always happening, señor. The petrol they bring in. God knows from where. Sometimes it has water in it. Sometimes there are whole tins which are nothing but water. Thus they cheat the Movement."

I got him to hold a torch while I unshipped part of the carburettor and worked the priming lever of the petrol pump. Petrol flowed out into my hand and in the light of the torch I saw that it was half water.

"You'll never get this thing started until you drain the tank and put in fresh petrol."

"But what do I do, señor? I have to take you to the hotel?"

He was a good soldier. He had orders and wanted to carry them out. Now, in an emergency he wanted fresh orders. The Movement had need of his kind. No resource. Just order-followers.

I said, "You hang on here. The *Singing Heart* or the *Sputnik Special* will be taking leave parties back later. You can get a tow. I can walk to Acaibo. It's only a couple of miles."

I left him there and went on up the hill. At the top there was a large saman tree. I stopped under it and lit a cigarette. Below me were the lights of Acaibo.

I went down the roadslope. It was hot walking in the still

air and after a few hundred yards, where the road took a turn to the left through a small cutting in the hillside, I came to one of those stone troughs let into the side of the road. A thin trickle of water came from an iron pipe above it. I went over to it to take a drink. The water came straight down from the hills. I bent over the trough to get my mouth under the pipe, the box file under my arm. As I bent I heard a movement from the road behind me; a swift shuffling sound, no more perhaps than a fast-moving snake might have made in the dust, but it was enough. I began to straighten up and saw on the star-reflected water of the trough the dark loom of a figure behind me. I turned and met the full force of a blow on the side of the head. I went down, crashing backwards against the stone edge of the water trough.

WHEN I came round the negro driver of the *Singing Heart that Never Tires* was crouched over me, splashing water in my face. My left temple throbbed viciously and I could feel the whole of the left side of my face stiffened up as though with frost-bite. I pushed myself up a little and he helped me to sit on the edge of the stone trough. My trousers were wet through from the overseep to the ground from the trough. I waved a feeble hand at him to stop him from splashing more water over me.

"You mus' sure be drunk, boss, to get right up here in this fix. Man, you sure want to see your face . . . !"

I couldn't answer him. It was coming back now fast. I groped in my pockets for a cigarette. The packet came out damp and sodden.

He fixed me with one of his own cigarettes, even lit it for me.

"You mus' been here when I take early leave party back. Didn't see you, though. Lights only hit this bit of road coming back. You all right . . . ? Here, take little more pain killer."

He pulled a bottle from his pocket and offered it to me. It was rum, strong hard rum, and it burnt me all the way down, but it pulled me round.

I stood up and swayed a little.

I said, "What time is it?"

"Just after midnight."

I must have been there about two hours.

"You got a torch?"

He went over to his taxi and came back with a torch. I flicked it around on the ground by the trough. I knew I wasn't going to find anything, but I had to do it. A black desperation was building slowly in me. There was nothing to be seen except the damp ground and a confusion of foot prints. No sign of the box file. I was still silly in the head from the blow. I could kiss that goodbye, I thought. Kiss forty thousand goodbye and with it all the other goodbyes. . . . The pain behind my eyeballs was suddenly shot with red streaks. I swayed and he held me.

"You lose wallet or somethin', boss?"

"Something," I mumbled. "Get me back to the hotel."

He helped me across to the taxi and eased me into the back. I flopped out against the leather like a sack of wet rice.

"Here." He had the rum bottle at my mouth but I shook my head. Rum was no good. Already I could see Drea looking up at me as I crossed the terrace of the Hotel Montana; knowing at once that I was returning empty-handed—no hotel, no future in St. Thomas. I cried out inside myself, fiercely, murderously against the vision. . . . He offered me the rum bottle again and this time I took it. It wasn't going to happen . . . I'd tear this island apart first.

He began to drive me back and I lay there, coming and going in waves of brief clarity and then long troughs of confusion. Half-way down the hill I made him stop and I vomited over the side. When we went on I lay there with my body shivering violently for a while until I got angry at myself for being all body. The anger did more for me than the rum but as we reached the hotel I was still in a bad way. I had a recollection of three or four officers playing some drunken wrestling game in the hotel hall, and a bottle being slung between them. In the dance room the music was pumping away.

Singing Heart was a good boy. He stuck with me all up the stairs, taking my weight and clucking like an old rooster.

I found my room and flopped on to the bed.

"I get your friend, Miss Eglantina's man."

He went out and I lay there in the darkness, coming back fast, and trying to sort it out, and with the coming back I could feel myself hardening up, not just in the mind but in the body as well. Whatever slack there was in me was being taken up, sweated right up taut, and it was like a kind of medicine, no cure for the real ill, but bringing me back into shape.

Monk came in after about five minutes. Eglantina was with him. He switched on the bedside light and stood over me.

He just stood there looking down at me without speaking for some time. He didn't really need to be told. He said to Eglantina without turning, "Get some hot water and some plaster."

She went out and I could see the thin shoulder blades working in the deep vee of the back of her red dress. Monk bent over me and his fingers turned my head gently sideways.

"Christ, what a bruise. Not badly cut though. Fix you up all right. Drink?"

I shook my head. He lit a cigarette for me and put it between my lips. Everything was going through my mind, everything that hinged on the loss of my money. Already I had murder and God knows what else planned.

Eglantina came back with a bowl of water and other stuff. She stood behind him while he fixed me up expertly. And it was expert. The real Monk touch. I'd never thought that I would become one of his waifs . . . but I was at that moment. A waif, and well astray. Eglantina stared down at me with eyes as big as eggcups.

Monk, easing plaster over the temple cut, said, "You were paid tonight?"

"I was."

"No trouble?"

"Not to begin with. The car broke down outside town. I walked."

"Into trouble."

"For me, and a lot of other people."

"Who was it?"

I didn't answer, my eyes on the scared, fascinated face of Eglantina.

"In my room you'll find a clean shirt or two. Bring one here," he said to her.

She went.

I sat up and rolled my legs off the bed. The damp linen clung to me.

"Who?" he asked.

"Sardi. He was quick but not quick enough."

"Sardi, eh? But he couldn't work this on his own."

"I'm damned sure he didn't. He's just hired."

Eglantina came in with the shirt. As the door opened music pumped in and I heard the officers shouting below. Outside in the square a drunken handful of soldiers were murdering some song and the church bell gave a cracked boom to mark the half-hour. I stood up and stripped off my shirt. Eglantina held the clean one for me like a jacket. She gave me a timid little smile as she slid around me.

Monk said, "What do you think you're going to do?"

"I'm going out." Eglantina had slipped back in front of me and was doing up the shirt buttons. With everything I had on my plate now, the really big stuff, I couldn't help noticing small things. She'd painted her nails silver and her hands worked neatly. She belonged to Monk and now, since I was part of Monk, she belonged to me. If I'd let her she would have tucked the shirt into the top of my trousers. I put my hands on her shoulders and eased her away.

"Eglantina," I said, "get downstairs and fetch me some cigarettes and a bottle of whiskey."

She looked at Monk and he nodded. She went.

"Where are they?" I asked him. "They didn't check in here."

"They got rooms in a house by the church. But if they did this job they won't be there."

"They might. If they thought I hadn't seen them. Anyway I've got to try it first." I walked over to the window, tucking my shirt in. I was easing up now, my body was coming back under control.

Monk said, "Hang on here a moment."

He went out and I waited. Eglantina came back with the cigarettes and the whiskey.

She said, "You better now, boss."

I nodded. "Too much drink. Slipped and cracked my head."

She didn't question me.

Monk came back after a while and said, "Okay, let's go.

And you—" he patted Eglantina on the bottom, "get back to your singing. Just going to walk Señor Marchant for some fresh air. And remember with that blues number, keep your eyes down. Till the last chord and then give it this—" He did an exaggerated impression, throwing his arms wide and flinging up his head. She giggled and went out ahead of us.

Outside the hotel he handed me a revolver and a handful of shells.

"It's loaded. I swopped two from the dance hall shelf and left a couple of our sub-machine guns in exchange. They'll sort it out."

The house was only fifty yards away across the square. We went in without meeting anyone and up to the third floor to a room overlooking the square. We didn't stand on ceremony. Just pushed the door open and went in with our revolvers ready, snapping on the light.

The room was empty. Two little folding cot beds, American army pattern, stood one against each wall. Everything was neat and tidy and unlived in.

We went downstairs and got hold of the *portera*. She was a big, sleepy-faced negress in a stained old wrap and her hair done up in twists of newspaper. The Hueica brothers had paid their rent and left early that morning. She didn't know where they had gone.

Monk said, "How did they go? Just walk out carrying their cases?"

On the *Mara II* they had each had a couple of cases, carrying their fortune and their furnishings with them, working their way back to Guatemala, to be big shots when they got back to Guadaloupe, or wherever it was. I could see them for the rest of their lives sitting around in some *cantina*, shuffling their feet on the pine-needle strewn floor as a juke box thundered out its endless *pasos dobles* and the tide went lower and lower in the bottle of *aguardiente*. In luxury for the rest of their lives on some substantial cut from my money.

The negress said, "They go by car, boss." She couldn't keep her eyes off my face and the sticking plaster.

"One of the taxis?" I asked.

"No, boss. In Lieutenant Ocampo's car. This mawnin'."

Outside, unsurprised, I said to Monk, "They must have been pretty sure they weren't going to be spotted. Or else General Lemaza didn't care a damn if they were. He never intended me to have that money." I laughed. "Except one way. I could have invested it in the revolution. I think he was honest about that. The bastard!"

Back in my room Monk poured some whiskey for us. I sat on the bed and he stood by the window, a big, bulky figure whose simple presence there was a great comfort to me.

He said, "Got to handle this carefully. No good steaming up to Lemaza with a revolver in your hand."

"I don't mean to. I'll tackle him through Katrina and Angelo. Damn it, the thing's so obvious. He's employed the Hueica brothers to rob me. I'll swear it. They must be on the island still. God, if I ever get hold of that Sardi——"

"Sardi, and Lemaza particularly, will deny everything. You were robbed by one of your own men. That's Lemaza's line."

"He won't be able to make that stick with Angelo. He's no fool. And he's honest." I finished my whiskey and slapped the glass down on the bedside table. "To think I fell for that petrol-water trick!"

Monk came across to me. He had the whiskey bottle in his hand and he filled his own glass. He held the bottle towards mine but I shook my head.

"Got to face one thing. You may never get this money back. What then?"

I stood up and began to unbutton my shirt front.

"That isn't going to happen, Monk. No bloody tin-pot dentist jumped up to Generalissimo is going to do that to me."

"Be careful."

"I'm going to get it. One way or another."

"Better have another whiskey. You won't sleep."

I didn't have more whiskey. But he was right. I didn't sleep. I lay there hearing the church bells ping out the hours and half-hours and I went over the whole thing, over and over again. I worked at it in the darkness and played it in my mind all the ways I could imagine it might go and I found

128

an answer for them all, an answer that would put me back to the point where I was walking again with the money under my arm and Drea on her way to meet me in Haiti. It had to be like that. Just had to be.

*   *   *

My face wasn't so bad the next morning. There was a big bruise running out from under the plaster to the top of my left cheek bone and the ache in my head was no more than a man might have from a mild hangover. I shaved and put on a clean shirt and suit and went out into the square.

The market stalls were up, brightening the morning with their reds, yellows and greens of tomatoes, maize and beans. An old man came through the crowd, whacking at the rump of a donkey piled high with bundles of cut bamboo, and a couple of old girls on a hardware stall shouted some good-natured obscenity to me as I passed. Yes, the world was stirring and full of vigour and happiness. Caramanga would soon fall and the future was bright with the prospect of free land and easy hours.

The *Singing Heart that Never Tires* was parked by the church and Singing Heart himself was asleep in the back. I woke him and told him I wanted to go to General Lemaza's headquarters.

"Man," he said, "you sure look fresh again. Powers of resistance. You sure got that. Yes, boss, you sure got to have that in this world. Now me, when I'm drunk, I'm drunk, man. Two, three days."

I got in the back. He went on talking most of the way but I didn't listen.

When we got to the gateway of the drive to the villa the sentry stopped the taxi. Unless I was in a military car with a military driver he couldn't let me through without a pass. I argued for a while but he was adamant. He did, however, tell me that the General was not up at the villa. He had driven out a little while before and gone towards the barracks. We went down there and this time I got Singing Heart to go and talk to the sentry at the entrance to the enclosure. He came back and told me that the General had been at the barracks for a while but had now gone up the road towards the air strip.

We motored up to the little group of huts by the stone jetty and I told Singing Heart to wait for me. I got out and walked towards the Nissen hut at the end of the strip. The six Furies were all up there now, wingless, propeller-less, and with a bunch of mechanics working around one of them. A sentry stopped me short of the hut, but I saw Parkes by the hut and shouted to him. He wasn't glad to see me, but he did as I asked, and ushered me past the sentry, biting the man's head off when he began to make a protest.

I asked him how things were and he said, "Not bad, not bad. But they're slow and you have to watch every move. What happened to your face?"

"I fell down the stairs."

He gave me an old-fashioned look but didn't pursue the subject. When we got to the hut he nodded inside. I'd told him what I wanted and he said, "You'll find His Nibs in there. Counting the screws and the spare parts."

I went into the great hut. At the far end, past the work benches and the piles of stores was a small glass-partitioned office. Generalissimo Lemaza was inside with Lieutenant Ocampo. They saw me coming; the General himself came out to meet me when I was about three-quarters of the way down the hut.

I gave him a good-morning and didn't waste words with him. I told him exactly what had happened, except that I didn't say that I had recognized Sardi. That was something I was keeping for Katrina and Angelo. He listened to me with patience and when I had finished he said—

"So, señor, I am sorry. . . . But what is there I can do? You have no description of the man. If you had I could have a search made for him. But it could be anyone. A Movement like this attracts all types . . . adventurers, the scum of the world. They are good fighters but when they are not fighting they are what they have always been . . . thieves, murderers. . . . But I feel for you. It is an unfortunate thing to happen."

Unfortunate, I thought, was a mild word.

I said, "I need that money. I mean to get it back."

"Naturally, señor, you feel like that. But what can I do?"

"There's one thing. I want to see Señorita Katrina. But I can't get by the sentry at the villa without a pass. You could give me that."

"But of course."

He turned, leaving me there and walked to the little office. A few moments later Lieutenant Ocampo came out and over to me. He handed me a pass, admitting me to the villa. General Lemaza was in the office, bending over a table. He didn't give a glance in my direction.

Ocampo said, "Your pass, señor."

His neat, dark little face showed nothing.

I went out and heard Parkes roaring at one of his men for smoking near a large dump of petrol cans on the runway.

Back at the taxi Singing Heart was standing on the jetty talking to a fisherman who had just come in with a motorboat and had thrown him a rope to make fast.

I gave him a shout and we started for the villa. I sat brooding in the back.

The sentry let us through this time and Singing Heart took me up to the front of the villa. There was an orderly at a small table in the hall and I went straight in to him.

"I'd like to see Señorita Katrina," I said.

He stood up politely.

"I'm sorry, señor. She is not here."

"Where is she?"

"She went early this morning to San Pedro."

"San Pedro?"

"Yes, señor. With her brother, the Leader Libertad."

The cunning bastard. No wonder he'd given me the pass so easily.

"When will they be back?"

"I don't know, señor. Two, three days. Is there anything I can do?"

"No . . . its nothing. I was here to dinner last night and I left my cigarette lighter. If it's all right with you I'll go through and get it. I think I know where I left it."

131

"Certainly, señor."

He sat down and I went over to the door of the large lounge. I shut the door behind me but I didn't waste any time in the lounge. The door of the General's office was unlocked and I went in. There was a safe in the wall opposite the window but it would have taken a better man than me and the right tools to get it open. Anyway that wasn't the way to do things. I wanted a case against the General that I could put before Angelo. Something that couldn't be ignored.

His desk was neat, both his In and his Out baskets empty. A half-empty box of Elvas plums stood by the telephone. The waste-paper basket was empty. Sometime last night I was sure either Sardi, but more likely Ocampo, had come into this room with my box file. The dollars would be in the safe. But the box file might not be. It wasn't, however, anywhere in the room.

I went back into the hall through the lounge, held up my lighter to the orderly with a smile and then walked out to Singing Heart.

I leaned on the door and said, "You know this house well, Singing Heart?"

"Yes, boss. Owner of sugar plantations live here before. I done jobs around this place when I was a boy. Before I got up and coming and get brain. What for, boss?"

"What do they do with the junk they throw out?"

"What you want that for, boss?"

I pulled out a ten-dollar bill.

"Just answer the questions, Singing Heart, and then forget they were ever asked. You'd do that for me?"

He grinned. "For any man with a ten-dollar bill in his hand, boss." He took the bill and said, "Get in, boss."

A hundred yards down the drive he stopped the car.

"Over there. Behind them bushes."

To the left of the drive was a large growth of bamboo flanked by two or three oleander bushes. Behind them I found a small gardener's shed and to one side of it a brick-sided incinerator with a tin top punched with ragged holes. A couple of cans of wet rubbish stood alongside and two sacks of old paper and cartons. I lifted the lid of the incinerator. It was empty except for a few black ashes at the bottom. No fire had been lit there that morning. I went through the first sack of papers without any luck. Half-way down the second sack I found my box file. It was dry but stained with mud where it had fallen on the ground by the trough. It was empty, too. I took it and went into the shed which was full of hoes and long-handled spades. I pushed the box right up under the thatch where it was out of sight.

Singing Heart was a good boy but General Lemaza had more ten-dollar bills than I had. Sometime during the day the rubbish would be burnt. I wanted the General to think the file had been burnt, too. It was tucked away where I could find it when the moment came.

I went back to Singing Heart and he looked at me puzzled.

"You all that interested in trash, boss?"

"Sure, some people have made a fortune collecting rubbish. I knew a man once who made himself an aeroplane, just out of stuff he picked up from dumps."

He laughed. "That's for me."

We went back to Acaibo and I was feeling better. I was going to get the General up against a wall, squirming in front of Angelo and Katrina.

There was a little telephone booth at the back of the hotel hall. There was no directory or instructions on how to make calls. I picked up the receiver and after a while a man's voice answered. I told him that I wanted to make a call to Army Headquarters at San Pedro. Privately, I didn't expect to be able to get hold of Angelo, but there was a fair chance that I might get Katrina.

The operator said, "Who is this calling?"

"Señor Marchant at the *Hotel de la Reina*."

"Ha. . . ." I could hear the sigh of recognition and he went on amicably, "The señor who brought in the planes?"

"That's it."

"I am sorry, señor. Maybe you do not know the rules? Calls from civilians are restricted to a radius of five miles of

Acaibo. It is an Army Order. For a civilian to speak outside that radius he must have Army authority and use an Army telephone. Application for this may be made to Lieutenant Ocampo, the town commandant. In your case, señor, I should think that there would be no difficulty after all you have done for us."

"Thank you."

I put the receiver down. In my case there would be every difficulty. I didn't mean even to try. They would have to come back. Singing Heart had told me that in a few days' time the People's Democratic Movement would be celebrating the fifth anniversary of the outbreak of the revolution. Angelo Libertad was due in Acaibo for this. Apparently there was a review of troops in the town square and a blessing of colours service in the church. Not once in five years had he missed this, for it was in Acaibo that the fight had started originally. All I had to do was to sit time out patiently. It meant that I would be later than I had anticipated getting to Drea.

I picked up Monk and told him what had happened and then we walked down to the harbour for a drink at the *Cantina del Morro* before lunch. We got there just in time to see the *Mara II* going out.

We watched her go and I could see the small figure of the captain on one of the bridge wings.

In the *cantina*, Da Silva was playing cards with the flyers. He gave me a brief nod over their heads. If they thought they'd enticed a sucker into their school they were mistaken.

I said to Monk, "Where does Da Silva hang out?"

"Tino's given him a room over this place, I believe."

"I'd like to know what he's after."

"That's easy. These people have got planes. Success around the corner. The big boys want to invest. Da Silva comes from them."

"The General would go along with that. But not Angelo. Not if they promised him a dozen Sherman tanks and two cruisers. He's doing this on his own."

"Da Silva wouldn't be staying if it were all that hopeless."

Tino brought us our drinks. He looked at my piece of

plaster and clucked his tongue. "It is a bad place that *la Reina*. Always fighting."

"I slipped on a banana skin."

He smiled and on his way back to the bar stopped to fiddle for a moment with the vase of flowers in the broken juke box. Today there were white marguerites.

We drank and Monk was quiet, rolling a cigarette.

After a time I said, "I've been thinking of that place you said Eglantina's brother had."

"Why?"

"Because of Lemaza. He must know I'm waiting for Angelo to come back. He's no fool. Something could happen to me. I could slip and go over the harbour side. An Army truck could side-swipe me. I could make a list a page long. Both of us should get away."

Monk nodded. "Good idea. Eglantina's brother's place is on the north side. We could go there tonight and keep low. Walk it. No trusting *Singing Hearts* or *Space Sputnik Specials*."

"That's what I think." General Lemaza was king around here. Anything could happen.

Monk fished in his back pocket for his notebook and with his pencil drew a little sketch of the north coast. I could follow it because I'd driven along the road with Singing Heart.

"I was up there yesterday with Eglantina for a drive," he said. "We'll go tonight."

Somewhere out at the mouth of the bay the *Mara II* suddenly sounded her siren . . . a long, derisive hooting that came wailing back to us as she hit the open sea.

* II *

AFTER lunch I went up to my room and had an hour's sleep. It was the best time to sleep really. The heat cleared the square and Acaibo dropped off into the quiet of a long siesta. At night the place was full of noise from the leave parties that came swarming in after six o'clock. It was nothing to have drunken officers or men blundering into your room at two and three in the morning. You couldn't stop them because all the bolts and locks on the doors had long been broken from constant battering. And even when the leave parties cleared off the radio was usually left on in the hall, nattering away all night.

When I woke it was about three o'clock. I lay on the bed and gradually became aware that something was different. A truck rumbled through the square and I heard men shouting. There was silence for a while, and then another truck came roaring into the square and pulled up with a screech of brakes somewhere near the church. I heard the clatter of heavy boots as men jumped down from it. Orders were shouted and there was the sound of running footsteps. House doors slammed. Another truck burst through the square and I heard it revving away on the hill beyond the harbour.

I got up and went to the window. There was an open army truck by the church. Two men squatted behind a machine gun which was mounted on it. At intervals around the square soldiers were posted, carrying their rifles at the ready. A squad of four men came out of the house where the Hueica brothers had lodged and went into the next house. Farther up the square I could see another party working from house to house.

From the hallway of the hotel I heard voices and the clatter of feet. I leaned out of the window and saw that there was a soldier on guard at the hotel entrance. As I drew back from the window the door of my room was pushed open. A soldier came in while another one stood in the doorway and covered me and the room with his rifle.

"What the hell——" I began.

The soldier in the room said curtly, "Just stay where you are, señor."

I stood where I was.

The soldier went over to my bed and looked under it. He went then to the small curtained recess that hid a hand wash-basin. He jerked the curtain aside. He turned back to the door.

"Nothing," he said to the other soldier. They went, slamming the door after them. I heard them working their way through the other rooms on the floor.

A little later I saw them come out of the front of the hotel and disappear down the square. I went along to Monk's room to see if he knew what all the fuss was about.

Eglantina was sitting on Monk's bed. She was wearing a loose yellow silk wrapper and underneath was stripped to her bust bodice and pants against the sticky heat. She pulled the wrapper close to make herself decent. The movement sent two or three shirts balanced on her knees to the floor. A tobacco tin full of odd buttons was on the bed at her side and she had a needle and thread in one hand. She gave me a grin and said:

"Every time this man put on shirt he busts off buttons like shelling peas."

"Where is he?"

"Harbour. Every afternoon he plays 'bout with that motor-boat of my brother. Gonna fix it so one day we make trip to Caramanga. . . ." She glanced at the open door and shrugged her shoulders. "Like things go now, though, maybe we won't need it. Go there by road in one, two months' time."

"What's all the fuss about outside? And these soldiers? Were they here?"

"Sure. They didn't tell you?"

"No."

"Them soldiers looking for that one you bring in. That John MacIntyre Albano man. He done a skip from the barracks. They look all over for him."

"He's out?"

"Sure, he's out. One of those soldiers is friend of my brother. Tell me 'bout it. Got away two hours since. Hit the guard over head when his food is brought, take his clothes and walk straight out pass all them sentries."

"Well, good for him. But General Lemaza will have someone's head for this."

"Could be. You need anything fixing, buttons or something, while I got steam up?"

"No thanks, Eglantina."

I went out and downstairs, thinking I'd go and find Monk, but I wasn't allowed to leave the hotel. There was a sentry outside and nobody moved anywhere until they had finished their searching. The way they were going about it I didn't think Albano would have much chance—unless he'd got smartly into the hills behind Acaibo. Once there he might have a chance. . . . I had my own troubles and they didn't leave any room for his. It was a pretty selfish attitude, but then I was in no mood to think about other people except the ones who were making it difficult for me to get what I wanted. Concentrating on one thing can give you a narrow view of life, like walking along with blinkers and only seeing right ahead of your nose. That may be all right for a horse in shafts but it doesn't help any man. In my business you don't want any blind areas. To keep healthy you need a hundred and eighty degree arc of fire. This job had me committed right up to the neck. It just couldn't be allowed to flop. It had to be successful because I had the biggest stake in its success. I couldn't pay enough attention to all the little straws that were being blown in the wind. A straw at the right moment can trip a man as surely as a tautly stretched wire. Placed as I was I needed the kind of vision which could "look into the seeds of time and say which grain will grow and which will not." Nothing was going to stop me from getting my money and meeting Drea in Haiti.

Meeting Drea in Haiti. That was my future. Towards that one point I lived. Back in my room, lying on my bed and listening to the noises from the square, I thought about her and our first meeting, of the first moment when I had seen her on the deck of the old stern paddler going up to Bogota. It was the rainy season and the river was in yellow flood. She'd come past me, wearing a white mackintosh, her chestnut hair free to the wind, and my eyes had followed her, but right from that moment it had not been the idle compulsion of watching an attractive woman. I watched her go by to the stern and then come back, walking with that grace which was peculiarly hers, and I don't think she even saw me. Later that day the steamer had broken down. It was always breaking down and usually at well-regulated calls in some river port where the captain could spend a pleasant three hours drinking while his engineer sweated. This time it broke down in mid-stream and there were a few minutes of panic while we drifted on the flood into the bank, crashing into the overhanging trees, and then were finally made fast. After six hours the captain announced that no repair could be made until he sent up-stream for spares. The steamer would be delayed for at least twenty-four hours. Most of the passengers, country people for whom time meant nothing, elected to stay on board. Bogota was two days upstream. What did it matter if it took four days? Or six days? It mattered to me. I wanted to get to Bogota in a hurry. I knew this part of the country, so I decided to go ashore to walk to a village a couple of miles inland where I thought I could get a car.

As I was going off the steamer Drea came up to me.

"The captain tells me that you want to get to Bogota in a hurry and you're going to hire a car?"

"I think I can get one in San Juan—that's a couple of miles away." It was the first time I had heard her speak and there was a slight huskiness in the voice somehow so right with that controlled puma-like grace of her body.

"Can I share it? I don't want to be stuck here a couple of days. I know these boats."

"If you don't mind the walk. It's rough going."

She got her case and came with me We didn't speak much, and a few minutes after we left the steamer it began to rain. It took us an hour to make San Juan and we were wet and muddy when we reached it. It was almost dark and we went to the one hotel, little more than a *cantina*. I asked the proprietor about a car and he said that there was one. His brother drove it, but he was away with a wedding party and wouldn't be back until the early morning.

I turned to Drea and said, "There's nothing we can do. It's this or back to the steamer, and frankly this is no night for walking. The car will be here in the morning and we can make Bogota by tomorrow evening."

"This," she said.

I asked the proprietor if he had rooms for us and he nodded. He took our cases off and we dried ourselves in front of the fire. There was a kind of stiffness, almost shyness, between us which made talk difficult. It was as though we were both waiting for the other to say something pertinent and revealing which would allow us to be easy with one another. The place was dead, the bar empty and the proprietor's wife killed a couple of small chickens and made supper for us. The chickens were the toughest I'd ever had. We had a couple of drinks and a bottle of wine, but they did nothing for us. I had the feeling all the time, that much as she attracted me, we could easily finish up by disliking one another. One or other of us only had to say the wrong word. The right word didn't seem to exist.

Later, when we decided to go up to our rooms, we discovered that the proprietor had taken us for man and wife. He only had one room and he showed us into it. It had a big double bed with a crumpled blue silk spread. We stood in the doorway looking at it and I think the proprietor took our silence for admiration, for he nodded at the bed and said, "Very beautiful, no? I am married in it. Anita has all our children there. Seven, señor. All married now."

I told him that we weren't married, but if he could find me a couple of blankets I'd sleep by the fire in the bar.

He was embarrassed about his mistake and spent a long time apologizing. Drea said nothing but I noticed that she was smiling.

I said good night to her and went back to the bar. I had a last drink and the proprietor's wife brought me in some blankets and cushions and I made myself comfortable. I lay

140

there by myself in the glow of the fire, far from sleep and thinking about Drea. I was puzzled by the barrier to even the most ordinary conversation between us. And then after an hour she came down in her dressing-gown.

I sat up as she came over to the fire.

"What's the matter?" I asked. The fire gleams on her hair caught my eyes and I could feel my heart beginning to pump rapidly.

"Bed bugs," she said. "They came out of the mattress like an army. I couldn't cope with them. Have you had trouble?"

"None."

She stood over me and said, "Do you mind if I share the fire with you?"

"Of course not."

She lay down on the blankets beside me and put her hands behind her head, staring up at the smoke-brown ceiling. For a long time she was silent and then, suddenly, without looking at me she said, "We don't seem to have much to say to one another. Why?"

"I don't know. There's a lot I want to say. I think I'm scared . . . of saying the wrong thing. It must be something new."

"Is there anything new?"

"I think so. . . ."

She half-turned her head and looked at me. Her eyes were very close to mine. Then she nodded her head and said, "Yes, I think there is. I think so."

I moved enough to reach her and put my lips on hers. She let me kiss her, but it was cool and unrevealing and after a second or two she lay back and stared at the ceiling again, smiling. I put out a hand, to find hers. She shook her head.

"Not yet," she said. "There's lots of time ahead."

I relaxed, not looking at her, but knowing she was there and that slowly the right words would come, that no matter now what we said or did it would be beyond our power to escape. And it had been like that. Not that night. Not the next day when we got to Bogota. But it had come and there was no more that I wanted. Nowhere else in the world was there anything that I wanted more than Drea and our love.

* * *

It was two hours before they took the guards off the square and we could move about freely. Eglantina had found a couple of light bags for us and we planned just to take these with a few necessities and leave the rest of our stuff in our cases at the hotel. I kept my revolver out handy. Of the four sub-machine guns we had brought (the Hueica brothers had handed theirs over to us when the *Mara II* had docked) two had already gone in exchange for revolvers. Of the others Monk and I had one each. I packed mine in the bottom of the case I was going to leave at the hotel, together with the tear-gas grenades. We planned to leave about an hour after darkness. The place then would be jumping with parties and no one would pay any attention to us. When I was all ready to go, I sat down and wrote a letter to Drea. I kept it short, merely explaining that the job was going well but that I might be delayed a few days before getting out. Then I walked down to the *Cantina del Morro* and gave it to Tino. He knew all the skippers who came in and out. If he could find one going to Haiti so much the better, but anywhere with a postal system would do. He just looked at the address, Hotel Montana, Port-au-Prince, Haiti, and said, "Nice place. If you can afford it."

With luck, I thought, as I walked back through the thick swift-gathering dusk, I might be there before the letter. Monk was in the bar and we had a drink together.

I said, "You heard Albano's out?"

"Yes. They were down the harbour. Going over all the boats. He knows this country. He'll be up in the mountains. They're offering a reward for him—alive. If he weren't the son of the Minister of Defence it would be dead or alive. Lemaza doesn't want any assets spoiled."

I said, "I wonder where Lemaza laid up the Hueica brothers?"

"In the barracks would be my guess."

"I'd like just ten minutes alone with Sardi. My God, I would."

142

"If you get it, make sure he hasn't a knife in his hand."
He looked at his watch. "Another half hour and we should
push off. I've fixed the motor-boat up. Could have taken
that and had a nice trip round. But with this Albano business
they've got their eye on all the boats." He patted his belly.
"Walk'll take this down. Nice night for it too."

We passed the half hour in the bar and then Monk said,
"Time to start. I'll go first. Meet you by the water trough on
the hill. From there we'll start being careful."

He went out and I stayed, finishing my drink. Eglantina
was singing her blues number. I couldn't see or hear any im-
provement in her act. There were quite a few dancers but
the place hadn't started to warm up yet. I gave Monk ten
minutes and then I went up to my room to get my bag.

I pushed open my door and went in. The light was on.
Lieutenant Ocampo was standing by the window. There
was a soldier standing just inside the door and another bending over my bed and on the point of closing the lid of my
case.

Lieutenant Ocampo said, "Good evening, Señor Marchant."

The soldier by the door slid behind me and blocked the
way out. On the top of the dressing-table close to Ocampo
were four grenades, the sub-machine gun, my revolver and
a pile of ammunition.

"What the devil are you doing here?" I demanded.

Ocampo gave a neat little shrug of his shoulders and he
pursed his lips primly before answering. He looked too damn
satisfied with himself.

He said, "The standing orders for civilians in Acaibo are
posted in the hotel lobby, señor. You have read them?"

"No, I haven't. The whole place is crumby with notices
for this and that. Anyway, what's it got to do with me? You
don't consider me a civilian, do you?"

"Why not, señor? While you worked for us, no. But your
work is finished. The standing orders state that all civilians
must hand over their arms to the Town Commandant.
These"—he jerked his head towards the dressing-table—"I
shall have to confiscate. Ordinarily there would be a fine for

143

the breach. But in the circumstances, I think we can dispense with that, señor."

"I should damn well hope so, after what I've done for you. Now, do you mind getting to hell out of here?"

He didn't like my attitude and I didn't mean him to like it. But he didn't rise to it.

He said to the soldier by the bed, "Corporal, search him."

The soldier came over to me. He had a revolver in his right hand. With his other hand he felt over my clothes, and then stepped back, shaking his head.

"Good," said Lieutenant Ocampo. "Then let us go."

"That's all right with me," I said angrily. This jumped-up popinjay was getting under my skin; the whole place was getting under my skin. I'd done a job for them and they'd welshed on me. I had to be careful to keep my thinking about it within limits otherwise I knew I should start breaking something. "The sooner you get out the better."

The Corporal went to the dressing-table and packed the arms and ammunition into a small canvas bag. Then he stood smartly alongside Ocampo. The soldier at the door opened it and stood to one side.

I waited for them to go. But none of them made any move.

Ocampo motioned towards the bed, on which lay my case and the light bag packed for my trip with Monk.

"You will want those, señor?"

I stared at him.

"What are you talking about?"

He gave a sigh then as though he were losing patience with some dumbwitted child.

"Since you are leaving, señor, you will naturally want to take your things."

"But I'm not going anywhere. Look, what is all this?"

He raised his hands slightly and rubbed the palms on the smooth leather of his belt. He had rather a fancy revolver holster studded with brass rivets in the shape of his initials, A. O.

He said in his patient-parent voice, "Señor, my instructions from General Lemaza were to make this as least

144

embarrassing to you as possible. After all we are grateful for what you have done. It is for this that I did not come to you in the bar, where the scene would have been too public. My instructions are to see you aboard with every courtesy."

"Aboard!"

"Yes, señor. Those are the instructions from the General." A hand slid up to his tunic breast pocket, and he began to fiddle with the button to bring out his instructions.

"Don't bother," I snapped. "Let me get this straight. You're going to see me aboard? I'm being kicked out?"

"If you put it that way, señor."

There were a lot of ways I could put it. I didn't need it in words of two syllables. I wondered if it were worth-while trying to make a break for the door. I stood there, seething with frustration and anger. If Ocampo had come half an hour later I would have been away.

I said, "I want to see the General."

Ocampo gave his neat shrug. "It is impossible, señor. He has gone up to San Pedro this evening. My instructions are to put you aboard the *Aciano*, which is leaving tonight. Your case, señor." He waved his hand towards the bed.

I said, "What about the rest of my party?"

Ocampo said, "My instructions concern you only, señor." He gave me a brief smile which was about as warming as a cold draught.

Sandwiched between the two soldiers I went down the stairs. It was on the stairs that I'd already decided to take my chance, drop my cases and jump for it. If I could reach the square I might get away. But Ocampo's instructions covered the possibility that I might try to escape. There were two more soldiers in the hotel hallway, just by the door. I went down, decided to do nothing.

Outside the hotel his car was waiting. I was put in the back between the soldiers and he sat in front with the driver. The two soldiers from the hall stood, one on each running-board. No chances were going to be given to me. A few people outside watched us curiously, and I saw Singing Heart standing by his cab near the church. Up at the water trough Monk would be waiting for me and wondering what

145

had happened. . . . I owed Monk three thousand dollars for his work. Forty thousand dollars. And Drea in Haiti. Inside me there was a volcano waiting to blow its head off. I thought of the letter I had written to Drea. It looked as though I were going to beat it to Haiti . . . I'd walk in to the hotel and there would be Drea waiting. She'd take one look at me and she would know.

The warm night air pressed against my face as the car swept around the curve of the harbour, past the row of red bulbs over the door of the *Cantina del Morro*, out towards the dark plug of the Citadel. There was a length of quayside there where the schooners and motor-craft of the gun-runners, the petrol carriers and all the other black-market stores came in.

The *Aciano* was a refurbished torpedo boat, low and squat and painted a pale sky blue. Three men leaned over the starboard rail and watched our little procession. One of them was wearing a high-crowned Mexican hat and had a guitar in his hand. The other two were in dirty singlets and greasy trousers. One of them had a long, naked woman tattooed the length of his right arm. I was taken forward to the old ward-room, which was about the size of a good hen hut. A young man with a pink and white face and a yachting cap at an angle opened the door and I was invited to step in.

I had the place to myself and one glance showed me that the ports were too small to let me out. Ocampo stood at the door and rubbed his palms again on his leather belt.

"This boat sails in an hour," he said. "There will be a guard on the door until she sails. You will be confined here until she is outside the three-mile limit."

He was about to close the door on me when the pink-and-white-faced youngster said cheerfully in English, "There's whiskey and cigarettes on the side there, chum. Help yourself. Don't try anything because these bastards mean business."

The door closed and I had the place to myself and my luggage.

There were a couple of bottles of Four Roses on the sideboard. I helped myself to a large whiskey, neat, and flopped into a cane chair, my feet and legs sprawled out, and let the savageness in me run free. It took a long time and I had to keep telling myself to stop thinking about what had happened, stop killing Lemaza and Ocampo in my mind, but to chuck away the past and get down to the future. I had to have my forty thousand. Some way I had to have it. . . .

An hour later I heard the engines start up, heard men call and move about the deck. By that time I'd calmed down a bit and was beginning to think. To think ahead.

*   *   *

The *Aciano* moved away from the quayside and a little later I felt her begin to lift and swing as she met the sea outside the shelter of the harbour. She was running easily, not pressing her motors. After about half an hour the door was unlocked. The young man with the yachting cap came in and gave me a grin.

"Rimmy will be down in a minute," he said.

"Who's Rimmy?"

"The captain." His grin broadened. "You're taking it very well. Not nice to be kicked out. I'd be out for blood."

"I'm saving that," I said. "Marchant's the name."

"Yes, I know. Sea Furies."

He went to the sideboard and helped himself to a drink, saying over his shoulder, "I'm Foxton. You must have stepped on someone's toe. Big three-star toes. The higher the rank the bigger the bastard. Brief military service taught me that one."

"You're English?"

"No. Everyone thinks so. Swedish. The name isn't, but then it isn't my name. If they think you're English," he gave a shrug, "might as well go along with it."

He came back with a glass of whiskey so full that it reminded me of the one Katrina had first poured for me. He knocked back half of it in a couple of swallows and smacked his lips. Seeing me watching him, he said:

"No drinking in port. Rimmy's orders. Sound, too. Mostly we're at sea. Get drunk in joints like Acaibo and there's always some bastard trouble."

147

"Where are you heading?"

He shrugged. "Don't know **until Rimmy** says. Last time it was Curaçao. Help yourself to a drink." He took another pull at his whiskey, and went on, "Where do you want?"

I got up and helped myself to a whiskey.

"I want Acaibo," I said.

He shook his head. "Rimmy would never wear that one. . . ." He tipped his chair back and switched on a radio on a shelf above his head. Some American station flooded the ward-room with dance music. He relaxed with his glass cuddled on his belt and began to sing the words gently.

I sat and waited for Rimmy.

He came down a little later. His procedure was the same as Foxton's. He went straight to the sideboard and poured himself a whiskey. He took a swig at it as he stood there, back to me, and then turned.

"Sorry about this. Don't hold it against us. If I hadn't taken you the General would have made trouble for us. We've got all we need of that." He spoke English, but it was much more accented than Foxton's. He was a big man, well in his fifties, with short blond hair going a little white over the ears, a big bushy beard, and a fine, strong body showing no signs of flabbiness. He looked the hard, carefree type who could float happily on a balso raft for half a year to prove something about sea currents. He wore a lightweight, high-necked blue jersey and white trousers. Big toes stuck out through the open ends of leather sandals.

I said, "What are they paying you to take me?"

"Two hundred dollars. It's not a long trip so you can't eat or drink into too much of that. Hundred and eighty left by the time I land you." He came over, flopped into a chair by the table, and reached back and turned the radio down to a whisper.

"They paid me forty thousand dollars for bringing in the Sea Furies, paid it, and then hit me over the head and took it back."

He shook his head sadly. "What is it they say? When you sup with the devil use a long spoon? Lemaza is a sharp business man. Me, I never unload until the money has been

148

paid." He nodded at a safe in the corner of the ward-room. "Lock it in there before the hatches come off. Don't deal with him much, though. Only our second run here . . . iodine, sulpha drugs, bandages, quinine. Could have a red cross painted on the deck, eh?" He laughed gently to himself.

I said, "I've got to get back there. I need that money and I know how to get it."

He looked at Foxton, who held up his whiskey glass and squinted through it.

Rimmy said, "It would mean we couldn't come back here again."

Foxton said, "Plenty of other markets, Rimmy. He's in our league. We ought to help, what?" He got up and went to fill his glass. Over his shoulder he said, "Who's got the wheel?"

"Joey. There isn't a rock between here and South America he doesn't know. Sure," he put his glass down on the table, "we ought to help. But what is help?"

I said, "Two hundred and fifty dollars. Take me up to the north coast and put me over in a dinghy half a mile from shore. Just before dawn tomorrow."

"Dinghies cost money. We wouldn't see ours back."

"Three hundred." I had just about that in my wallet.

"Not just the money, Foxton knows that. It's you, brother-worker. You'd only get yourself in a mess and still no money."

"It's his neck," said Foxton. He'd drawn a whiskey to match Rimmy's this time, right to the brim of a tumbler. He was a nice lad, but even though he was on my side I knew that I had been landed with a couple of soakers. I wanted to get things fixed while they could still give the crew a few orders. Foxton took a pull at his glass to prevent it slopping as he walked. He went back to his seat carrying the second bottle with him and put it by Rimmy's glass. Rimmy topped his glass up and poured a healthy shot into mine.

"It's his neck," said Rimmy. "But I don't like people getting into that kind of mess. Quixotic. What chance have you got?"

"I just want five minutes with Angelo Libertad. He's due back tomorrow or the next day. A few words with him or his sister who came over with me on the *Mara II* and I can have the pressure put on Lemaza. I've got a friend ashore, waiting for me in a hiding-place."

Rimmy cocked an eye at Foxton.

Foxton said, "His neck. But he's got it worked out. I think we should for two-fifty."

"Three hundred," said Rimmy, grinning. "It's a beautiful dinghy. Mahogany fittings, clinker built, silver rowlocks and a built-in radio. Couldn't replace it for a hundred."

They both laughed together and I could tell that the drink was working fast. I took a sip at my own glass. Heavy drinkers don't like to see you hanging back and I needed all their goodwill.

"Three hundred," I said. "And I can look after myself."

"Can you?" Rimmy scratched at his blond beard. "You've already looked after yourself forty-thousand dollars down. Maybe you need protection. I don't like people I like to get messed up."

"I was day-dreaming before. Now I'm awake and coming back fast. Let me worry about myself." I had to get him soon because there would be no shaking him in fifteen minutes. He'd be full of drunken philanthropy and father-love for me, determined to save my neck.

Neither of them said anything for a while. They took their whiskey glasses down to well below the plimsoll line, topped them up before they hit bottom, and considered the situation in silence. I'd met some heavy drinkers before, but these two were all-time champions and they had the champions' knack of never letting the bottom of the glass dry out. Curious thing was, they both looked so damned healthy on it.

"Where'd we take the next cargo?" asked Rimmy out of the blue. "No welcome at Acaibo."

"Heard Batista's boys were starting up in Cuba and places. Could try that," said Foxton.

I said, "Where are you heading now?"

"Curaçao," said Foxton.

"Aruba," said Rimmy.

"Both Dutch," said Foxton. "Nice, clean Dutch. Eat off the floors."

"Wherever it is," I said, pulling out my notebook, "ring this number in Barranquilla and speak to Señor Barrau." I scribbled his number as I spoke and tore out the page. "He's got a stake in the forty thousand. He'll fix your next cargo."

"Barrau?" Rimmy took the paper.

"Yes. He does your kind of business."

"Barranquilla?" Foxton leaned back and put the radio up a shade. "Wha's like?" It was the first shade of slipping I'd heard from either of them.

"A paradise," I said.

"A paradise on earth, eh?" Rimmy nodded to himself. "I'd like that."

"We'll go there," said Foxton. "Yes?"

"Yes," said Rimmy, and looking at me, he went on, "You come along, too. Can't miss a paradise."

Foxton, on my side still but fast easing off, said, "He wants Acaibo. Remember?"

"So?" Rimmy's hand went out for the bottle.

Foxton was silent for a moment and then with a sudden spurt of brightness he said, "Know what? Let's put it to the vote. Acaibo or not for him. Eh?"

"Good idea," said Rimmy. He was smiling gently at his half-full glass. "All those in favour of Acaibo for the señor raise right hand."

Foxton put up his hand and Rimmy kept his down. I raised my right hand. Rimmy looked around at us and then said, "O.K. Carried two to one. Democratic decision."

I raised my glass and drank to them and they acknowledged the toast, and while the goodwill stirred strongly in them I said, "Maybe you should get your helmsman Joey down and give him instructions now."

"Okay. Okay," said Rimmy.

Foxton leaned back and pressed a push-button switch close to the radio. A horn sounded on deck. A few minutes later the man I had seen with the high Mexican hat on deck came into the ward-room. It took about ten minutes for him to get his instructions from the two of them, but he showed no surprise or concern at their state, and he was dead sober.

When he went Foxton said, "First-class chap, Joey."

"First-class," said Rimmy.

"Officers drink at sea. Crew drink in port. Excellent system," said Foxton.

Half an hour later they were both as drunk as I'd seen anyone for a long time. But they were still sitting up and taking it, talking now to one another in Swedish. I left them and went on deck and they didn't know that I had gone.

*　　　*　　　*

Two hours before dawn I went down to the ward-room. The radio was going full blast. There were three empty whiskey bottles rolling gently about the floor, clinking now and again with the odd glass. Rimmy was asleep in a cane chair, snoring hard. Foxton was lying on the floor with his head pillowed on a pile of old magazines. He was breathing evenly and looked the picture of health. I counted out three hundred dollars from my wallet and left them on the table with a scribbled note of thanks. I picked up my case and light bag and went on deck.

Joey was in the wheelhouse, his face just touched with the light from the binnacle. He pointed away to the port hand and said:

"Red light. That's on palm tree at air strip."

I could see it dimly, losing it now and again as we swung in a swell that was coming in from the north-west. We were around the eastern tip of Cordillo and running steadily up the north shore. But I couldn't see any land. The night was overcast. We were running without lights except the one in the wheelhouse over the binnacle.

Joey said, "Captain sleep?"

I nodded.

"Good man, captain."

"Is he always drunk at sea?"

"No. Only first three days. Señor Foxton two days. Not so tough."

"How long have you been with them?"

"Five year. Everyone here five, four year. Not same boat though. You got trouble in Acaibo?"

"Yes."

Up forward I could see the shapes of two men getting the lashings off the dinghy. Now and again a lick of spray came back over the bows, flecking the deck briefly with dying phosphorescence.

"I had trouble in Mexico once. That's why I leave. You got gun?" He looked down at my cases.

"No."

"Need gun? German Mauser pistol. Twenty-six rounds. Always keep clean since Mexico but never use. Fifteen dollars."

I bought it. It would make me feel more comfortable when I got ashore.

We ran for another half hour and then I told him to take the *Aciano* in. We stood in for about a mile and then he cut the motors down so that we just held our way against the run of the sea.

"No farther, señor. Bad coast." He nodded to the fore-deck where the two men were waiting. *"Adios. . . ."*

They lowered the dinghy and held it while I went over. My case and bag were handed down. The man with the tatooed woman on his arm pointed obliquely to the south-east. "Keep her heading that way. The wind and tide will take you, señor."

They let go and the dinghy slid down the port side and in a few moments was astern of the *Aciano*. As I unshipped the oars the motors roared and there was the quick white creaming of foam above the *Aciano's* screws as she turned away and went out to sea.

I didn't hurry. I had plenty of time and darkness and I wanted the light to be just breaking as I closed in to the cliffs. I rowed easily for half an hour, and then the first grey loom of light began to ease up like a long bruise along the eastern horizon. A little later I could make out the low line of cliffs, their tops fringed by tall palms. Once I saw the headlights of a truck or car come snaking along the cliff-road making for Acaibo.

I found a small V-shaped beach running sharply back
into the cliffs and put the dinghy ashore on hard white sand.
She hadn't got the *Aciano's* name painted on her. I pulled
her up the sands and dragged her into a rock cleft. The beach
didn't look as though it were used much. In fact, at its head
there was no path up to the cliff top. I had a fairly easy
climb up through shrub and rocks. Half-way up I hid my
case under a rock and piled dead palm fronds over it. I
wanted to travel light and my bag was enough. The sun
lipped the eastern sea as I reached the top. The coast road
was about fifty yards away through a grove of king palms.
I sat down and had a look at Monk's map. So far as I could
make out I had to go about three miles westwards along the
road and then take a small path up into the mountain country. About a mile off the road Eglantina's brother had a
small plantain holding which hadn't been worked for three
years. Whether Monk would be there or not I couldn't
know. He would have waited for me at the trough for a
while and then certainly have gone back to find out what
had happened. If he had stayed in Acaibo I would have to
get in touch with him.

Monk wasn't there.

12

THE path ran up into the mountains, following a steep valley which had been cut into terraces in the usual *barranco* fashion to make small plots of ground for cultivation. It was obvious that there had been no work on the terraces since the beginning of the revolution. Everything was overgrown. I passed a couple of drum-shaped concrete water reservoirs. They were empty and given over to lizards and ghekkos. The hut was about a thousand feet up and built of timber and bamboos, the palm thatch gone in places. It sat back squatly against the mountainside, screened by shrubs and backed by a clump of immortelle trees, their flaming blossoms vivid against the blue sky.

Monk wasn't there. It was just one large room and then a sort of lean-to construction at the back which housed the cooking quarters. Against one wall of the main room was a rough wooden bunk with a mildewed canvas mattress.

I fetched some water from a small trickle that came down the hillside not far from the house, made a fire, and gave myself a shave and a swab down. Afterwards, I sat at the hut door and smoked, watching the path. Now and again, very faintly, I thought I could catch the rumble of distant artillery fire up towards San Pedro. I sat there for a couple of hours and it began to be clear to me that Monk wasn't coming. Once he had heard what had happened to me there would be no reason to come out here. He had far too much sense to go and make trouble with Ocampo about my deportation. He might even begin to question his own safety in Acaibo. More than likely he would decide that it was time for Eglantina and himself to clear out and would be working hard to get the motor-boat fixed up. I decided to give him until mid-day. I sat there and watched the sun climb higher. The heat increased and my only company came from a

couple of fork-tailed kites that circled in the air currents
high above the valley.

By now, I thought, Drea was on her way to Port-au-
Prince, could be there even. It was curious that it should
have been Port-au-Prince and the Hotel Montana again.
Once before she'd walked out on me; not being able to say
then what she had said this time. I'd been frantic, not understanding, knowing only that I had to find her. I had caught
up with her there. It had taken me a month to find her. As
I had got out of my taxi, she had come down the steps. There
was a tall, a little too-plumpish blond man with her, wearing a flowered shirt and beautifully creased lavender slacks,
and a Cadillac was parked just ahead of my taxi.

She saw me, but she said nothing. Neither did I. They
went past me to the Cadillac. I followed and the man in the
flowered shirt had turned and said, "You want something?"
He was holding the door of the car for her.

I said, "Yes." I looked at her, at the open door of the car.
All she had to do was to get into the car. She knew it, and
I knew it. Then she turned away from the car and came
towards me. For a moment I thought he was going to take it
badly. Then he saw her face as she came to me and with a
sudden shrug of his shoulders he got into the car. We never
saw him again. What would it be like, I wondered, this
time? Just wanting her wouldn't be magic enough this time.

*   *   *

At mid-day there was still no Monk, so I decided to move.
There was an old straw sun hat on the wall of the hut. I put
this on. I had a blue shirt in my bag. I ripped it here and
there and rubbed some dirt into my drill trousers and turned
them up a few inches at the cuffs. I was brown enough to
pass for a near-white if no one looked too closely. My shoes
were too good, so I changed them for a pair of white canvas
shoes from my light bag. I went on up the valley, hoping to
strike across and meet the San Pedro road which would take
me down into Acaibo on the harbour side. I was in no hurry
because I didn't want to reach Acaibo until it was dark. I

carried my Mauser in my bag, right at the top where I could get at it quickly. My one anxiety was that there might be parties of soldiers out in the hills still looking for Albano. I didn't want to get mixed up with them.

It took three hours to reach the San Pedro road, three hours of hard, gruelling going. I needn't have bothered to mess myself up before starting because the climb up the valley and down to the road achieved the tatterdemalion effect I needed. There was a certain amount of traffic on the road, mostly lorries going up to San Pedro. I headed for Acaibo, shuffling along in the roadside dust and keeping my head down, giving a very good imitation of a work-worn peon. Two miles down the road I had luck. Just off the road under a group of tall palms was a long tin-roofed cabin with a couple of trucks pulled up outside it. A green-and-white board over the door said—*Cantina de las Fuerzas Armadas Libertad.* I could see that this complimentary gesture to the Armed Forces of the Revolution had been painted crudely over some previous name. But the thing that interested me more than my thirst for a drink was the fact that a set of telephone wires ran up from insulators at the side of the cabin to join the wires that were slung down the roadway on poles.

There were four soldiers drinking beer at a table just inside the door, and a black-faced mountain of a woman behind the bar with her head wrapped in a yellow handkerchief. Talking a bastard Spanish I ordered a bottle of beer and, after a bit of trouble, managed to get some bread and a tin of sardines. The Armed Forces weren't interested in food. No one took any notice of me as I sat at a table at the far end of the counter and waited for the soldiers to go. The telephone was on the wall by the door. I was pretty sure that the place was well within the five-mile radius of Acaibo. After the beer and the sardines I felt better. Since leaving the hut I had moved in a dull, unthinking mood; not concerning myself much with any problem except the immediate one of contacting Monk. I had plans for the future beyond that but I kept them stowed well away.

The soldiers went and I bought another bottle of beer and

got some coins for the telephone. The woman sat behind her counter and closed her eyes against the heat, which was almost unbearable because of the tin roof.

She looked up briefly as I went to the telephone and then relapsed into her dozing.

I called the *Hotel de la Reina* and got through without any trouble. I asked for Eglantina. She was usually around the place most of the day. I had to wait five minutes before she came.

I said, "Eglantina, is Monk there?"

She was a bright girl. I heard her breath go and she gave a little "Oh, Lordy," as she recognized my voice.

"Tell him," I said, "that I'll be in Acaibo at eight tonight. I'll be in the church. Just inside." I rang off without giving her time to say anything.

* * *

I went down the road about a couple of miles until from a high bluff I could see Acaibo at the foot of the hills. I turned off the road and found a spot overlooking the sea. I slept in the shelter of a cane break, content to wait until the daylight went. I only had an hour's walk to Acaibo.

I slept like a log, a thick, dreamless sleep. When I woke the light was going fast. I started for Acaibo, feeling stiff. As I hit the outskirts I heard the church bell strike the half-hour. Lights were showing from the houses and from the few craft at moorings in the harbour. People were sitting outside their doors catching the coolness after the heat of the day. I moved along, head down. A party of soldiers came up the harbour side with a couple of girls between them. I stepped out of their way.

A few moments later I was in the square. There was the usual noisy evening parade going on with the leave parties. Both taxis had gone from the front of the church. I went in and slid into a seat just inside the door. The place was in gloom except for a few lights over the figures of saints in the side chapels. Four great candles flickered in the draught at the altar at the far end of the church. I tucked my hat on

158

my knees and half bent in a devotional attitude. There were two figures in similar attitudes close up to the altar and a woman, her head black-shawled, came down past me, her lips moving noiselessly. As I sat there, waiting for Monk, I thought of my parson father. Right up until the time I had left England I had gone to church regularly, without question. In the last five years I could count the times on the fingers of one hand. He wouldn't have approved of this occasion. With a little bit of shock I realized how far away I'd slipped, not just from him, but from a lot of things which had been me. All that business of the body renewing itself completely in seven years was nothing compared with the change that went on in the mind, in one's real self. Little by little one changed and woke up to find oneself a different character. Here I was in Acaibo, determined to get my money, thinking of nothing else. If there had been no Drea, I would probably have cut my losses and gone. Five years ago I would have done this. But not now. The money was vital because of Drea. And Drea, without question, was vital for me. There was no questioning that. We had come together and the thing was complete. Unanswerable. Changing us both. She was for me, and I was for her. Only now, some growing, irrefutable sense of self-preservation, fatigue, if you like, from the forces holding us, had made her impose a condition.

Alongside of me Monk said in a whisper, "You're a damned fool, but I'm glad to see you. Excuse me." He leant forward and I knew that he was praying. I'd have given a lot to know what he said in those few moments.

His head came up after a while and he said, "We can't talk here. I've got lodgings for you. Eglantina's outside. Go with her. I'll be along."

I got up and went out.

Eglantina was outside, a large silk scarf draped over her shoulders, a high comb in her hair, and the edges of a white gown held up daintily in one hand. She looked very conspicuous.

"Mr. Keith, you come my place. No trouble there."

She began to walk up the side of the square. A few doors

beyond the house where the Hueica brothers had lodged we turned into a dark doorway. She stopped and handed me a key.

"Top floor," she said. "The door with three brass monkeys. Go in. There's candles on the wash-basin. Don't run to 'lectricity here. Here——" From under her shawl her hand came out holding half a bottle of whiskey.

I said, "What if I meet anyone going up?"

She chuckled. "You won't. But if you do nobody's goin' to be nosey about a man going to my room. Only wish I could get Mr. Monk up there. Seems he don't like a girl to say thank you no way."

She went. The stairs were in pitch darkness and I went up until I could find no more stairs. I struck a match and found a door with a small brass knocker in the shape of the three wise monkeys. See all, hear all, say nothing. That suited me. I went in.

I struck a match and found the candles on the wash-basin. It was a small, rather long room, and one could only stand upright well away from the window because of the slope of the roof pent. By the window was a bed with a patchwork quilt, the brass head-rail hung with a collection of gaily coloured tourist dolls. A white plaster figure of the Madonna was on a bracket against the wall over the bedhead. A radio and a record player stood on a table behind the door and there was a coloured photograph, taken from some magazine, of Ella Fitzgerald stuck above the wash-basin. Two chairs were piled untidily high with clothes. I fixed myself a whiskey and sat down on the bed.

Monk came in after about fifteen minutes. He stood just inside the door, pursing his thick lips and frowning at me, a big, unshakeable-looking man. It was good to have him there.

He said, "You must want those dollars bad. I'd written mine off."

"You don't have to. They owe us the money. I got the chaps who took me out to put me over the side in a dinghy. Went up to Eglantina's brother's hut to look for you."

He went to the wash-basin and rinsed out a glass and then

reached for the whiskey bottle. "What do you plan to do?"

"Wait for Angelo and Katrina to come back. Then I'll give them the whole story."

"Katrina's back. Came into town this afternoon. Not her brother, though. He's up at San Pedro still with Lemaza. They come back tomorrow afternoon. Some big parade in the square here."

"The anniversary of the start of the Revolution. It's going to be an anniversary day for Lemaza, too. I'll tackle Angelo when the parade's over."

"How are you going to get to him?"

"I don't know. Go up there at night. The only sentry is at the drive gate. I could go in the back way, across the fields."

"Just walk in?"

"Why not? With Angelo and Katrina there Lemaza could do nothing. I don't have to think about his feelings."

"He'll deny everything. You were robbed. Period. You started to be a nuisance so he kicked you out. Period. He'll stick to that."

"I've got the box file. Can he talk himself out of that?"

"He'll try."

"It won't come off. Angelo knows him too well."

Monk picked up a pile of clothes from a chair and dumped them on the bed.

"Girl's as untidy as hell. Like me." He tossed the whiskey back and reached for the bottle. He saw me look from the bottle in his hand to him and grinned.

"Don't worry. I was beginning to feel like it. But now you're back I'll hold it. They haven't picked up Albano yet."

"He's well away by now."

"Won't make Lemaza any sweeter."

"Who cares? I can't wait until tomorrow evening."

"You've got to up here."

"What about Eglantina?"

Monk smiled and stood up. "She has the bed and you have the loft. Unless you come to some other arrangement."

He got up on the chair and pushed up a wooden trap in the slope of the ceiling. His head out of sight through the trap his voice came to me muffled. "We've stuck a palliasse up here. Couple of blankets. You can use the room during the day." His head came into sight and he got down from the chair. "She'll see you get food. There's a way on to the roof at the end of the loft. You can sun yourself out there, but keep out of sight. Anything you want?"

I shook my head. I just wanted tomorrow evening to come quickly.

He went to the door. Standing there, he said, "I met Parkes today. He was clearing his stuff out of the hotel. He was erupting. When Albano slipped away he refused to go on with his work. Ocampo gave him two hours to decide whether he'd go on or stand against a wall and be shot. Parkes voted for work. He's living up at the strip now."

"We've all got our troubles."

Monk grinned. "I'll tell him that. Should make a big difference."

A couple of hours after he was gone I climbed up through the trap and bedded down for the night. It was hot with the accumulation of the day's heat under the roof, so I pushed open a small square door at the end of the loft and had a view of the sky and an angle of chimney pots silhouetted against it as I lay on a hard palliasse. I woke once, around three o'clock, to hear Eglantina come in. She was singing to herself and clattered between bed and wash-basin for what seemed hours. Then I heard the springs of her bed go and there was silence.

*　　*　　*

I was awakened the next morning by Eglantina. Her head came through the trap and she pushed a cup of coffee to me across the joists.

"You sure sleep well," she said. "Snorin' hearty. I lay there for half an hour listening. Sounded good to have a man almost in the room again. What you care for to eat?"

"Some rolls and butter?"

"I'll get that." Her brown face smiled at me from floor level. "Yes, Mr. Keith, is very good to have a man about. 'Fore Mr. Monk came was always a man up here with me usually. But since he come I sort of lost the habit. Just happy to go to bed to sleep at nights. Don't make so much money, of course, but I sure feel brighter in the mornings."

She withdrew and began to sing about the room below. I lay there and drank my coffee, watching the morning sky through the roof door. Later the rolls came up with more coffee, and after that Eglantina said she was clearing out and it was all mine for washing and shaving. I took my time over it because I had nothing else to do. While I was shaving I switched on the radio and got the Caramanga station. There was a long military bulletin, mostly about the fighting in the San Pedro area, but it didn't amount to anything. There was a brief mention of the fact that the *Mara II* had docked at Caramanga the previous day. I imagined that the station had instructions to play this down. There was no point in reminding people that Angelo Libertad now had their planes. Neither was there any mention of Albano. Which meant that he probably hadn't made his way through the lines yet. I shut the set off when it started to play dance music. That wasn't my mood. And anyway Eglantina kept me going with all the song I could take.

* * *

I went up on the roof for about an hour, but it got too hot up there so I came down. I'd just pulled the cover over the roof trap and had stepped down from the chair when there came a light knock at the door. No one knew I was back in Acaibo, so I was not worried about search parties. But I wasn't keen to be seen in Eglantina's room by any stranger. I took no notice of the knock and began to move quietly towards the curtain of the hanging cupboard in the far corner of the room.

Before I could reach it the door was pushed open. Katrina came in. I stood there like a fool, wondering where in hell she had sprung from. For a few seconds we faced one another without movement or words. Then she came flying across to me and was in my arms and her head against my shoulder, calling my name, and her hands on my back shaking me gently. I don't know why it should have been so, but it seemed the most natural thing in the world for her to do. I held her close to me and kissed the top of her head gently. For more than one selfish reason I was glad to see her, but to my surprise I was also just glad . . . in the way, I supposed, that a brother might be glad to welcome a favourite sister after a long absence. She was a nice girl and I was very fond of her, and there was something about the spontaneous way in which she had come to me that touched me. She leaned back from me and her eyes were shining and there was a curious pleasure in me as I held her weight. She had a slip of a summer dress on, and she was warm and soft and unexpected. But for all her knee-length dress and long arms, the nearness of being a young girl still in all her movements, she was a woman. My salad days were over and at this moment I couldn't afford to be green in judgment. I kissed her lightly on the cheek, which wasn't at all what she wanted, and I released her.

"Keith," she said, not managing her breathing very well, "I never thought I'd see you again."

"You can thank your brother-in-law for that. How did you know I was here?"

"Monk told me."

I gave her a cigarette and watched her hands shake a little as she held it.

"When did you see him?"

"Just now. I came in to do some shopping and he was in the square."

"He told you why I'm here?"

"No. Just that you were here and wanted to see me. What is it all about?"

"Someone may have seen you come up here."

"No, I just slipped in. Anyway I'm told Eglantina does a little dress-making at times. I could be coming to see her. What's happened, Keith? Why are you hiding here?"

"Because," I said bluntly, "General Lemaza robbed me of my money the night I left you. Within an hour."

"I can't believe it!"

164

"It's true. Why do you think I'm up here, hiding? He arranged it neatly. Couldn't bear to part with all those lovely dollars——"

"But you should have come to me, to Angelo. Oh, it's not possible!"

"The next day I did try to get in touch with you or your brother, but he fixed that. And then he shipped me out."

"And you came back."

"Of course. I need forty thousand dollars. Remember?"

She was silent for a moment, then nodded and said, "For her."

"For me. This evening after the parade I'm coming up to see your brother. He's getting the full story."

She walked away towards the bed and her hand went out absently and played with one of the toy dolls.

"Lemaza," I said, "is one kind of man. Your brother's another. In a way. I can even sympathize with Lemaza's point of view. He's got to find the cash and the supplies. He must have plenty of headaches."

She turned and said firmly, "There's no doubt you'll get your money when my brother hears."

"I'm sure of it. But it won't improve things between the two of them. However . . . for the time being you haven't seen me and you know nothing of this affair. Don't go talking to your brother. Let me do that. You promise?"

She nodded and then went on, "No matter how difficult money matters are, Siles shouldn't have done it. Angelo will be furious. A bargain is a bargain. . . ."

I didn't say anything. There was no point in making trouble for her by saying that in my opinion Angelo would always have difficulties with Lemaza. The two just couldn't pull in harness together. Even less would they be able to do so when they got to Caramanga. Señor Da Silva wasn't sitting in Acaibo for nothing. Apart from my trouble, I was sure that some deal had been made by Lemaza for the future. . . .

"This is the first time you've been with your brother for some years, isn't it?"

"Yes. Why?"

"Do you think he's changed at all?"

She looked at me, just the edge of her teeth biting gently at her lower lip as she thought it over. "Yes, he has. But not in the way you imagine. Oh, I know you're cynical about ideals and the men who live for them. But that hasn't changed. He's just the same. But he's older, inside, simply because of fighting for what he believes in. I suppose if you live with a burning truth, and for it . . . well, it makes its mark on you. He's the noblest man I've ever met. . . ."

She waited for me to say something, to disagree, to argue, but I didn't want to do any of those things. From the way she said it there was nothing one could do but accept it.

"You don't believe it. You think there's something of Lemaza about him?"

"No. I believe it. It just is. and you must see this, that noble men make all the others uncomfortable."

"Oh, no. I've just come back from San Pedro and I've seen how the men up there worship him. In a way it was quite frightening. They look up to him, he's everything they believe in. Having to carry all that is a tremendous strain. That's why—whatever you and I may think about Lemaza —he has to have other people to take the smaller things off his shoulders. And, of course, they take advantage of him— but only in small ways. Nobody can touch what he really is. You know. . . ." She came back to me and I was seeing now no girl, but a woman, shaped and impressed and accepting a whole new world of experiences. "You know, there were times when it was hard to believe that he was my brother. . . . He seemed to have gone beyond any relationship like that. To have become what he believed in. Just a force. Does that sound far-fetched?"

"No . . . I suppose not."

"He doesn't think of himself. He doesn't even look after himself. He wouldn't let me go anywhere where it was dangerous. But he goes everywhere, just carrying that stick of his. No one up there can stop him. . . ."

Somewhere, flickering in my memory, came up a shadowy lithograph of General Gordon at Khartoum facing death at the top of the steps, cane in hand. I wouldn't disillusion her about her brother, because I couldn't, and didn't, in fact, have anything to disillusion her with. Maybe he was right out there in front, in the Gordon class. But if he were then I knew that somewhere in the men around him there must be those who would hate him simply because they couldn't stand the sight of a goodness they could never emulate, couldn't live with his kind of shining truth . . . not in this day and age.

I put my arm around her shoulders and began to lead her towards the door.

"You look after him all you can," I said. "When you find someone who means so much to you, hang on. Don't argue with yourself about it, just hang on. In a way I envy you."

She turned, lifting her small nicely ovalled face to me, and said, "Do you? I thought you had someone like that. Isn't that why you're still here?"

I laughed. "Drea. . . ? Yes, I suppose she is. But I wouldn't put her in Angelo's class. She's the other thing that men are ready to die for."

"Die?"

"It's a figure of speech. Now remember, you know nothing about me until I turn up tonight."

"All right. I'm sorry, I shouldn't have said anything about her. It's just that I'm jealous. I can say that quite frankly. I'm jealous." She gave a little laugh. "And I won't say anything. About the other thing."

Just for a moment her hand touched mine and then she went. From the window, I watched her come out and cross the square towards the harbour entrance. She looked very small, a girl walking slowly, her dress a bright splash of colour against the dusty stones of the square.

I went to the wash-basin and got a glass and poured myself a bottle of beer. A few minutes later Eglantina came singing up the stairs with a straw bag full of tomatoes in one hand and a bowl of dressed crab in the other.

13

I WATCHED the anniversary parade from the roof top. During the morning working parties had strung lines of bunting and the revolutionary flags along the fronts of the houses. Everywhere you looked was the yellow and scarlet blazonry of the eagle carrying its rifle. Most of the housewives had left their coloured bed covers hanging from their balconies. A platform of wooden planks had been erected on timber baulks just in front of the *Hotel de la Reina* and the front of the stand had been decorated with great swags of poinsettias and stiff bunches of wild arum lilies. There was a microphone on the stand and a couple of amplifiers were slung on a wire across the square. From just after mid-day an army truck with a broadcasting system relayed gramophone records at full volume. The whole square was vivid and shrieking with colour and noise. By two o'clock the square was packed with people who were held back four and five deep against the houses by a cordon of soldiers.

It was hot on the roof, but not so hot as it was in Eglantina's room. Seeking for shade I moved along to the right about fifty yards, scrambling over a couple of low parapets until I found a tall clump of chimney pots. I sat down with my back against the brickwork and had a fine angled view of the square. Monk and Eglantina were keeping away from me that afternoon, but I could see them with some other people on one of the hotel balconies across the square.

I don't know who was responsible for the show, probably Ocampo, I guessed, since he was Town Commandant, but it was done with great precision and smoothness. It didn't surprise me for there was nothing the Latin-American liked better than a good, colourful show. Their fighting was mostly guerilla and mountain warfare, so they jumped at the chance of formal parades.

Two companies of infantry marched in and formed up in

front of the church and facing the platform. Then came a couple of staff cars and I saw Angelo Libertad, Generalissimo Lemaza, and three other high-ranking officers get out and take their places on the stand. A great cheer from troops and the crowd greeted Angelo. From the other staff car came Katrina, Lieutenant Ocampo and two more officers. Katrina went to the back of the stand, a little to the left of her brother.

When the cheers had subsided General Lemaza came forward to the microphone and began to speak. He really let himself go, for this was the kind of occasion he was born to enjoy. Above the square the amplifiers cracked and spat and whistled and it was hard to catch what he was saying. Not that there was any need to know because it had to be, coming from him, a paraphrase of everything martial which had been said before and so much better. . . . *Now thrive, the armourers, and honour's thought reigns solely in the breast of every man. . . . He which hath no stomach for this fight, let him depart. . . .* But one thing was certain with Lemaza running things, the departing would get no passport, and no crowns for convoy would be put into his purse. He went on and on, ten minutes too long by my reckoning, and the cheers of the crowd which had punctuated his speech, strophe, and antistrophe, weakened and lost gusto.

Lemaza stopped at last, but Angelo did not come forward. From the far end of the square a convoy of six armoured cars rumbled through and Angelo raised his hand to take the salute from them. Following the armoured cars came a couple of bren gun carriers, freshly painted, a troop of twenty-five pounders, lorry after lorry, canopies stripped, full of erect, green-bereted soldiers, three tanks which I could not identify, a truck towing a water tank which had been decorated with yellow and scarlet flowers and had a papier mâché figure of the revolutionary eagle perched on it . . . on and on, men, vehicles, roaring and stamping across the square . . . And most of them, I guessed, would be on their way back to San Pedro that evening.

More troops marched into the square, darkening the yellow dust. The packed crowd on the church steps parted to let through a priest in full canonical dress. With him went four boys in white surplices swinging censers. After Angelo had spoken the troops were to be blessed. There it all was below me, the world in little . . . the soldiers, their guns, the Church, its blessing, the people, their betrayals. . . . Only one type was missing. . . . I wondered where Señor Da Silva was passing the afternoon. Taking a siesta, probably; lying on his bed working out the swift moves that must follow victory, for victory in any revolution is a sitting duck for a shot from the curtained East or the debentured West.

I moved along a little to follow the shade and lit myself a cigarette. As I did so I happened to look sideways, further along the run of roof tops with their crumbly parapets and shabby, paint-blistered pents and gables. On the roof of the house which formed the far corner of the square on my side, I saw a man come through the doorway of a pent-house. He was about a hundred yards away. His back was to me and he was bending down, dragging out something which was masked from me by a run of parapet. As he came into the sunlight another man followed him, bending also and helping with the load they were managing. They dragged whatever it was to the edge of their roof parapet, then straightened up and went back to the doorway. They stood just inside it, the sun striking down at them.

There was no mistaking them . . . the neat linen suits, the splash of flowered ties, and the dark, smoothly greased hair. Not more than a hundred yards from me were the Hueica brothers. If they could see me it would be no more than my head and I was wearing my old straw hat so they would have taken me for a spectator of the scene below. I sat there, wondering what I should do. Pretty obviously Ocampo had kept them hidden up since robbing me. My whole instinct was to go over and grab Sardi . . . but a few moments' thought showed me that this would serve nothing. I could have the satisfaction of beating him up . . . but that would ruin everything. I edged back a little to be less in their view. The Hueica brothers would keep until after I'd had my interview with Angelo.

It was at this moment that I heard the noise from the

north. It was thin at first, then beat up against the hot blue sky into a familiar pulse. All the heads in the square below swivelled upwards. I looked up, too. It came in over the town from the direction of the air strip, flying too damned low, and its new roundels of scarlet and gold flashed in the sun. It went over with a mighty throaty scream. Above the harbour it climbed, much too steeply for its age and performance, rolled at the top as it turned, and came back again in another shattering explosion of speed and sound. As it flattened away out of sight, the crowd in the square became one mouth and throat, one pulsating roar of approval and delight. The first of their Sea Furies was in the air. It didn't come back again. I could guess why. Up at the strip Parkes and his men must have worked like beavers to get it in trim for this celebration flight. This must have been its first time off the deck. No test flights. Parkes would have fought every inch of the way against such a dangerous first demonstration. Lemaza and Ocampo would have over-ridden him. They needed the sign of victory in the air.

Angelo was waiting for this moment. The noise echoed away in the square and I saw him step forward to the microphone. The priest was on his right now and Katrina was half-hidden by the boys in their white surplices. I saw, too, that at some moment she had been presented with flowers for she stood, holding to her bosom, a great sheaf of the wild arum lilies. This was a great moment for her, to stand behind her brother and watch the adoration in the eyes of the crowd, to be near him, and to see his work after the years of separation. Maybe I was wrong, I thought. Maybe he would turn out to be different. Maybe he would know how to handle peace and to plan prosperity. Maybe he was one of the few who knew the right moment to shave off the mountain beard and to make guerillas become good neighbours . . . maybe. For her sake I hoped it.

He began to speak, not raising his voice, giving the amplifiers a chance . . . a tall, thin figure, dressed in green trousers and a khaki shirt, his body a little stooped on one side as he rested a hand on the thin rattan cane . . . and he spoke without any pomp, without any flourish, a quiet voice that drew

171

the square and its people and its soldiers in to him, the voice of a brother and a good husbandman giving his report.

"Five years ago, the struggle for freedom began in this square. Since then we have all fought and made our sacrifices. Today I do not mean to go back, to recall our triumphs or our bitterness. You have all seen—" his hand went up to the sky briefly, "the token of our coming victory. It is certain. It is waiting for us within the next few weeks."

The crowd roared and he waited for them to quieten down.

"Today, I want us all to think of what victory is going to mean. When the fighting finishes, the work begins. Victory must be turned into peace, and peace must be turned into order, prosperity and justice. To do this will take longer than all the fighting we have known; to make the name of Cordillo respected will mean more sacrifices, more struggles, and all the good will and good sense that are ours because we are human beings and wish to live with one another as human beings, in faith, in love, and in pride of our country. It is useless to call for a blessing on our arms if that blessing does not touch our hearts. Victory will bring no exaggerated rewards. Our house has been shattered. We must mend the walls and the roof before we think of luxuries. . . ."

He meant what he said. He stood there and in their taste of coming triumph he had the courage to point to the future and its hard promise of labour and sacrifice. Nobody was going to get an unfair share of the cake. There would be no cake. Bread and sweat. He meant it.

He stood there on the platform, well out in front of the others, a quiet man, talking firmly to his people. I wondered what Lemaza and Ocampo and the others grouped at the back of the platform were thinking. After victory the loot. After war the feast.

Angelo raised a hand, pausing in his speech, and for a moment the square was so still that I could hear the gulls crying out over the harbour and the bickering of sparrows on the roof tiles behind me.

Then he cried with a sudden passion, his voice full of command, "Take this then to your hearts, people and soldiers of Cordillo! No matter what lies in the future, no matter what happens to us as individuals, we are one body, one mind, one heart and one resolution——"

They were the last words he spoke. From my right I heard the single crack of a rifle shot. So absorbed was I in Angelo and the square below that for a moment there was no awareness in me of what had happened. I saw Angelo stagger, almost fall, and then steady himself on his cane. His head came up and he shook it as though he were shaking off some unexpected dizziness. The rifle was fired again and this time he dropped, falling forward on his knees, smashing into the microphone stand and finishing with his head lost in the bank of flowers along the front of the platform.

Away to my right, the figure of Sardi with a rifle rose from where he had been crouching by his roof parapet. In the doorway behind him was Tomez. Sardi turned and he dropped the rifle to the ground at the foot of the parapet and then went quickly back and through the doorway. I jumped to my feet, pulled myself round the chimney pot so that I was out of sight of the square and began to run across the roof flats. As I did so, from the square, as though some anguished animal were trapped down there, came a great howl of despair. I ran, not thinking, not planning anything, following the simple instinct to get hold of Sardi before he got away. I went over the dividing parapets, round the junky penthouses and stucco-walled water tanks and finally reached the doorway through which the Hueica brothers had disappeared. As I came up to it, I saw the rifle lying over by the far parapet, and close to the rifle the recumbent figure of a man.

I pulled up then. With an icy suddenness thought and common-sense gripped me hard. The man was lying on his side with his face towards me. It was a face which I recognized immediately, athletic, fresh, squarish, with a tiny scar at one corner of the mouth. His fair, sun-bleached hair fell forward over his forehead. It was John MacIntyre Albano in a crumpled blue blazer with silver buttons and dirty white trousers and many days' growth of beard on his face. I saw him stir a little and heard a faint groan.

173

I didn't wait for more. Understanding, if not complete, at least enough to put me on my guard, was coming to me. Through the doorway I caught the sound of footsteps and men's voices. I swung away from the door, away from the square and raced around behind the penthouse and to the far side of the roof. Below me was a stretch of waste ground and then the backs of the buildings which faced the harbour. Away to the left the ground rose steeply to one shoulder of the headland which guarded the eastern edge of the bay. There was no way down and no way back to my room which I could take before people would be on the roof. But in the far corner of the roof was a decrepit pigeon loft, wire-netting over wooden frames, empty of birds now, and the floor strewn with boxes. I ran into it and threw myself on the ground behind a couple of low boxes. I just had time to pull one of the boxes in front of me for better cover, and then a bunch of men came through the penthouse door.

I lay there, holding my breathing down, and watched them through the thin gap between the two boxes in front of me. All hell had broken out in the square. I could hear men shouting, women screaming, and now the quick revving up of vehicles, and above it all somebody was roaring unintelligible orders over the amplifiers.

There were five men on the roof. It didn't surprise me to see who they were. I was gone a long way past surprise now. I was beginning to understand Lemaza more than ever before and I had no more curiosity about Da Silva. And though I had always considered myself hard-boiled enough for most things, this was making me feel sick.

Lieutenant Ocampo, two soldiers, and the two Hueica brothers were on the rooof. The Hueica brothers kept well back out of sight of the square. Ocampo gave no orders. The pantomime had been well rehearsed. The two soldiers went over to Albano and lifted him to his feet. They lifted him and held him so that he could be seen by all the people in the square below. Holding him they shook him, gripping his arms and shoulders as though he were struggling with them. He had no more struggle in him than a mouse long paralysed by a cat's play. A great roar of anger billowed up from the square at the sight of Albano.

The men turned and dragged him, upright still, towards the door. As they disappeared through the door Ocampo turned towards the Hueica brothers. He smiled at them and nodded. They faced him, their backs to me, two neat, tidy figures, not a crease out of place on them, efficient, obedient Tweedledum and Tweedledee. . . . Oh, they were going to be big shots when they got back to Guatemala, men full of the profit from darkness, their hiring days over, nothing to do but sit in the sun and blink and drink the hours away. I had my Mauser in my pocket and, against all thought for my own self-preservation, it was hard not to let them have it from where I lay hidden.

But I didn't have to do it. That equally efficient couple Lemaza and Ocampo had got it all arranged. As Ocampo smiled at them, the brown warm smile of commendation for filthy work well done, his right hand which held his revolver came up swiftly and he gave them their reward. He fired four times, twice at Tomez, dropping him where he stood, and twice at Sardi as the little man turned and began to run. He hit him twice; once as he ran and once as he stumbled. Sardi skidded on his chest across the roof and finished with his head not three feet from the loft where I lay.

A soldier came through the doorway and I heard him say: "Shall we take them down, lieutenant?"

"Leave them until the square is quieter. Vermin. We have the one who really counts. Keep a guard on the house door and come up for them later."

He went through the door and out of sight. The soldier stood there for a moment, lit himself a cigarette, and then went to Tomez. He rolled him over with his foot and I saw the blood patterning the flowery tie. The soldier went through Tomez's pockets and then stole his wristlet watch. He came over to Sardi and did the same for him, humming gently to himself. Then he went back to the penthouse and disappeared, closing the door behind him.

I gave him two minutes; two minutes during which I lay there with Sardi's face a few feet from mine. He was on his side now, facing me, his dark eyes wide open, his mouth slack in death, and even in death he didn't look any different . . . just a dark, quiet, intent little man who had nothing to say, no thoughts which could be trusted to the world. But there was nothing he needed to say to me.

*　　*　　*

Five minutes later I was back in Eglantina's attic. There was no one in the room below. I dropped through the ceiling trap and fixed myself a drink. My hand shook as I held it and walked to the window. Outside, the square had been cleared and a cordon of soldiers was posted at intervals all the way around. The platform was empty. So long as the square was guarded neither Monk nor Eglantina could get up to me. I lay down on Eglantina's bed with my drink. This was the kind of thing which went on everywhere, part of the cynicism which kept me the way I was. I lay there while the afternoon died, while the soldiers patrolled the streets, while the lorries and armoured cars rolled back through the square, while somewhere Katrina sat mourning, and somewhere Lemaza and Ocampo toasted themselves in private triumph that out of a live and dedicated Leader they now had created a martyr, a figure of legend for whom every soldier would fight harder than before in order to bring them the victory and the fruits which were to be piled high into only a few chosen bowls.

And then, over the other thoughts, came sweeping in the picture of Drea waiting in Haiti. A little while ago I'd been confident of getting my money. Now Angelo was dead. Lemaza was king, and in one stroke I was out in the wilderness . . . a couple of rifle shots had killed Angelo—but they had also taken Drea from me, robbed me and committed her. It was a bonus result which would have made Lemaza smile. It filled me with a heavy, murderous blackness.

*　　*　　*

Just as it was getting dark the soldiers were withdrawn from the square. Life came back to it slowly. I stood at the window, waiting for Monk and Eglantina, and watched. *The Singing Heart that Never Tires* and the *Space Sputnik Special* came back to their stands by the church. The church bells began to beat out a long-paused note and a queue of people, marshalled by a couple of soldiers, began to form outside the church, stretching away around the corner into the harbour. Angelo, I guessed had been taken into the church, was now laid out, and the people of Acaibo were moving past him to pay him their last respects. Lemaza was wasting no time.

Eglantina came up first.

She stood just inside the doorway and said, "Oh, Mister . . . ! Oh, Mister . . . !" I could see she had been crying. "He was a good man."

"Sure. He was a good man. Where's Monk?"

"Come in a minute. You want some food?"

"No thanks."

She went over to her hanging cupboard affair and began to ferret amongst a pile of stuff on the floor. Finally she came up with a black headshawl.

"No dancing or music this night."

As she draped the shawl over her head and turned back towards the door, I said, "After you've been to the church, Eglantina, keep away from here for a while. I've got to talk privately to Monk."

"Yes, Mr. Keith."

"And when you do come back, I want to know if Miss Katrina is in church and whereabouts."

"Yes, Mr. Keith. You sure you don't want food?"

"No."

Not long after she had gone Monk came in. He went over to the bed and sat down, resting his great head on his hands.

"Christ, what a thing!"

"There's a damned sight more to it than you know."

"Not that I can guess. I wasn't born yesterday. You should have seen that poor Albano bastard when they brought him down. Took them all their time to stop the crowd from ripping him to pieces. Saw that happen to a man once. Bloody crowd went over him like swarming bees. When they cleared off there was nothing left. . . ." He got up and went and helped himself to a whiskey. He took a large shot but I didn't say anything even though I knew from the moment he came into the room that he had been drinking.

"I was on the roof. I saw it all. . . ."

He came back to the bed with his drink and sat silently while I told him all I had seen.

I finished, "Albano was framed. They had him lined up for this from the moment I brought him in. He was a gift, my gift to them," I said bitterly.

"And the escape from prison?"

"They just took him out and cached him away in that house. Said he'd escaped. Up there he was lying drugged or something. He couldn't have had any idea of what was going on. God, you've got to hand it to Lemaza. The Hueica brothers pinch my money and hand it back to him. Then he gets rid of me. Then he frames Albano to assassinate Angelo —and the Hueica brothers get paid off. Two bullets each instead of the handful of cash they looked for. Not even Sardi was expecting that. Not even his dark mind could place Lemaza with that stroke."

"Poor old Tomez. I liked him."

"You're wasting your sympathy."

"Maybe. But I've got plenty to waste. . . ." He looked up. "You had the radio on? No. Well, it's started already. Blasting away. Lemaza is taking over. Everything Angelo stood for will be accomplished. That'll keep 'em going until they reach Caramanga. Nobody like a martyr to stir the troops to fighting pitch. Angelo's worth as much dead as alive. And now they know it was Albano who did it—son of the Minister of Defence on the other side! He's in the soup."

"They won't touch him yet," I said. "He's too good a pawn to wipe out quickly. They'll go through all the rigmarole of a People's Court and wring every drop of propaganda from it they can first. Meanwhile. . . ."

Monk levered himself up from the bed and went for more whiskey. I still said nothing.

"Meanwhile, what?" he asked.

"We've got to do something."

"You're crazy! There's nothing you can do. Nothing. Angelo was your trump card. He's gone. Keith, boy, you're in a situation familiar to us both. One that is always liable to happen. Everything's blown up in your face. *Stay Quiet* and *Get Out*. They're two good hounds for this hunt."

"Not for me," I said grimly. It was there inside me, the hardness which had been forming for hours in this room. "That bastard Lemaza has too much owing on his slate."

Monk drank, shook his big head, and said, "Forget your dollars. I've got the motor-boat fixed up. We can get out."

I shook my head. "I'm staying. There are things to do."

Monk frowned. "For God's sake, know when to quit. You can't touch this man. Cut your losses and go. Lemaza is going on. The race has been rigged. He'll have Cordillo. He's too big for you to handle. Only Da Silva's people can do that—and they will if he doesn't play ball." His hand went out for the whiskey bottle.

I went across to him and I took the bottle from him. He let me without any protest. I knew my Monk and he knew me. He knew, too, what was going on inside me.

I said, "Listen, for a lot of reasons that seem good to me, though I can't line them up nicely, I'm going on. I can try it by myself, but I'd rather have you with me. If you want to be with me, you've got to knock this off. I know the way you're heading." I held up the bottle between us. "You just say if you want it back."

For some time he didn't say anything. He leaned back, his large, brown, capable hands spread on the wash-basin for support. He watched me, rubbing his thick lips together as though he had a sour taste in his mouth. Maybe he had . . . the bitterness that comes with a conflict between friendship and common-sense. I wouldn't force him.

Finally he said, "You're a stubborn bastard."

"Call it that."

"Have you got any ideas?"

"A few."

"Could they work?"

"With a bit of luck."

"That's a great comfort. Got to have luck."

"It can be promoted. With good planning. Do you want this?" I offered him the bottle.

He straightened up and took the bottle from me. Then he tossed it gently on to the bed. "Let Eglantina have it as a night-cap. Okay—what do we do?"

"We go to see Parkes," I said. "But it might be a rough visit. Can you get the motor-boat out of the harbour?"

He looked at his watch. "Yes. There are four or five fishing boats go out each night. In another hour. I can go out with them."

"Bring it round the headland. There's a beach where the headland tails away into the long straight stretch up to the barracks. I'll be there at midnight."

"No more than that?"

"Not for the moment. I've got some thinking to do."

"Okay, you do that. Think. I'll concentrate on the luck. Whatever you've got in mind we're going to need it, and I can't think why the hell I've agreed."

"Put aboard all the spare petrol you can. How big's the boat?"

"Take four or five. Small cabin."

"Can you get enough petrol to make Haiti?"

"I guess so—if the north-east trades aren't too strong. Why Haiti?"

"We've got to go somewhere."

"Sure. Anything else?"

"Yes, a spare anchor, plenty of rope and a small marker buoy. Something that looks like a lobster pot marker."

"What do you want that for?"

"It's the beginning of an idea. Depends on Parkes. But get it, anyway."

He spread his arms and rolled his eyes and then said humorously, "Why should I worry? I was forgetting. I'm not going anywhere. Nobody's waiting. It's better to do something crazy than nothing at all."

He went and half an hour later Eglantina came in.

"Miss Katrina's still in church, Mr. Keith. Way at the back on the left. There's a pillar with some flags hanging on it."

"Good."

"You hungry now?"

I was going to say no, but I changed my mind. "You make up some food, Eglantina. Take it down to Monk. He's with the boat. Be quick."

"You leaving?" Her small face came up to mine, suddenly shadowed with anxiety.

"Not without you. Take some things with you and tell Monk I said you were to go out in the boat with him."

"You mean take my things for going away?"

"Sure—and not a trunkful, either. One small bag."

"Oh, Lordy!" Her face broke into a smile. "All I want of this place could go in one pocket, Mr. Keith."

14

THERE I was in my old straw hat, ragged shirt and trousers, shuffling along in my canvas shoes down the side of the square to the church. Just beyond the church steps I saw Ocampo's car parked, the driver sitting on the running board. Two soldiers stood guard at the top of the steps, but the queue had thinned now to just a trickle of people moving quietly in and out of the church. There was some wind going, hot and filling the air with whipped-up dust. The platform was still standing outside the *Hotel de la Reina* and groups of people were clustered about it, talking and moving slowly, held by it, describing no doubt to one another that moment of death under the bright sun. I could see the white trumpets of the lilies against the dark boards.

My head low I shuffled up the steps past the two sentries and went into the church. Hat in hand I stood just inside the entrance, dipped my fingers in the holy water and crossed myself.

Right up by the altar was a catafalque on which Angelo Libertad lay. It was guarded by four soldiers, their arms reversed, and six tall candles stood around it, their flames burning stiff and straight in the still air. People were filing by slowly and there was a sprinkling of men and women sitting in the nave, heads bowed. From one of the side chapels came the sound of a priest praying, his voice a low, broken, almost querulous mutter that went on and on. I went slowly up to the catafalque, keeping my head low, and joined the slow file about the body. Only for a moment or two did I raise my head and then it was to see Angelo Libertad's face.

He lay under the scarlet and gold of the Army flag, just his face visible. He lay there as though sleeping, his face relaxed and expressionless, no sign on it of the way of his death, no shadow of any last thought or emotion. Had he known in those last few seconds of the treachery around him? Had he had time to take the bitterness fully to his heart? Maybe he had known for years that it could always happen so could never surprise him. He was as Katrina believed him to be . . . *not for the fashion of these times where none will sweat but for promotion*. I had long been out of touch with such men, but that did not now prevent me from taking some of the bitterness of his end and cherishing it as an anger in me. It was a new kind of anger for my kind. But it was there and I knew that I was going to have to follow it. And if in doing this I served my own interests, too—and I meant to —then that would only be more humiliation and bitterness for Lemaza. I could have been paid and gone days ago with my forty thousand dollars. Now, forty thousand dollars would be the symbol in his mind for as long as he lived . . . the symbol, maybe, of a lost kingdom. For the want of a nail, of a shoe, of a horse . . . the kingdom was lost. For a few hours of scheming to cheat me, one of Lemaza's own kind, one of the sweaters after promotion and money like him, he was going to have his own bitterness to live with.

I went shuffling down the far aisle and found the pillar which Eglantina had mentioned. Halfway up it was hung with dusty banners. Katrina was sitting on a chair a few yards in from it. She wore a black dress and there was a black shawl pulled over her bowed head and shoulders. There were a few other people sitting in the benches and chairs, but they were well away from her. She sat alone with her grief and everyone respected it.

I stood by the pillar in the gloom. Up by the altar the candles threw a pale wash of yellow against the grey stone vault of the nave and transept arches. I stood there and watched her and I knew that in a little while she would know that she was being watched. And after a time she did. Her head came up and slowly round. She saw me. I made no sign but I stepped back from the pillar and into the semi-darkness of one of the side chapels.

It was so dark that when she came to me I could hardly see her face. I put out a hand and took hers. We said nothing. But her hand was there in mine and I held it and knew that for the moment it was all she wanted. After a moment she said, "Keith, you shouldn't be here. . . ."

"I know," I said. And then, inadequately, as it must always be, I went on, "I'm sorry about Angelo. . . ."

She raised her head a little, but didn't trust herself to words.

"Listen," I said, "I've got a lot of things I must tell you. But I can't stay here with you now. Can you meet me to-morrow? As it gets dark?"

She nodded.

"Good. There's an old plantation reservoir on the hill behind your villa. I'll meet you there."

"Keith. . . ."

"Don't say anything about me. Just be there."

I let go of her hand and I left her. As I got to the church door Ocampo came through, short and dapper in uniform. I stepped back to let him pass, my head going down, my body cringing in an anonymous movement of deference to the Army, my straw hat pressed against my chest, the upper rim over my chin and mouth. He went by without seeing me.

I passed down the church steps and walked away from the harbour, across the square and towards the road that led up the hill past the water trough where I had been robbed.

*   *   *

The wind was fresh from the north-east, slapping a choppy run of waves against our starboard bow as we went up to the air strip. We carried no lights and kept well out. She was a solid boat, tubby, and high decked with one small cabin forward and the wheel just aft of the cabin break. Not built for speed, but a good plugger. Away on our left a few lights showed from the barrack buildings and against the night sky I could see the high loom of the mountains inland. Eglantina was in the cabin to escape the occasional wave crest that broke aboard. Monk had the wheel.

As we drew level with the barrack lights Monk said, "Why do you need Parkes?"

"I need his advice."

184

"He doesn't love you. Not to distraction. Maybe he won't give it."

"I think he will. If he won't I'll work it out myself."

"Work what out?"

"Forty thousand dollars."

Monk laughed gently and then after a little silence said, "You don't have to do it, you know. You could cut your losses and go. Drea wouldn't want you to go on."

"I've got to go on. I need that money."

"Because you think it's going to solve everything? Maybe it is. But is the risk worth it? Why don't you chuck it in?"

I wasn't really listening to him. He wanted to help me, genuinely—but he didn't know everything. I had to have the money. He thought that Drea would change her mind. Women did.

I said, "I've got to have that money. I know how Drea feels . . . I know exactly where I stand."

Monk shrugged his shoulders, and said, "Then you're unique. Most of us know what we want. But few of us know what we are. That's the thing that counts."

I shook my head. "I know what you're after, Monk. But it's too late. I'm going through with this. I've got to. Nothing can stop me from trying. Don't waste your breath."

Monk said no more.

A little later, as a few lights began to show from the group of houses at the small harbour by the air strip, I said, "Beach her on the sand just the other side of the strip. And keep it quiet."

We ran in with the engine cut down and I could hear the wash of the waves creaming over the sand. To our left was the sharp silhouette of the houses. An oblique rectangle of light came from the open doorway of a small *cantina* and I began to catch the sound of a radio, a man's voice going on and on . . . *propaganda, Cordillo, the death of kings and dictators, the martyrdom of innocents, we must, you will, victory, defeat* . . . pounding away through the air, the sky charged with it all, and no truth, no truth that wouldn't need dynamite to blast it out. Just at that moment I envied Monk. He wanted nothing. He asked for nothing. He was just himself, untouchable . . . needing no one. Then I saw Drea, walking like a puma, saw the shift of light on her tawny hair and heard the rough-touched voice, and had more strongly than I had ever had the aching fierceness for her, the thirst and the hunger and the need for possessing.

Eglantina's head came out of the cabin and she said softly, "You boys wan' anything I can get? Drink? Food?"

I said, "No. You stay here while we're gone. In the cabin."

I went forward and took the small anchor on its rope. When the launch hit sand in about two feet of water I jumped down and waded to the beach. A few yards up I drove one of the flukes deep into the sand.

When Monk joined me, I said, "How's the tide?"

"Coming, for another two hours. She'll be all right. Eglantina knows how to handle her."

We went up over the lip of the sand dunes to the end of the air strip. The nissen hut was about two hundred yards away. Farther on, at the far end of the strip, I could see the red light burning, marking the edge of the palms.

We moved off, across the strip and then along a little path that ran towards the nissen. As we got closer to it I saw that there was a light showing through the window of a little lean-to affair at the back of the hut. I left Monk and went on alone.

Avoiding the light cast from the window, I went round to the narrow wooden door. I tried the handle and it moved easily under my hand. I pushed it open enough for me to slide in and then closed it behind me.

Parkes was lying on a wooden bunk that ran along the far wall. He was half-sitting up, reading, a pair of spectacles perched on the end of his nose. He was wearing thick blue and white striped pyjamas. He looked across at me and said nothing. A pressure lamp on a packing case a yard from the bunk hissed quietly. Parkes just cocked his head in my direction, his sandy hair tousled, bright eyes considering me deliberately.

Then he said, "You might have knocked." He put the book down flat on his chest.

"This is a private visit. I apologize."

"Private? I see. What the bloody hell do you want? I thought you'd left Acaibo."

"I came back."

"I can't think why."

"We won't go into all the reasons. Just a few of them."

"Which ones?" He was very self-possessed, neither hostile nor friendly to me.

"The ones that concern you and Albano—and General Lemaza."

"That bastard."

"It's an accurate description. Do you believe that Albano shot Libertad?"

"He might have done. Depends whether his Spanish blood had the upper hand."

"He didn't do it. I was up on the roof and saw it happen. Albano was rigged. General Lemaza arranged everything very neatly."

"Maybe you did it," said Parkes coldly. "For money, I guess."

"I'm not in that class yet. Give me time."

"What are you after? Out with it."

"I'm arranging for Albano to get out of prison and off this island. I thought you might like to leave at the same time."

He didn't say anything for a while. He just looked at me, his weight now on one elbow and one hand rubbing at his stubbly chin. Then with a gruff little chuckle that had no real humour in it, he said, "You thought I might like to go, too. Did you now? And so I would. But Mr Bloody Marchant I think you expect me to pay for my passage. Eh?"

"Naturally. But the price isn't high. I don't want to upset you, but unless we all co-operate a little Albano's going to be stood against a wall and shot for something he didn't do. He's a nice lad. I don't think that should happen to him."

"Neither do I. But let's face it, he's where he is because of you. You beginning to have a conscience?"

"Call it that if you like. But to do anything for Albano, I've got to have a few cards up my sleeve before I go and see General Lemaza."

187

"Do that and he'll have you smartly up against a wall, my lad."

"Not if it's handled properly. How are the planes going?"

"Another week. They made me rush one for the parade today. I didn't expect to see it come back in one piece."

"He did a half loop and a roll over the harbour."

"The bastard."

"General Lemaza has got to have those planes in the air. All I want from you is the key of the nissen hut. You just tell me what parts to take away—parts that can't be replaced—to keep the planes on the ground."

He lifted the book and closed it with a snap.

"So that's it. You're going to bargain with him. Parts against Albano. That it?"

"That's it."

"Anything else."

For a moment I hesitated. Then I let him have it straight because there was no hope of deceiving him.

"He still owes me money. That comes with Albano, too."

"We're frank, aren't we? And tomorrow when the balloon goes up how do I explain that my key was used?"

"You don't have to. You can come with us now. There's a launch at the bottom of the air strip. We can make Haiti in a couple of days. You can fly home from there. Your company wouldn't expect you to stay, in the circumstances."

He considered this for a while. Then he said, "Nobody's going to touch me. I shall get away in time. What happens if I tell you to scarper off."

"I'd go. But first I'd have to give you a crack over the head to keep you quiet while I took your key. The parts I'd have to figure out for myself. I know something about aero engines. You just say the word which way it is to be."

He shook his head like a man tired of arguing with some childish demand.

"You're mad to try it—one way or the other. There's four crates of spare parts in that shed. You'd never sort them out. Still . . ." he paused, a crinkled grin slowly spreading over his face, "I don't altogether dislike you. Don't alto-

gether blame you. Seen too many of your kind—from the
moment they begin to take too much gin in the mess until
they start forging cheques. I suppose it's something about
bein' up there that gives a man different ideas. Big ideas.
Some can handle 'em. Some can't. Anyway, you needn't
worry about me. Or my key."

"What do you mean?"

"That you don't need my key. There's a sentry round the
front of the hut. He's got a key. He'll be sitting in his box
smoking if I know him. And as for the parts to take, you'll
fall over them—just inside the door on the right. Only things
we haven't got spares of. Typical. But you'll have trouble
carting and hiding them."

"Leave that to me."

"I am. I'm going to finish my chapter and have a good
night's sleep. Just where do I meet this boat of yours and
when?"

"Tomorrow night. You be in this hut from the moment
it's dark and I'll send someone for you. And thank you."

"For what? I'm doing nothing. We just had a little chat.
Just is, that since you're in the mood for cracking heads I
don't see why it should be mine. He's the only sentry there
is. The relief comes on in about two hours."

*   *   *

We had no trouble with the sentry. Parkes had been right.
He was sitting in his sentry box smoking. He looked up as I
moved quietly around and in front of him. I hit him hard
with the butt of my Mauser on the side of the head. He
slipped sideways, grunted, and then tried to come up at me.
I hit him again and the second time he went down and
stayed down. We took the hut key from him and opened up
the door. Just inside on the right I found the parts which
Parkes had mentioned.

Monk flashed his torch on them and said, "They'll take
some carrying and hiding." Laid out on the floor were the
five propellers from the Sea Furies which still awaited complete assembly. Spare parts of practically everything else, but

no spare propellers. I could see the flicker of disgust on Parkes' face as he had mouthed the word—*typical*.

It took us five trips to get them down to the beach. A good hour's work since it was too dangerous to use the direct path. We went across the strip, past the still shapes of the Sea Furies, and into the bushes on the far side. The sentry showed signs of coming round when we had cleared the third propeller so we hauled him into the nissen, and roped and gagged him. When we came back for the fifth propeller he lay there, his dark eyes flickering at us anxiously.

On the beach we carried the propellers out through the light surf and dumped them aboard the launch. Within an hour and a half of my leaving Parkes the launch was heading out to sea to round the north-east tip of the island. Clear of the land we turned westwards and began to run up the coast. After about a quarter of an hour I picked up the shape of the island off which I had been dropped from the *Aciano*. A hundred yards east of the island we roped the propellers with a twenty foot gap between them and, moving gently, lowered them over the side into about two fathoms of water. The last one went over and I paid out on the rope and finally cast it off with a lobster pot float.

We went round to the north of the island and ran into a small cove with bamboo and palms growing right down to the water edge. We took the launch in as close as we could get her to the rocks at the head of the cove. Monk and I went ashore and brought back bundles of dead palm fronds and branches which we spread over the decks and superstructure for camouflage. By the time we had finished the dawn was beginning to show signs and Eglantina had coffee ready. When we had finished we all went ashore and lay down under the palms to get some sleep.

15

IT was a long day, hot and breathless as the sea wind dropped. We kept away from the launch, sticking to the cover of the trees on the island. For a time, around mid-day, I walked across to the landward side of the island. I could see parts of the coast road up to San Pedro, but nothing of the air strip which was masked by a rising bluff of ground some miles away to my left. A few lorries went by on the coast road, but there were no signs of any special activity. Parkes would have kept his mouth shut I was sure, but by now the propellers would have been long missed and the sentry would have identified myself and Monk. Ocampo would be working hard going through Acaibo. If the launch were missed then Ocampo's men would certainly begin to comb the coastline. But there was a lot of it to search. And anyway, for all they knew, we had headed right out to sea with the propellers without any intention of ever coming back. Just south of Acaibo, about a couple of miles offshore there was a small group of islands and sand cays which it would take half a day to search thoroughly. I hoped Ocampo would be concentrating on them first. I sat under a palm by myself and watched the dust trails rise as the occasional lorry went along the road. Lemaza wouldn't advertise the loss of the propellers. The search parties would be at work but the public wouldn't know what they were looking for . . . and sometime during the afternoon there would be Angelo's funeral. Lemaza and Ocampo were going to have a busy and disturbing day. I could imagine them both. . . . Ocampo snapping around like a terrier, and Lemaza big and full of outward confidence, but inwardly knowing that the props, if they weren't found, meant the end of his ambitions. I wondered how long it would be before Da Silva, sitting quietly in the *Cantina del Morro,* found out. No props, no triumphal entry into Caramanga, and no support from Da Silva's employers. It was going to be a bad day for Lemaza, a long bad day and if I could have made it a forty-eight hour one for him I would.

And well within forty-eight hours, I thought, I would be at sea and on my way to Haiti, to Drea. . . . All I had to have was a little luck, no more than any man could reasonably count on, and to keep my head. By now, Drea must be long in Haiti, and getting anxious. I leaned back against the tree and thought about her. Once in the past she'd walked out. Once in the past we'd come together again. I imagined her waiting for me now, sitting at this very moment possibly on the hotel terrace, looking down over Port-au-Prince. I saw myself walking on to that terrace when the moment came. She would turn and watch me and she would know right away. If I had failed she'd go because she had more courage than I had ; a courage that made her face facts, let her see clearly how the future would be. And I would deserve to lose her because I saw now how obsessed I had been with my own selfish view of our love.

I stood up, disturbed by my thoughts, my feet making the dead palm litter crackle. Suddenly, I heard away to my right the sound of a plane. It was low at first, mosquito thin, and then welled up into that big, throaty roaring, into that scream and shriek of wings and propellers which had always been music to me. . . .

It was the one Sea Fury which remained operational. It came low over the far bluff that hid the air strip three miles away, climbed steeply and then levelled out and flew up the coast. I watched it. It flew at about four hundred feet, following the coast line and in a few seconds was gone out of sight to the west. But almost as soon as the noise had died, it began to grow again. The plane came back and this time it was flying low, no more than fifty feet above the water and retracing the line of the coast. It flashed by the island, a half a mile away.

I ran through the trees and joined Monk and Eglantina.

"Hide," I called. "Get down in the bushes. He's sure to come out here."

As I finished speaking I heard him coming back. We

crouched in the undergrowth, deep in the tree. He went over so low that the wind of his passing shook the top hamper of the palms. He came back in another pass over the island, low again, too low, I thought, and I prayed that the camouflage we had piled on the launch would fool him. I would soon know. It was not easy to make up your mind at the speed he was going that you really had seen something. If I'd been up there and fancied I'd seen a camouflaged launch, I would have come back for another, and then, maybe, even another look.

We waited as the noise died, waited for it to well up again. But it thinned away and there was only the sound of the sea lapping gently on the rocks. For the rest of the afternoon Monk and I kept watch on the landward side of the island, watching the coast road and the beaches for any sign of movement. But the day passed uneventfully.

* * *

When it was dark enough we went aboard the launch, took her around the island and straight across to the coast. We hove-to about twenty yards offshore. It was a calm night with a great blaze of stars above, so still that I could hear the occasional crackle of bursting seed pods in the shrubs on the cliff side. The three of us were in the well behind the cabin. Monk said, "I don't like this at all. You can't manage it by yourself."

During the afternoon I had told him what I intended to do and he had been arguing about it ever since.

I said, "I've got to manage it. And I think I can. I need you with the launch more than with me." I patted my pocket in which I carried a torch that came from the launch. "I'll signal with this from the beach below the air strip. You've got to be standing off there all night. If you don't get a signal by an hour before dawn you know what to do."

All he had to do was to go back to the propellers. He and Eglantina could haul them up between them and head out to sea. Far out, they could dump them where there would be no hope of finding them. I wasn't being heroic. It was just common-sense. If anything went wrong then I would be the only one to suffer. And Albano—but he had to take his chance of standing against the same wall with me and facing a firing squad. Parkes and Katrina would have no connection with me that Lemaza could trace.

"Eglantina could handle this boat easily," he persisted.

"But she couldn't pull up the props by herself."

"She could cut the buoy. Nobody would ever find them."

"They would if we didn't come back. They'd make us speak. Given time. No, you stay here."

He didn't argue after that. He took the launch in a little closer and I dropped overboard into about two feet of water and waded ashore with the phosphorescence creaming around my legs. On the beach I turned and watched the launch go out. A few minutes later I was up the cliff and over the road, breasting the climb to the top of the long bluff that hid the air strip away to the left. Once over this all I had to do was to follow the line of the foot of the hills that stretched away towards Acaibo. I reckoned that it would take me about an hour of cross-country going to reach the reservoir above the villa.

I passed through the trees about two hundred yards up the slope from the red warning light at the end of the air strip. Over the bluffs the ground was badly broken with rocks and thick shrub and it was hard going. It was a warm night and in no time I was sweating all over. The only company I had were the mosquitoes that rose around me from every shrub I brushed.

After a while, I had to work up the hill slope to avoid the broken run of a small gorge. I caught a glimpse of the harbour lights at Acaibo. I couldn't be far from the villa now. I skirted the gorge and then came down, low enough to be free of the shrubs and trees, and found the edge of the old cane plantations. An overgrown path ran along their top side and I followed this. After a while I saw the rounded edge of the old water reservoir come up sharply against the blaze of stars some way ahead of me. I slowed up and went cautiously. Down to the left a light shone in one of the windows of the villa. Along the road beyond it a car beetle-crawled, its headlights probing through the night. It went up over the hill and disappeared on the dip to Acaibo.

Ten yards from the reservoir I stopped. The path ran around the lower side of it through a clump of trees. Nearer me I could make out the tufted crests of a patch of bamboo. I stood there listening. This was the true beginning of the night's work. From now on I was going to walk on edge and there had to be no slip.

I moved quietly towards the bamboos. It was an hour and a half after darkness now and Katrina, if she were here, must have been waiting some time. A mosquito whined close to my face and I brushed it away with a slow movement of my hand. As I did so something moved in the darkness at the base of the bamboo clump. I dropped my hand towards my pocket and the Mauser but I did no more than touch the cloth of my jacket.

She came out of the darkness, swiftly and silently to me and it was exactly the same as it had been in Eglantina's room. Her arms went round me and her head was against my chest. I could feel her hands gripping the looseness of my jacket shoulders. She didn't say anything; she just held to me and I wrapped my arms about her to still the shaking of her body. After a moment she raised her head and I had the paleness of her face below mine and the soft dark line of her lips. Without thought I kissed her as a man kisses a woman who offers herself to him. Then I held her away from me. I had no wish to offer even the edge of any promise. I concentrated on what had to be done. But perhaps there was an unnatural harshness in my voice which went on misleading her though it rose from a desperate need to ensure that she came to no harm. Time had a wallet at his back all right. . . . *Wherein he puts alms for oblivion.* Well, these few moments had to go in and *be forgot as soon as done.*

I said, "You've got to make me a promise. And you've got to keep it. Whether you like it or not."

I still had my hands on her arms and for a while I don't think she really took in what I had said. She leaned back a little from me, looking at me. Through the darkness I could see her eyes shining and catch the sound of her breathing, a sound that still carried the pulse of her exaltation and wonder.

"Promise," I said. I gave her a little shake.

"Anything."

"You'll do exactly as I say, even if what I'm going to tell you makes you feel you must disobey me."

"I promise, Keith. Oh, Keith. . . ."

I shook her again gently, ignoring all she wanted to say. Cursing myself for those few moments. Right now I was going to drive her hard. She had the spirit and fire of her race and there would be murder in her when she learned what Lemaza had done to her brother. Her hand would reach for knife or revolver. It had the instinct worked into it now. She would go to him with the cold passion of a woman who is possessed by revenge.

"You'll go down to the villa before me."

"You're going there?"

"Yes. But don't worry about me. You'll go quietly. Pack yourself a small bag and then slip away. Go up to the beach below the air strip. Don't let anyone see you. Are you taking this in?"

"Yes, yes, of course. But Keith——"

"Go up to the beach. Take a torch with you. If I'm not there three hours after midnight you flash it on and off three times. . . ." I went on, telling her what to do to get Monk, what to do to get herself away from this island, and all the time her hands were on my arms, not wanting to break the contact with me.

I finished, "Is Lemaza in the villa?"

"Yes. But why are you going there? What do you want from him?" Katrina was hanging on my arms, her face tilted so that I could catch the small points of star reflection in her eyes.

I moved, releasing one of her arms, but still holding her with one hand, and began to walk her towards the trees below the reservoir. I said, "I want my money. But there's something else. You're leaving this place with me and Monk. There's nothing here for you now that your brother has gone. General Lemaza will take Caramanga and from then on

196

everything will be different. . . . You wouldn't want to be here to see it. You, particularly, since you are his sister."

"Why should it be different? Angelo's gone . . . but his work remains. Every soldier now is more determined. Cordillo, the new Cordillo, is going to be his monument. . . . In the church today one only had to see their faces. . . ." She broke off and I felt her hand grasp mine more tightly.

I said, "I was up on the roof of Eglantina's place when your brother was shot. I saw everything. I saw how it was done and who did it. I saw Albano——"

"Keith, please. I don't want to talk about it."

"But I must. You've got to understand."

"Understand what?"

"That Albano didn't shoot your brother."

"Albano didn't shoot my brother?" It came flatly.

"No."

"Who did?"

I said: "The whole thing was arranged. Albano was framed. Lemaza was behind it. He betrayed your brother, had him assassinated——"

"Lemaza!"

I nodded.

"Oh no! I can't believe it."

"I was there——"

Before I could say anything more four shadows rose out of the periphery of gloom that held us beneath the trees. A carbine was jabbed into my back and my arms were seized. A familiar face came between me and Katrina. Two men pulled her back, wordless and shrinking with them into the darkness, the only sound the reluctant scuffle of feet as they went. Lieutenant Ocampo's hands went over my body and I was relieved of my torch and my Mauser. And for good measure as he stood in front of me with his trophies, he raised the Mauser and whipped me across the side of the face with it. I raised my right foot and kicked him in the groin. He doubled up for a moment, groaned, and then slowly straightened, coughing, while the two soldiers held me from behind. He moved safely to one side of me and hit me again.

* * *

I didn't see Katrina. They must have taken her down ahead of me. They tied my hands behind my back and I was marched down to the villa between the two soldiers. Ocampo came behind me and I could hear him coughing and spitting occasionally from the blow I had given him. Ocampo's car was in the driveway and his driver beside it. The man came to attention as we passed. My head was still muzzy from the two blows I had received and I walked, awake, but as though still half held by some recent dream. An outside light was on over the door at the top of the house steps and a scattering of moths fluttered around it like snow flakes. An orderly opened the door to us and we went across the hall. The orderly, after a knock, opened the door of the Generalissimo's room.

I was marched in and halted a few feet from his desk. The two soldiers were dismissed. Ocampo went past me and placed on the desk my Mauser and my torch. General Lemaza, who was sitting behind the desk, looked at them briefly and then ignored them. No word passed between him and Ocampo. I had the impression that they too were all part of a wordless dream. In a moment they would come into the realm of sound and reality.

General Lemaza looked up at me and he smiled; a smile of genuine welcome and pleasure, I decided. He had been looking forward to this moment, had played some slender hunch in the hope of picking me up, not expecting it to work, maybe, but delighted now at his combination of luck and perspicacity. There he was, the bluff Father Lemaza, showing me his tartar-free dentist's smile, confident and beautifully dressed as usual in his coffee-coloured shantung tunic, the room lights winking on the silver buttons with their flying rifle-carrying eagle, the close-grained walnut pigskin of his face, lotion fresh, and one big, ringed hand, lightly touching the top of a box of Elvas plums. I waited for him to take one, but he held himself back, promising himself one, no doubt, as a reward after he had finished his business with me.

The General got up from his desk and walked around to stand in front of me. He hawked a little in his throat, like an amplifier crackling, and then the sound came on.

"Señor Marchant, you have been very unwise. Tenacious, admirably tenacious, but wholly unwise."

It was a good beginning. Nice rounded phrases.

Lemaza's right hand came up and he hit me. It was a powerful hand and I went over and backwards to the floor and lay there for a moment dazed by the brutal shock.

Ocampo came to me and kicked me hard in the ribs.

"Get up," he said calmly.

I saw no point in it so I stayed where I was.

"Get up," repeated Ocampo and he kicked me again.

I lay where I was, breathing hard, so hard that it sounded to me as though I were sobbing.

General Lemaza pulled a chair forward.

"We should be a little more polite, perhaps?"

He bent down and with Ocampo's help lifted me into the chair. He made me comfortable with another blow alongside the face, nicely calculated so that it did not knock me off the chair. I saw his face smiling at me through a blood-shot haze and I licked at the corner of my mouth to taste the seaweed tang of blood running from some cut on my face.

"Unwise," he said with parental concern. "But not unintelligent. Intelligent people learn quickly."

I was sagging a little sideways in the chair and he hit me on the side of the face to correct the sag and save me from falling. He was all consideration and I was beginning now to be ready to shut my eyes as the blow came and take the shock.

He stepped back a little and examined the knuckles of his right hand, brushing them lightly with the finger tips of his left hand. A dentist, I suppose, must look after his hands, and that was all the future he could hope for—to go back to dentistry. He reached back to the desk and picked up a long, black circular-sectioned ruler. He stood in front of me and tapped the end of it into a palm which he intended to have well greased for the rest of his life.

I said, "You've had enough exercise."

"Ha. . . ." Lamaza's face beamed. "You wish to talk. That is an excellent decision. Force is repugnant to me. You realize that? It is peasant's work. You and I are reasonable men, though occasionally you have curious lapses into indiscretions. However, Señor Marchant, we shall be delighted to listen to you. You know, of course, why you are here? The sentry at the air strip recognized you. Let us confine our talk purely to the subject of propellers."

"It's not as simple as that——"

The ruler flashed out and cracked me over the shoulder, jarring my collar bone.

"It must be as simple as that, Señor Marchant. The propellers."

"I've got them," I said. "If you want them, you've got to pay for them."

General Lemaza rested his bullock-sized backside against the edge of the desk. He said to Ocampo, "Get Señor Marchant a drink. The best business is done over a drink."

Ocampo went to a wall cupboard. He came back and held a glass to my lips. It was brandy and I took it. I was in no position to refuse hospitality.

"You will, of course, be paid," said Lemaza. "We both appreciate the enormous importance of these propellers. Normally, after you had told me where they are, I would have you shot. But I have no personal animosity, and you did bring the planes in originally. In view of all these circumstances, you shall be paid. The price is your freedom. You will be put on the first boat leaving Acaibo. Whichever way you consider it, a handsome arrangement."

"It stinks," I said quietly. And then as he moved the ruler I went on quickly, "Lay off that for the moment. I'm not in a position to run away. But you've got to know the facts."

"And what are the facts? Simple. You came back to Acaibo because of your money—taken from you through no fault of ours. You steal our propellers so openly that it was clear you would come to me with some kind of blackmail offer, Señor Marchant. . . ." He paused for a moment, smiling, and then went on: "In all fairness I must give Lieutenant Ocampo full credit for your present position. He suggested that before you got in touch with me, you might try to contact Katrina. . . . You would want to know where to find me, to be sure of a word with me. So, all day we have watched her. I never believed it would be successful." He half-turned to Ocampo. "My congratulations, Lieutenant Ocampo."

Ocampo's dark face creamed with a happy smile.

"You should make him a captain."

Lemaza chuckled. "It is already in hand. Let us get down to these facts of yours."

I said, "If I tell you where these propellers are you won't let me go. We must be realistic about that. Don't bother me with it again. And get this straight. They're hidden and there are two people with them. If I don't return to them by dawn the propellers will be destroyed. You'll never have them." I looked up then, directly at him and the smile was gone from his face. "Whether you believe it or not, General, I can hang out until dawn."

It shook him. There was no doubt about it. He leaned back against the desk, frowning at me and then his hand went back and he put the ruler down and absently reached for the box of Elvas plums. He put one in his mouth and sucked on it and then began to chew.

Then he said sharply, "Maybe we can't get you to talk in time. That's possible. But we can still find these people and get the propellers."

"You can't find them before dawn. By then they'll be away. And they're taking something with them, General— not only the propellers. But a story the press of the world would like to hear. A story that unless you get to Caramanga and become President or whatever it is you want—you'll never be big enough to deny. A story that will make Da Silva's people pull out, money bags and all."

"What is this story?" he asked.

"I was on the roof top the day of the anniversary parade. I saw Angelo Libertad shot dead. I saw Tomez and Sardi Hueica shot. And I saw Albano too drugged to know what was happening. It's a hell of a story. My friends know it. You can never handle it unless you get to Caramanga. And you can't get there without planes. One isn't enough."

I leaned back then, letting my head drop away on my shoulders, feeling the brandy inside me fighting against the bruising ache in my body. I didn't care a damn for him because I knew he had to make a bargain with me.

He straightened up, rubbing one hand over his smooth chin. Ocampo stood to his side like a dark whippet.

"This is a fantastic story. Completely and scurrilously untrue."

His emotions worked in clichés too, but they couldn't help him.

"Save that stuff for your victory speech in Caramanga. Your troops won't believe it here. The only thing that can save you is having planes in the air. I'm willing to trade in those propellers—for a few considerations. It's your choice."

It was some time before he said anything. He walked around and sat at his desk and took another plum. He sat there, looking across at me, chewing the cud like a cow and I knew that underneath his fine uniform he was giving houseroom to a flock of private agonies. Fame may be the spur, but the steed is ambition and it's a horse that takes a lot of handling . . . but he had capable hands, dentist's hands, and he knew when to rein in for a spell.

He said bluntly, "What do you want?"

I said, "My hands untied first. I can't bargain in the attitude of a trussed fowl."

He considered this for a moment and then he picked up my Mauser from the desk in front of him and slipped it into his pocket.

"Ocampo."

Ocampo came over and behind me, looking like a man well out of his depths.

16

OCAMPO cut the cord from my hands. It was a bad moment for me. Until then the cords and the pull of my bound hands behind me had given me a tension and restriction which had acted as a support. As I brought my hands in front of me I could feel my aching body crying out to be allowed to relax. I bowed my head forward as I chafed at my wrists, giving my body a few moments' grace. Then I pulled out my handkerchief. It was damp with salt water which had seeped up my trouser legs from wading ashore. I wiped my face and stood up.

They said nothing. But they watched me, Lemaza behind the desk and Ocampo standing now by the drink cupboard. I fished for my cigarettes. They were damp, too, and I threw the packet into a waste paper basket by the desk.

"Ocampo."

The little dark lieutenant, soon to be captain, took a packet from his pocket, came forward a couple of steps and handed them to me. He stood there with his lighter poised.

The first hungry draught at the cigarette made me feel better.

Lemaza said bluntly, "What do you want?"

"Two things to begin with. Forty thousand dollars from that safe behind you."

Lemaza smiled sourly. The situation had changed and he was accepting it.

"I have them," he said. "It was purely a matter of good business. Revolutionary house-keeping. You shall have them. The second thing?"

"Albano," I said. "I brought him here. I'm taking him out with me. You can always pretend he escaped again." I nodded to the telephone on his desk. "Ring the barracks and have him sent here."

I saw Ocampo stir, rather like a fussy woman wishing she

could dare to butt in on some bold policy of a determined husband.

It was some time before Lemaza said anything. He was marching step by step with me. I knew that with every yard he went he was searching around for some tripping point, some unwariness on my part which would give him the advantage.

He said, "It could be done. And in return?"

"In return you get your propellers."

"How, Señor Marchant?"

"Albano comes here. You dismiss his guard. You give me my money—and then we all walk out. You, Ocampo, the whole bunch of us. We take Ocampo's car and drive to the coast. You won't know where until we reach the place. A boat will pick us up and take us away. As I leave the beach I'll tell you how to find the propellers. The moment we leave this place, of course, you will hand over any arms you carry."

"I see. I am to hand over the money, and Albano. Give you a safe conduct—and then trust you at the last moment to tell me what I want to know."

"What you must know if you want to get to Caramanga."

"Why should I trust you to tell me where the propellers are hidden?"

"Because you damned well have to."

He eased himself back a little in his chair and then looked from me to Ocampo. Almost casually he said:

"Captain Ocampo, what would you do in my place?"

Ocampo wasn't a man for this kind of decision. He shuffled uncomfortably.

He plunged, "In a few hours we could make him speak, Generalissimo. Why should he tell you where the propellers are when he's free to go?"

Lemaza's eyes came back to me. "He's a fool," he said quietly. "A good officer, but a fool when it comes to matters like this." He reached out for the telephone.

I said, "Say one word more than is necessary and the bargain is dead."

He just looked at me without bothering to reply. He got through to the barracks commander and instructed him curtly that he wanted Albano brought to the villa under the guard of one officer and one private. "He must be here within fifteen minutes." He put the telephone down.

"When they come, dismiss the officer and the soldier back to the barracks."

Lemaza smiled. "You should have taken command of our air strength. It is a pity there is something in you which only lets you go so far. The remnant of a conscience, maybe?"

"Anything you said about my teeth I'd believe," I said, "but leave my conscience alone. It's outside your field."

He laughed then, though I didn't expect him to laugh. Maybe it was his way of riding an insult.

"The dollars," I said.

He got up and went to the safe.

He brought out a shabby brown brief-case and put it on the desk.

"They're all there. Just as I took them out of the box file when they were brought to me." It was his first open admission of the theft, and the fact that he made it without emphasis or excuse showed me that the game was really running now, high-staked, and wide open. I only had to make one slip and he would have me up against a wall with six carbine mouths ready to roar a quick farewell.

I went forward to the desk and opened the bag. I tipped the money out and I counted it. Then I put it back and lifted the case over to the chair on which I had been sitting.

Watching me do it, he said reflectively, "Angelo was right. I should have paid you. He was always so right. You can go on being right for just so long as discretion demands. If you take it too far people end up by hating you. There was always a bullet waiting for him in the years ahead. I did him a favour. He died with everyone loving and respecting him. Not with everyone hating and fearing him because he wouldn't give them what they wanted."

I said, "You don't have to make two funeral orations in one day for my benefit."

It was then that I realized that he was looking right past me.

I spun round.

The side door in the main sitting room had opened quietly while I had been talking. Katrina stood just inside the room. She wore a black dress with a large shawl over her shoulders. Against her bosom I saw the length of chain with its gold cross. In her right hand she held the small revolver which I had first seen on the *Mara II*.

"Katrina!"

I made a move towards her but she brought the revolver up a little and for a moment it included me as she shook her head.

"Stay where you are, Keith. Stay where you are. He had my brother killed." She broke off and came forward a little into the room. Out of the corner of my eye I saw Ocampo's hands poised against his hips. A quick move would put his hand on his holster. Lemaza stood behind the desk, his finger tips resting on his blotter.

Keeping my voice calm, I said, "Katrina, if you kill him now you'll——"

"Don't talk to me, Keith. He killed Angelo. He knows I'm going to kill him."

I didn't say anything. She was going to kill him. She was going to walk a few more paces towards the desk so that she couldn't miss, and when she fired she was going to bring everything down in a great crash around us. Albano would get his bullet, so would I, and so would she.

She wasn't watching me. Her eyes were on the silent Lemaza. I reached back behind me slowly and felt for the brief-case on the chair. I got one of the handle loops and I slung it out from me and towards her. She had a lot to learn still and I hated teaching her.

The case caught her on the right hip and jolted up her right elbow. I jumped for her and got her wrist and the impetus took us to the floor. When I stood up the revolver was in my hand.

I reached down and helped her up and she stood in front of me, dazed. Suddenly her head dropped and she began to sob.

Lemaza dropped back into his chair and I saw his big shoulders collapse.

"Thank you, Señor Marchant," he said.

"Don't thank me. You've got a bullet coming to you one day. And now, just to show how much you trust me I'll have the rest of the armament. My Mauser and Ocampo's revolver."

They handed them over. I kept my Mauser and dropped the other two into the case. A simple movement. But then they always are, the little movements eating up only a few seconds of time, but loaded, loaded down to the gunwales, with the freight of the future.

There was a knock on the door. I looked at Lemaza.

"That'll be Albano. Let me do the talking."

Katrina's head came up and I saw the tightening of her lips, the flash of returning spirit in her eyes. She was coming out of her trance fast.

"For this," she said bitterly, "I'll never forgive you. Never."

The knock came on the door again. I nodded to Ocampo and he went over.

*　*　*

A captain brought him in while the soldier escort stood at the open door. Albano came into the middle of the room. His blazer was ripped and dirty and he hadn't shaved for many days. He looked around him suspiciously. They had been keeping him without adequate toilet facilities. The dirtier and more disreputable he looked the better showing it would have been at his trial . . . a young desperado. His face was puffy and cut below the right eye. It looked as though they were still keeping him drugged. If they were I might have trouble getting through to him.

Lemaza said, "All right, captain. You can go back to the barracks. I will telephone you when you are needed."

The captain saluted and turned away to the door.

As the door closed I said, "What have you been doing to him? Softening him up with rifle butts so that he'll remember his lines for the trial?"

Lemaza stood up and the muscles of his face tightened.

"I've put myself in your hands, Señor Marchant. I don't

207

want this business prolonged by any discussion of our prison methods."

And then, astutely, beginning already to hedge the future, prompted to it by the knowledge that the captain would go back to the barracks and talk and set people wondering, he went on, turning towards Katrina:

"This man killed your brother. The rest is lies. I am being forced into a bargain by Señor Marchant which I must accept."

Katrina said nothing.

Albano moved and looked at me and then he said slowly as though each word were an effort, "What is he talking about?"

I said, "I'll explain later. You're coming with me. Away from Acaibo. It is part of a bargain."

"Bargain?"

I nodded.

He shrugged his shoulders, awake but not really with us. And I was glad that I didn't have to go into the details of the bargain with him. Even in his present state he would have resisted any bargain that put the Sea Furies into the air against his side. I went over to the cupboard and poured him a glass of brandy. He took it and held it cupped against his chest.

"Drink it," I said.

He drank obediently.

As he did so I turned to Katrina.

"We're going now," I said. "You're free to stay here or come with us."

"She will stay here, of course," said Lemaza quickly. "There is no reason for her to go. Katrina——"

"Let her speak for herself."

She looked from me to Lemaza and then at Albano. Then she said to me, "What do you want me to do?"

"It's your decision. Not mine. You know the facts."

She shook her head. "What do you want me to do?"

If only I could I would have wiped out those few moments at the reservoir. Already they had put on me a weight I didn't want to carry.

208

I said, "You must come with us."

"With you?"

"With us," I repeated firmly. "I'm not going to be alone in the boat."

"All right."

At once, Lemaza said, "I can't allow this."

"She's coming with us," I said. "You don't start giving orders again until the bargain is completed."

Albano said, "I don't understand any of this at all."

I didn't bother to help him. I turned to Ocampo who had been standing in shocked silence at Lemaza's impotence, and I said, "Go and clear the orderly from the hall and then stand by the car. If there are any of your men outside clear them off. And, remember, don't try anything. I'm going to be right behind you General. . . ." I lifted my Mauser.

Lemaza said, "Captain Ocampo, you will do exactly as Señor Marchant orders." And then as Ocampo moved towards the door, Lemaza turned to Katrina, "Katrina, I beg of you to reconsider this most hasty——"

"Skip it," I said. "Her mind's made up, and you haven't got a cliché in you that will change it."

17

WE went across the hall and out to the car. Ocampo was the only person in sight.

I made Ocampo drive and the General sat alongside him. The rest of us got into the back of the car and I sat directly behind the General.

"To the air strip," I told Ocampo.

At the end of the drive the sentry on duty saluted smartly and then we turned north. Away on our right I could see the pale line of wash from the waves rolling up the beaches. The wind had got up a little and there were patches of small cloud racing across the star-loaded sky. It wasn't midnight yet. I was glad of that because the more hours of darkness we had at sea for a start the safer we would be. Once Lemaza knew where his propellers were he would send a boat out from Acaibo after us. I couldn't stop that, but I reckoned that two or three hours' grace would be as much as we needed in the launch, for no one would know which course we had taken.

Katrina sat alongside me and, knowing the emotional burden that hung between us, knowing, too, that the longer I let it rest there the harder it would be to support it, I said easily, "What happened to you after we were caught?"

She was staring straight ahead of her and for a moment I thought she wasn't going to reply.

"What happened?" I asked.

"I was locked in my room," she said. "Lemaza was to see me later. They didn't know you'd already told me. Keith——" Her head came round and I could tell she was going to change the subject.

I put my free hand on hers and said quickly, "It's all right. You don't have to say anything. How did you get out?"

"On to the verandah through the window and then back

into the house through my . . . through his room. . . ." Her head turned away from me and her hand tensed under mine.

The lights of the barracks came up on our right and as we passed the entrance I saw the *Singing Heart that Never Tires* drawn up and some leave men getting out. I don't know why but the sight of the taxi, reminding me of my first days in Acaibo, served to point the fact that now, very soon now, I would be getting out, and taking with me the money I had earned . . . not honourably, maybe, but certainly earned. And I was going, too, without leaving any responsibilities behind me. It wasn't often that life handed you a nice profit and also left your conscience untroubled. . . . The weight of the brief-case on my knees was pleasant and I think I should have been completely happy had it not been for Katrina at my side. She was in love with me. She was going to have to work it out for herself, gain a little more experience. . . .

But although I was beginning to feel easier I didn't let that tempt me into any carelessness. Lemaza would be watching for the slightest advantage.

The barracks dropped behind us and then I saw the red light of the air strip. I told Ocampo to run the car up to the large nissen and round to Parkes' hut. There were two sentries at the hut now but Ocampo dealt with them.

As the car drew up Parkes came out of his hut. He had his panama hat on, a light overcoat and was carrying a small grip. Somehow the sight of him turned the whole affair into a commonplace departure. Mr. Henry Parkes all ready to leave for Balham or Tooting or wherever he lived . . . spare socks and shirt in his grip, passport and wallet tucked away in his jacket.

He came over to the car and looked at Albano. Although Albano was brightening up he still had a long way to go. Parkes must have appreciated at once what had been happening. He put a big hand out and gripped Albano's arm.

"Nice to see you, Mr. Albano, sir." And then to Lemaza he said roughly, "I'm leaving. What there is to do here can be done by your chaps. Also I won't tell you what I think of you. It would take too long and there's a lady present."

Lemaza said nothing.

Albano said, "You're coming with us?"

"Yes, sir," said Parkes. "We'll be all right." He stood on the running-board of the car for the short ride down to the beach and as he did so Albano said, "But what about the planes. Are they going to be in the air for him?"

Parkes said, "I don't know. That depends on Mr. Marchant here."

Albano turned towards me. "What about the planes?"

He was coming back fast and I didn't want any trouble with him.

"Sit tight," I said. "And be glad you're getting out. There's no future in facing a firing party." To Ocampo I said, "Run down the strip to the beach."

"But I want to know," Albano insisted.

"Sit tight," I said sharply.

A little later we were on the beach. I took the torch out of my brief-case and signalled. It was a good ten minutes before I heard the sound of the launch's engines. Soon afterwards her bulk rose against the night sky. She came into the beach and her bows grated on the sand about three yards out from the water's edge. Monk called gently to me from the bows.

"Hold her there," I said.

I stood at the back of the group, brief-case in one hand and my revolver in the other.

Parkes and Albano waded out and I watched Monk help them over the side. Katrina followed them. She ignored Lemaza altogether and he made no move or sound. He and Ocampo stood there with the waves fading up towards them and they watched me. I waited until Katrina was safely aboard and then I went down to the water, keeping the two covered.

It must have been an anxious moment or two for Lemaza. I could break my bargain easily. The water came up around my feet and Lemaza's eyes were on me.

He didn't say anything. He just waited, a big, smartly dressed man, his peaked cap tilted just slightly at an angle, the starlight glinting on his silver buttons. He was going to remember this moment and I didn't hurry to relieve his agony of mind. I waded back until the water was up to my calves.

It was too much for him then.

He said hoarsely, "I have kept my side of the bargain, Señor Marchant."

"Because you had to. Don't worry. I'm going to keep mine. Along the coast from here about four miles, there's a small island. The propellers have been roped together and sunk about a hundred yards east of the island. They're buoyed. You'll find 'em."

I think then, if he had thought it would be successful, he would have come for me. I could see the swift reassumption of command in him, bracing his body. But the Mauser kept him off. I stepped backwards, facing them all the time. But Lemaza didn't wait for me to reach the launch. He turned sharply, snapped something at Ocampo, and the two of them began to run up the beach, back to their car.

Above me Monk said, "Come on."

I turned and climbed aboard, holding the brief-case firmly. I found myself facing Albano. His damaged face was creased with anger.

"What you've just done, I'll never forget. You've given him those planes back, haven't you?"

"Yes." I was suddenly tired and near to losing my temper with him. "If you want to, you can go back and do something about it. Go on, if you want to."

I went by him and aft and found Eglantina.

"We could all do with a drink, sweetheart," I said.

*   *   *

We went north all night with a fresh trade wind slapping the occasional wave over our starboard bow. Some of the party slept, but I stayed with Monk beside the wheel and now and then Eglantina came up from the cabin with a mug of coffee. Towards dawn the sky clouded right over and when daylight came the sea was running grey and there was a sporadic sweep of rain squall at times, hissing across the dull waters. The clouds were down to about three or four hundred feet. I didn't mind the dullness of the day. It cut the visibility down and that was a help if anyone was searching for us.

Just after daybreak Katrina came up from the cabin and stood beside us. She looked pale.

"How are they down there?" I asked.

"Albano is sleeping. He had three glasses of whiskey and in his condition they've sent him off."

"He'll feel fine when he wakes. I shall have trouble with him." I gave her a grin. "He's another who isn't going to forgive me."

She shook her head. "We all say things we don't mean at times."

Monk nodded. "The hardest thing at any time is to say the thing you mean. Even when you know someone well you're always having to hide things from them."

"He's always like this in the early morning," I said to Katrina. I was feeling good and I didn't want to think about anything but Haiti and Drea ahead of us.

An hour later Parkes and Albano came on deck. Parkes gave us all a good morning, but Albano said nothing. He went and sat in the stern and Parkes kept him company. They didn't talk much. Albano was young, too, like Katrina. He was learning all the time.

Eglantina fixed up some breakfast and I took over the wheel from Monk while he went down to eat with the others.

Katrina kept me company. My hands on the wheel, I whistled gently to myself. I was happy, elation running firmly in me. I had my money and Drea was waiting for me. I wanted nothing else.

Alongside of me Katrina said suddenly, "You're thinking about her?"

I nodded.

She said, "I wish she didn't exist!"

I smiled. "I'm glad she does." And then, because I liked her so much and knew how she was feeling, I went on,

"Don't look so glum. In six months you'll be in love with someone else. Someone far more worthy than me."

She made an impatient movement of her head. I said no more. There was nothing I could say.

Parkes came up to us and said, "What's that?"

"What's what?"

"Listen."

He cocked his head, cupping one ear in his hand.

I listened.

It came up then, growing stronger every second; the sound of a plane's engine.

"Hell!"

Parkes' bright blue eyes were on me and then went up to the grey clouds. A few seconds later we saw it, skimming through the lower layers of cloud away to the east. It was the one Sea Fury which General Lemaza had in operation. It was about a mile away and there was a chance it might not see us. The sound of its engine brought the others on deck.

I grabbed Parkes' arm and swung him around to me. "Did you get as far as fitting the armament?"

"Ay, we did."

Two 20-mm. Bristol Hispano cannons in each wing. They could make a mess of this launch in no time.

I said, "Everybody keep down. No movement. He may not see us."

"And if he does?" It was Albano.

I said. "You know what those cannons can do. If he comes for us our only hope is to go over the side. Swim away and spread the target."

I put a hand out and took Katrina's shoulder. "If we go over, stick with me." I cut the engine dead. We didn't want to advertise ourselves with a wake.

The noise of the plane died and it was swallowed in a far bank of cloud. Then a little later it swelled up again and Monk said, "There he is."

He'd gone round to the north and was now coming back on a course to the west of us. I watched him. He came down a bit to be free of the cloud cover and I wondered which of the *Cantina del Morro* boys it was. They'd had him out of bed, out of drunken sleep and waiting on the air strip for first light. I watched him away on our left now. He took the Sea Fury down almost to wave level and then brought her back in a climb that carried him into the clouds. The bowl of sky above us echoed with the roar of the engine. General Lemaza had his propellers by now. General Lemaza was going to wipe us out, but not just us. He was going to wipe out a story, wipe out the need for any denials of the truth about Angelo Libertad. . . . And I'd had all the time in the world last night to remember the one good Sea Fury.

The noise above us deepened. He broke cloud about a quarter of mile astern and came down in a long shallow dive. He was down and over us with a great screech, clearing us by about fifty feet, the wind of his passing battering down on us. As he went away he waggled his wings, and I could imagine him, laughing to himself, sure of his identification as he swept up into the low cloud again.

"Get over," I said. "The next time he'll go into business." I heard Eglantina say, "Mr. Monk, you can swim?"

"Not as far as Haiti," he said.

"You stay around me. . . ." Out of the corner of my eye I saw her strip off her dress. If she had to she would swim all the way to Haiti dragging him.

I pulled off my jacket and picked up the brief-case and jumped over. At the stern I heard the splashes as Parkes and Albano went. I trod water, waiting for Katrina. She followed Eglantina's example and pulled off her dress. She jumped in and we swam quickly away from the boat. A hundred yards from the launch I stopped swimming and Katrina came close to me. The others were spread away on the far side of the launch. There was no sign nor sound of the Sea Fury.

Katrina's hand came out and touched my shoulder gently. I saw the run of her long brown arm, the water shine on her brown shoulders and a wet wing of dark hair clinging to her cheek. . . . She looked like a child then, like the girl I had first met.

"Stick by me," I said. "And if he comes our way, dive under."

216

The first time he came down out of the clouds about half a mile ahead of the launch. I watched him level out, hearing the scream of the engine, knowing in a quick turn of memory just how he must be feeling, remembering the times I myself had come down like that with a thumb ready on the button. . . .

Two hundred yards from the launch he let go and the air shuddered with the sudden wicked punch of his guns. He was a good boy and knew his stuff. He was back in his element with all the night's hangover dissipated, eyes clear, brain and body one. He came in slightly at an angle to widen his target and I saw the sea swiftly ripped into ragged white tears that flashed from fifty yards out right up to the launch and over it. He roared past and the launch jumped like some sluggish animal and the air was briefly slashed and dirtied around it with splintering wood and debris.

He did a long, lazy turn under cloud level and came back. This time he took the launch full on the beam. He was down and over chattering and roaring and the cannons tore furrows away to our left as he passed. I went under with Katrina, clasping the brief-case to my chest. When I came up the launch had lost its high cabin forestructure and was afire. A thin plume of smoke rose from it and tailed away in the wind.

I began to swim away from it further and Katrina went with me. There was water in the brief-case now, sogging through it and weighing it down in my hand. But I hung on to it. Wet notes could be dried.

He came back again, well away from us and this time he must have hit the petrol tanks. There was a mighty double pulse of explosion, beating for release against the surrounding atmosphere and then the boat blew up, bursting into an untidy flower of wreckage. And as he went what was left of the launch settled swiftly and then disappeared, leaving for a moment of two a spreading flare of burning petrol on the surface.

He came back again, over the spot where the launch had been and then turned in a tight circle. But his guns were silent. I watched him finish his turn a quarter of a mile away and then head back to us. We were well spread now. As he came I wondered . . . the launch was fair game and, if we'd stayed in it, so would we have been. When you've got a target nothing can keep your finger off the button as you come in . . . when you've got a target. But people struggling in the water weren't targets. When you ride high and fast on wings like a god then you have to act like a god . . . use your power to destroy or to spare. . . .

He went over us again and his guns were silent. He went over and up into the clouds and I trod water with Katrina's hand on my shoulder and knew that he was deciding. Up there above the grey pall, clear in the morning sunshine, with the cloud tops bright and floss-whipped, he was deciding still.

He came down from the east, faster than ever before, screaming towards us and flattening out until he was no more than twenty feet above the sea. Away ahead of me I could see the black spots of the heads of Parkes and Albano. A hundred yards before he reached them he suddenly pulled up steeply, dangerously, practically standing on his tail and then was over, streaking up and away from us into the clouds without firing. The noise of the plane died away and he didn't come back. He didn't have to come back. Our launch was gone and we could drown at our leisure.

*   *   *

But it had been decided somewhere that we had no drowning mark upon us. I remember thinking sometime during the long hours that perhaps my complexion was, indeed, perfect gallows.

With the going of the plane we all came together. But it was hard work staying that way. Different bodies drift at different speeds. Now and again I lost my temper, shouting at Monk and Eglantina to keep close. We drifted in our three double-headed groups, Parkes and Albano, Monk and Eglantina, and Katrina and myself.

Towards the afternoon, I saw that Katrina was weakening. She didn't speak, but her head kept dropping and her hand on my shoulder began to lose grip and now and again slipped from me. When it happened I grabbed at her with my free hand and helped her to catch hold of me again. I kept talking to her, because I could see that she was at the point of being really scared. From the moment she had come aboard the *Mara II* she had been changing and learning all the time. It had been all a bit too fast, too violent, too crowded. Experience wants to come slowly. For a while she responded to my talk and then I saw that she wasn't with me. Fatigue was now swamping her fears. . . .

An hour later Katrina gave a little cry and her hand left me and she went under. One moment her face was close to me and the next moment she was gone. The going struck a jolt of panic through me. I kicked round and porpoised after her. Somewhere in the green fog of water I found her, caught her by the shoulders and brought her up. She lay back weakly, her shoulders against my chest and I got both my hands under her armpits to hold her while I lay back supporting her.

I can remember talking to her, God knows what nonsense. Telling her to take it easy, to relax, let herself float while my hands kept her shoulders up. And sometime in the talk and the unreal passage of time I realized that in diving for her I had let go of the brief-case. I even looked around for it, wondering if it would float and then remembered that inside it with the money were her revolver and Ocampo's. *A thousand furlongs of sea for an acre of barren ground.* Well, I'd made my payment. It was then that depression came down on me. I'd lost everything. After all I'd gone through, I'd lost everything. I didn't care then what happened to me. Nothing mattered because nothing worth having lay ahead for me.

At ten minutes past four that afternoon a Puerto Rican schooner picked us up. She was on the run from Jamaica. As soon as we were aboard Albano demanded that the captain should arrest me. Personally, I didn't care a damn what he did. I think the skipper thought Albano was delirious. Anyway, he refused to involve himself in the charges.

It was Monk who arranged things. The next morning he got the captain to go off course northwards to the Baie des

Cayes on the south coast of Haiti. We lay off Cayes and got a passing fishing boat to take us in.

Parkes and Albano, leaning over the rail, watched us go. Parkes raised a hand in farewell, a short, solid figure, heading for Balham. Albano at his side gave no farewell gesture.

In the boat I said to Monk, "How did you fix it? Albano could have made trouble for me in Jamaica."

Monk smiled. "I talked to Albano. Just talked to him and he saw reason."

"You must have had something pretty powerful to say."

"I did."

"What?"

"I'll tell you later. He just saw reason."

We had to do a little fast talking with the harbour officials when we got in, but we had no trouble with them and by mid-day we were in a small hotel in the town. I had a few dollars from my wallet which I had carried in the back pocket of my trousers. I dried this out on the window seat of my room. Monk I knew had some money, too.

As I was laying it out Katrina came into my room. She was still wearing a jersey and canvas trousers she had been given on the schooner.

She stood inside the door and watched me. From the moment we had been picked up she had made no mention of my brief-case. But I didn't have to be told that she knew what had happened to it.

I straightened up and looked down at the money.

"It's not much," I said wryly. "But it's enough to keep going on for a week or two."

"What are you going to do?" she asked. Her voice was gentle, uncertain.

"Do?"

"You know what I mean."

"Yes, I know. I'm going to hire a car and go over to Port-au-Prince. It's only about ninety miles."

She came over to the window by me and looked out over the houses to the sea and the tufted crests of the palms along the coast. An old man in a straw hat and blue shirt was pushing a handcart up the rough roadway. The wheels, unoiled, creaked and sang.

She said, "The money meant everything, didn't it?"

"Yes," I said.

"Then why go?"

"Because I've got to go."

"Will you come back?"

I shrugged my shoulders. "I don't know."

She turned and left the room.

I let her go and then went along to Monk's room.

Monk was lying back on his bed in his underpants, smoking, while Eglantina was busy washing shirt and trousers in the hand-basin.

I said, "Eglantina, go and see the clerk downstairs. Fix me up a hire car for Port-au-Prince right away."

She reached for a towel and began to dry her hands.

"Sure, Mr. Keith." She gave me her brown smile and went out singing gently to herself.

Monk scratched the top of his head. "Something I ought to tell you. About the propellers. While you were ashore, Eglantina and I lifted 'em all. Hell of a job, but we did it. Dropped 'em, unbuoyed, a mile out at sea. That bastard Lemaza will never find 'em."

"Why did you do that?"

"Frankly, I didn't think you'd carry things off. Anyway— it was a trump card with Albano. He could have made real trouble for you. Now the whole thing will be forgotten."

"I've got other trouble."

"I know. But there's nothing I can do about that. Wish there was."

"To think that I had it all in my hands. I could see the future . . . all beautiful. Well, there it is."

"You don't have to go to Port-au-Prince."

"No, but I'm going."

"I know that. Maybe it's as well. Anyway, I'll be here. I've got a little cash. You need any?"

"No thanks, Monk."

Eglantina came back.

"Car right away, Mr. Keith."

"Thank you, Eglantina."

I went out of the hotel into the sunshine and to the car. The boy who was driving it was the dead spit of *Singing Heart*.

As I got into the car he gave a melon grin and let in the gear. We were off and before we had cleared the town he switched on the car radio and a thumping calypso began to shock the sunlit air.

*   *   *

We had two punctures on the way, and the engine gave trouble. I began to think that the delays were deliberate.

We got there just before six and the beginning was just as I had imagined it might be. She was sitting at a table on the terrace, close up against a wall covered with bougainvillaea. The canopy over the table was tipped to let the westering sun strike across her hair and I saw the reddish lights slide over it as she turned and watched me coming. She was wearing a white dress and my topaz brooch . . . Drea. There was no one else in the world for me. No world for me without her. But I was coming back with a broken lance and without the garlands of victory.

She knew that before I had reached her and sat down.

Her hand came across the table and took mine.

"Keith. . . ." The rough-touched, beloved voice.

"Drea. . . ."

We sat looking at each other silently.

Her hand left mine and she said, "It didn't come off?"

"No."

"Your face is awful. What happened?"

I said, "Forget that. Stick to us. All you have to say is Yes or No."

"What happened?" she repeated firmly.

"I was in a car accident. The driver called his cab the *Singing Heart that Never Tires*. Nice name."

But she didn't smile. She said, "You had the money?"

"I had it. In my hand. Then I dropped it."

"Why?"

222

"I was in the sea. I needed both hands."

Her eyes came down from my face to where my hands rested on the edge of the table. I saw the tiny movement of her shoulders as though she felt suddenly cold. Then her hands came out and took mine, holding them, gripping at them and without looking at me she said with a rush of words, her fingers tight over mine, "Blast you! Oh blast you. . . !"

I dropped to my chair and put my lips to her hands, and catching at any hope I began to beg. . . . "Anything. Blast me. . . . Anything. But don't go. . . ." Her face came up towards me and I stopped for I could see that there was no need to beg. The Drea who was holding my hands was my Drea. The truth was then sharp and inevitable between us; try as we might to escape it, or put conditions to it, we were its creatures, bound to it irrevocably. We had to go on together, knowing that nothing could be settled in advance, that love changes its course from moment to moment, and that we had to follow because we weren't just lovers, but a part of love itself, for better or for worse.